Praise for *Skin Deep* ... ₩augnn

"I absolutely loved this story! The settings are perfect and the banter among the characters keeps the story interesting."

– *Literary Nymphs*

"...an unusual and intense read and was never boring,"

– *Reviews by Jessewave*

"Wholly original, *Skin Deep* is a fascinating mixture of eroticism and intense suspense. It is incredibly compelling, chilling and brutal one minute, achingly tender the next."

– Lisa, *Joyfully Reviewed*

"S.W. Vaughn has created a wonderful world filled with passion, drama and intrigue that will keep you enraptured to the last page."

– *You Gotta Read Reviews*

"So much to read and absorb in the pages of Skin Deep by S.W. Vaughn—paranormal beings, suspense and violence, and, of course, love."

– *Sensual Reads*

Loose Id ®

ISBN 13: 978-1-59632-415-2
SKIN DEEP
Copyright © June 2010 by S. W. Vaughn
Originally released in e-book format in December 2009

Cover Art by Anne Cain
Cover Layout and Design by April Martinez

Printed in the U.S.A. by
Lightning Source, Inc.
1246 Heil Quaker Blvd
La Vergne TN 37086
www.lightningsource.com

SKIN DEEP

Chapter One

If Tess didn't stop looking at him like that, Will was going to walk out.

He didn't want to go on the air tonight anyway. He had a headache. He needed a cigarette. And he sure as hell didn't feel qualified to dispense relationship advice when his own was...well, a disaster. There. He'd admitted it. Lyle Thomas was the worst thing that had ever happened to him. Besides Brett, and Adrian, and oh-God-put-the-knife-down Yvan. His love life was one long fucking train wreck, and the tracks never ended.

He should know. He'd laid them himself. Was still laying them, every time he rolled over and took Lyle's increasingly brutal displays of tough love. His ass was still sore enough to ensure he'd do this show on his feet.

But Tess wasn't looking at his ass. She was looking at the bandage and the makeshift sling that supported his sprained left wrist. She was looking straight through his stupid excuses and directly at the ugly truth.

"Will."

He couldn't look at her. "Are you going to give me the prod notes or not?"

"Sit down, Will."

Her tone was soft, at once daring and heartbroken with concern. She knew he couldn't. He glared at her. "No, thanks. I'm in a hurry. Got a show to do, remember?"

"He hurt you. Again."

"I fell."

"Don't insult me."

He sucked in air through clenched teeth. "He didn't mean it, Tess."

"Stop it! Stop making excuses for him. Will, you need to go to a hospital. And you need to leave that crazy-ass bastard before he kills you."

"Hospital. Right." She knew just as well as he did how pointless it would be. How did you hurt yourself, Mr. Ambrose? Oh, I fell off my bed. Yeah, into a couple of fists. Ha-ha, clumsy me. Let's just call the police—what's that? Oh, your boyfriend is a cop? Well, you should go home and tell him all about it, then.

Filling out a restraining order against a cop—especially Lyle—would only ensure him a nice, comfy spot in a cell. Or a cemetery.

Fuck it. Fire me if you want. He pulled a half pack of smokes from his back pocket and winced at the resurgence of pain the slight contact caused.

"I saw that," Tess whispered.

"Shut up." Will managed to light up one-handed and deposited the rest of the pack on Tess's desk. "Look, just give me the notes, okay? Don't make me fall apart right before airtime. I'll do that after the show. We'll go out for drinks or something."

A frown graced the corners of her mouth. "Promise? Because if you tell me you have to go home to him or else, I'm calling somebody, Will. I'm serious."

"It's not like that. He's just...a little rough." *I think.* Lyle had insisted he didn't know how tight his grip had been when he threw him on the bed. He'd been appropriately apologetic, even tender, afterward. And Will—stupid, forgiving Will—accepted his advances, despite a cold suspicion that Lyle knew he'd pushed it and just didn't care. "I'm a grown-up," he said to Tess, as much to remind himself as to reassure her. "Lyle is my partner, not my keeper. And if I want to go out and have a few with my slightly overconcerned friend, I can."

He tried to crush a frisson of doubt with logic. They didn't have plans tonight. Lyle had just said he wanted to crash at Will's place because it was closer to work. He was probably asleep already. He hoped.

Tess laughed a little. "If I'm overconcerned, you haven't been smacked around enough."

"Okay. You want to finish me off?"

"Tease."

"Fag-hag."

"Will!" She colored prettily and pushed back from her desk. "Fine. We'll go out for drinks. But we're going to talk about you. No twisting the conversation to make me spill my guts so I'll forget about you spilling yours."

He flashed an innocent expression. "I never do that."

"Right. And I'm Oprah Winfrey."

"Does that make me your fashion designer, or your cabana boy?"

"Get out there and do your show before I fire you, cabana boy."

"Yes, ma'am." Will tipped an imaginary hat, took the pages she fanned at him, and left her office before she could lapse back into mother mode.

He made the short trip down the hall to the studio without bumping into anyone and slipped inside. At least he wouldn't have to try explaining himself again to the rest of the staff. He'd managed to convince most of them that he'd taken up skateboarding, a story that covered the occasional bruise or scrape better than any tone of foundation. Tess knew the truth because she knew him.

Will switched on the midlevel lights and sighed. A wrinkled wrapper lay on the edge of the console, leaking crumbs everywhere. No doubt courtesy of Liza Jewel. She hosted *Lovin' Ladies* in here from six to eight, and she always left some remnant of whatever excuse for dinner she'd grabbed at the corner store behind. And they said men were slobs.

He cleaned up the mess and glanced over the prod notes. They were brief—just his standard intro and a few lines inviting callers to phone in and spill their guts on the air. A couple of familiar riffs to fill gaps, if he had any. Open-question shows made things easier for him, since the callers did most of the talking. Sometimes Tess demonstrated moments of psychic foresight that astounded him, like tonight, when the last thing he wanted to do was struggle through a monologue and then defend his so-called expertise when the crazies started calling.

The ready light flashed a two-minute warning. Will queued the intro track, flipped three lines open, and jammed the cans on. He pushed the boom mic up a few inches to accommodate his standing position and shoved the stool away to prevent taking an unconscious seat during the show.

He passed two minutes not thinking about his throbbing wrist. When the on-air light came on, he rolled the intro, only half listening to the snippet he'd long since memorized, which started with a bass-infused beat and ended with a welcome to *The Truth Will Out*.

"And we're taking your calls tonight from all across the city." Will jumped into the flow over the fading strains of exit music. All three lines lit within seconds. No fill tonight, then. "Whether you're gay or bi, curious or tri, I want your questions and confessions."

Tess came through his ear. "Line one. A little sketchy, but try it."

He held the kill switch, said, "Gotcha," and opened the first line. "You're on the air. Question or confession?"

"I am?" A high-pitched and jumpy voice squeaked through the headset.

Will nudged the in-volume down to four. "Yes, you're on. Got something to say?"

"Oh. This is really Will Ambrose? I mean, I'm not talking to a recording…"

"No way, baby. I'm live and in person." Will forced cheer into his tone and rolled his eyes. Live call shows always ran the risk of drag, since the callers couldn't be scripted or edited. This one seemed like a dud already. His finger hovered over the disconnect. "What'll it be, question or confession?"

"Sorry. Question." The guy giggled. Someone shouted something in the background. "I saw your picture on the Web site, hot stuff. You available?"

Definitely a dud. He cut the call first, to preempt any wiseass retorts, and said, "Not for you, sweet cheeks. I'm a one-horse cowboy. But thanks for asking." He switched over to Tess. "You called that one. Got any more winners?"

"Line three." She was brisk, dismissive. "Sounds like he'll need a little coaxing."

"Great." He opened three. "Hey, you're on. Question or confession?"

Silence greeted him. Terrific. Two for two, and he'd been on all of sixty seconds.

He gave it one more shot. "Hello...anybody in there? You're on *The Truth*, my friend. Question or confession?"

"Confession."

The husky, restrained voice sent a shiver through him. His radio instincts deemed this call golden, but his empathy cringed at letting it through. The man was in obvious pain.

"Go ahead," Will almost whispered. "Unburden yourself. I'm listening."

A shuddering breath, perfectly timed. He couldn't have scripted it better. "I pay men for sex."

Gold. Will practically heard a thousand listeners sitting up straighter. He could go a few different ways with this.

Hoping to let the caller off the hook, he chose the lighter route. "Why's that, darlin'? You got a face made for radio?"

"If only. Attraction is not my problem. I've plenty of offers."

A sliver of disgust chipped at Will's empathy. Another God's gift, center-of-the-club drama queen. "Maybe it's that oversized ego of yours. But hey, true love is only an insecure slob away. Try lowering your standards."

He almost hung up before the caller said, "Men who love me get hurt."

"What?" Something in the delivery tore him apart. He tried to stay professional, keep it on the easy track. "Do they get hurt, or do you hurt them? Bet you're a real heartbreaker."

"I shouldn't have called."

"Wait." Will reflexively rubbed the bridge of his nose. "Sorry, man. You call me looking for comfort, and I tear you down. Let me confess something to you. I'm no Casanova myself, you know? So tell me your troubles."

The hesitation was exquisite. "I can't."

"Yes, you can. No one knows who you are, friend. Not even me." He spoke gently, desperate to rectify his own goading. Ratings be damned. "Let it go. Don't punish yourself. Whatever happened to your lovers, I doubt it was your fault."

"It is my fault," the caller insisted. "I'm cursed."

Cursed? That was a new one. Will floundered for something sane to say. "You just haven't found Mr. Right yet. Trust me on this. There's a man out there waiting for you to save him from the big empty, and he won't charge you for it. Take your time."

"Good-bye, Will." A scant breath sketched the words. The caller hung up.

Tears pricked his eyes, and for a moment he forgot Tess, the show, the hotlines, even Lyle. The caller's tortured confession filled his being. Those final words had seemed so personal. He wanted to be the one he'd told the caller to look for—Mr. Right, true love, no charge. He wanted to be hurt, and healed, by the owner of that haunted voice. And to heal his doubt in return.

Will shook himself. It was just a call, and there were more waiting. On with the show.

* * *

Cobalt glowered at the lump of plastic in his hand. The damned phone mocked him with silence. Why had he called? Stupid, to believe a voice he found pleasing would bring him comfort or salvation. He would have neither.

"*Don't punish yourself.*" Easy enough for Will Ambrose to say. But how could he not hold himself responsible? He'd driven two men to insanity and one to his death. A commitment to him spelled disaster. None of them were strong enough. None would ever be.

A knock at his door bled the contemplation from him. "Hey, Cobalt. Your nine o'clock's early. Want her to wait?"

"Yes. And tell her to buy a watch." Cobalt smiled despite his lingering bitterness. Apprenticing Malik had been one of the few things he'd done right. Most shops had turned down the youth because of his age—a barely legal eighteen—but in just a few weeks Malik had become indispensable at the Grotto. He followed every rule, without question, no matter how bizarre it seemed. Of necessity, Cobalt set strange rules. He could not risk discovery.

"You got it." Malik retreated into the shop.

Cobalt sighed and ran a hand through his hair. He hadn't planned to degrade himself with a whore tonight, but after his foolish indulgence in self-pity, he craved release. He reached for the phone.

It rang.

He frowned. No one had his private number. *Will?* Perhaps the radio host with the irresistible voice had lied about not knowing who he was—or at least where he was calling from. He debated not answering, but curiosity prompted him to pick up with a brusque "yes."

"Ciaràn. Have you found satisfaction?"

Cobalt closed his eyes against the needle of familiarity that lanced his belly. "I don't want to know how you found me. Leave me alone."

"It was not difficult. These human devices are simple enough."

He almost hung up then. After a decade of forgetting, contact with the Fae who had orchestrated his punishment after he'd left the bastard threatened to overload his senses. "What do you want?" he made himself say.

"Everything you denied me."

"I'm banished, Eoghann. Is that not enough for you?"

"You know it is not."

A shudder wormed through his core. He'd forgotten how cold Eoghann could be—his voice, his touch. Frigid as a winter wind. It took everything he had to reply, "My answer is the same. I won't be yours."

"Ah, Ciaràn." The reproach in his tone was unmistakable. "Ten years submerged in human filth, and still you deny your place. How much further must you be punished?"

"I'll not play this game with you."

"Things have changed. I have changed." Eoghann's voice softened to a purr. "Let me come to you. Invite me inside."

His heart stammered. How close was he? At least the Laws still held. No other Fae could enter the Grotto without an invitation from his lips. He would be safe. "No, Eoghann. I'll not see you. A thousand decades won't change my mind." He clenched the phone so tight, he feared he'd break it. "Don't contact me again."

He disconnected. An urge to destroy the device that had wounded him twice tonight came and left, and he dropped the phone on his desk. *Eoghann.* Why now? After ten years, the Unseelie queen's consort should have found another lowborn wretch to amuse himself with. Perhaps he'd just been feeling nostalgic and another decade would pass before he bothered to torment him further. Time meant nothing in the Fae realm. And Eoghann was too shallow and self-absorbed to expend much effort in the pursuit of one worthless plaything when there were so many he could choose to break instead.

Regardless of his plans, Eoghann couldn't touch him as Cobalt. He'd realize that soon enough and give up wasting his time. Ciaràn no longer existed.

Chapter Two

Will put a hand over the glass on the bar and blinked blearily at the bartender. "She really doesn't need another drink."

"Yes I do. Move, 'bana-boy." Tess leaned over and nearly fell off her stool. She laughed. "You need another one too. You're dry."

"No, I don't."

"Drink," she insisted. "Last one. Promise."

Will sighed and uncovered the glass. "Two more Jäger bombs. Please." At least the alcohol dulled his aches. After this, he'd take Tess home and drag himself to his apartment. And sleep until tomorrow night's show.

He watched the bartender flick liquid into glasses with practiced ease, then glanced at the neon clock behind the bar. One in the morning. Lyle would've expected him to come home two hours ago. He'd debated calling after the show, telling him he'd be late, but he needed to prove that he wasn't a kept man. He had to know that when he got back, there would be no shouting or accusations. Just two adults in a stable relationship, with a little rough stuff on the side.

Finished drinks materialized on the bar. Tess grabbed hers, sloshed a little. Jäger tentacles crept through the outer ring of Red Bull like the sweet poison it was. "Let's drink to you," she said. "To *The Truth*. May your ratings…rate."

"Rate?" Will raised an eyebrow. "You're drunk, Tess. Did you know?"

"Yep! So're you."

"Yes I am." No use questioning that little factoid. He lifted his glass. "To *The Truth*. May it rate. Or something."

They downed the bombs in tandem. Her glass clinked on the bar half a second before his. She grinned. "Wuss."

"Boozer."

"Killjoy."

"Reprobate."

Tess blinked. "What's that?"

"Dunno. Can't find my dictionary." He pushed his empty glass forward, dug in his pocket, and came up with two twenties to slap on the bar. "C'mon, I'll take you home."

She shook her head. "I got a better idea."

"Better than sleep?"

"Way." A crooked smile lit her face. "I've always wanted a tattoo."

"Huh-uh. No way." Will held up a finger. "One, you're wasted. Two"—he stared at his hand until another finger joined the first—"it's one. In the morning."

"And?"

"There's no place open."

"Yes, there is. The Grotto."

"You're crazy." He grabbed her arm and tried to help her down from the stool. She didn't budge. "Nobody gets in there. There's a three-month list. Besides, there's the eleventh commandment, y'know. Thou shalt never tattoo drunk." He formed the words carefully, aware of his own delirious intoxication. The last bomb was hitting hard.

"Y'mean *screw* drunk." Tess slid from the stool and into him. He had just enough presence of mind to turn away while he winced. "It's thou shill...that word. Never screw drunk."

"Close enough. They rhyme."

"Screw the tattoo." She snorted laughter. "No, seriously. I can get us in. My brother's roommate works there now. And you're famous, remember?"

"Sure. Beating off fans with a stick, that's me."

"You definitely make fans beat off, stud." She smiled, splayed a hand on his chest. "How many offers you get tonight?"

He staggered a bit. "Stop. Really, Tess, I've got to get home."

"Will." Her eyes narrowed. "You do not. That jerk doesn't own you."

"It's not him." Even as he protested, he knew it was. Lyle would be pissed. He hated the radio admirers, hated drinking, hated Tess. Hated everything that Will loved about his life. He was wrong for him on so many levels.

"Whatsa matter, William? Chains a little snug tonight?"

Something inside Will hardened. "You know me. I like it rough." He slung his good arm around her and steered her through the crowded bar. "Let's go see how much clout your brother's roommate has. Maybe we can get something pierced."

A sharp pain in his chest suggested his heart had started on the plan without him.

* * *

Will tried calling Lyle from the cab. No answer. He figured he must be asleep, which was fine with him. He really didn't want to face Lyle shitfaced and late after a night with Tess.

The cab deposited them outside the Grotto. Will had passed the place a few times—it was twenty blocks or so from his apartment in Chelsea. The front was unremarkable enough. It didn't even look like a tattoo parlor. Absent the flash art and neon signage, this plain brick building with the single wooden, windowless door could have been anything. But from what he'd heard, it was the inside that really set the Grotto apart.

Cool night air combined with anger and self-disgust had contrived to sober him more effectively than a cold shower. Unfortunately, it hadn't done the same for Tess. She stumbled along beside him, grinning like a conspirator. "Always wanted to come here," she said. "The Dub got his septal done at this place. Said they'd never do me. They're *exclusive.*"

Will stifled a groan. *The Dub* referred to Double X, Tess's on-again, off-again boyfriend and the occasional bane of her existence. Right now he was off. So this *was* a revenge tattoo. He couldn't let her go through with it, even if they somehow got in. She'd definitely regret it in the morning.

Before he could suggest a less scarring alternative, like sticking a hot poker up her ass, she threw the front door open and barreled inside.

He cursed and hurried after her. Beyond the door was a room with a wooden table and chair, and nothing else. Not even Tess. A stamp pad and an open notebook lay on the table. Muffled music entered the room through another door at the back. She must have gone in there.

He slipped through. His first impressions consisted of dark and nightclub and where-the-hell-is-Tess. After a panicked few seconds, he spotted her to his right, one arm slung companionably around a slight, dusky-skinned pretty boy who sported a bemused smile.

"Will!" She shouted above the music, much louder in here, and waved him over. When he joined the pair, she said, "This is Frank's roommate, Milk."

The boy laughed, held a hand out. "Malik," he said. "You must be Will Ambrose." A whisper of cultured accent flavored his words and made him sound older than he looked.

"Yes. Nice to meet you." Will shook quickly. "Hope we're not interrupting."

"Not at all. I've heard a lot about you." Malik favored Tess with a grin, and his eyes shifted to the sling. "What happened to your arm?"

"Crashed my board." The excuse slipped out automatically. He tried to relax and get a better feel for the place. His initial assessment hadn't been too far off. It looked like a nightclub in here, a Goth's dream of darkness shot with red and amber lights. Tables with cushioned chairs dotted the spacious room. Three vending machines stocked with vitamin water, energy drinks, snacks, novelties, and single-serve OTC drugs served as silent bartenders. Thick, velvet-bound books graced each table, attached to the center with heavy chains.

Will watched a nearby patron open a book. It was full of photographic images—tattoos and piercings from ordinary to erotic. Samples of work done at the Grotto. One image in particular caught his eye: a male torso with impressive musculature. A seven-point-star tattoo sprawled across the chest. Intricate knot work formed the center of the symbol, and tendrils radiated from the knot to twine gracefully around the edges of the points. The page bore a single word below the photo. *Cobalt.* Strange, because the design didn't contain any blue. Maybe it was the name of the pattern.

He looked up and forgot what he'd been about to ask when he finally realized what set this shop apart. Live entertainment.

Three immense panels stood spaced apart at the far end of the room, peep-show-style windows that showcased the artists at work. One contained a completely nude female having her back inked. In another, an older man grimaced through a Prince Albert piercing. But it was center stage that grabbed Will completely and refused to let go. Behind the glass, a tall and imposing artist worked on his subject with a knife.

He knew a little about scarification. Popular with the BDSM crowd, the method had recently gained some popularity in the general public. He'd even considered it himself, but there were few skilled artists and too many risks involved. And it hurt. Still, he'd heard nothing negative about the Grotto.

And that artist was a piece of work himself. Even from a distance, the man exuded sexuality in the curve of his stance and the fluid grace of his hands. At once, Will longed to see the face that went with the body.

Malik caught him staring and smiled. "That's Cobalt."

"Jesus. That's his *name?*" The idea struck him as intensely sexy. No Tom, Dick, or Harry for this guy.

"Yes. He owns the Grotto. The rest of us generally bask in his glory."

Will looked at the kid, trying to decide whether he was being sarcastic. He seemed completely sincere. "Right," he said. "Well, I think I should take Tess home now." He held his breath and hoped she wouldn't protest. He really didn't want to drag her out.

She blinked a few times at the mention of her name. "Gonna sit down," she murmured—and promptly slid to the floor.

"Damn." Will crouched beside her and touched her shoulder. "Tess. C'mon, we have to get going. Can you walk, hon?"

"Unngh."

"I'll take that as a no." He sighed, glanced up at Malik. "Sorry about this. Give me just a minute, and I'll get her out of here."

"I'll help you."

"No, it's okay," he said. Tess would be mortified enough as it was, if this little story got back to her brother. He should've insisted on not coming here.

Will flexed his injured wrist. The pain wasn't as bad as he feared—a good thing, since he'd need both arms to move her. He slid the knotted end of the bandanna sling off his shoulder, stuffed it in a pocket, and braced Tess with his good arm around her waist. "Up we go, darlin'," he said gently. "Ready?"

She didn't reply. He hadn't expected her to. He rose slowly, bearing her up with awkward jerks, and finally straightened with a grunt of effort. She moaned, leaned her head on his shoulder. And vomited all over him.

"Oh God." Will fought the violent urging of his stomach to follow her example. "Oh, shit. I'm so sorry. I'll clean this up. Can she just…?"

"Let me take her." There wasn't a trace of anger or disgust in Malik's voice. He scooped Tess away as though she weighed nothing, and guided her to a nearby chair. Once he'd settled her in, he turned and walked toward the back of the room.

Will stood frozen in place for a moment. Sensations battered him: the hot gazes of staring patrons, the rapidly cooling liquid soaking his shirt and pants. The stench of half-digested food and alcohol mingled with bile, and the throbbing burn of his embarrassment. He would never live this down.

He forced away the shock, determined to salvage what he could of his dignity. At least she'd mostly missed his jacket. He peeled it off, then lifted his soiled shirt up his back and over his head, turning it inside out. That done, he shrugged back into the jacket and gave the front of his pants a futile swipe. At least they were just wet. He knelt, tuned out his lurching stomach, and attempted to mop the thick puddles on the polished wood floor with his shirt.

"What are you doing?"

The voice behind him didn't belong to Malik. Will stiffened, grateful for the darkness that hid his flushed face and neck. "My friend wasn't feeling too good," he said with hollow cheer. "So I'm playing nurse."

"Don't bother. We're closing. Malik will clean that up."

The harsh words were knives twisting in his chest. He bunched the sopping shirt as best he could and slowly got to his feet. "I'm really sorry about this," he said. "Honestly, I don't mind taking care of it. If you have a mop, or..." He turned to face the angry voice and immediately wished himself dead.

Cobalt.

He'd never seen a more beautiful man. As exotic as his name suggested, the artist possessed waves of blue-black hair and dark blue, glittering eyes in a sculpted, golden-skinned face. Tribal tattoos graced the sides of his neck and caressed his jawline. One ear was studded with hardware from upper edge to lobe, while the other sported a single silver hoop. A lower lip piercing, a position Will had always found slightly repulsive, looked natural and stunning on him. Especially with his full, firm mouth set in such a deep scowl.

Next to this dark god, Will felt like a pile of shit. Probably smelled like one too.

Cobalt's brow furrowed, and then his features relaxed in surprise. "Will?"

The whispered word sent shudders through him. Recognition buzzed a few synapses in his addled brain and promptly fizzled away. "Do I...know you?"

"You're Will Ambrose." Somehow, the statement was an accusation.

He tried to shrug. "Most of the time. But tonight I'm just an asshole wrecking your place. I'm sorry. You don't have to close because of me."

"I'm done for the night." Cobalt glanced beyond him, into the shadows. "What are you doing here?"

"I..." *Making an ass of myself.* He became vaguely aware of Malik's shepherding people out the front door. Fresh shame coursed through him as he felt them blaming him for cutting their entertainment short. "My friend, Tess." He made a lame gesture in the direction of her unconscious figure, slumped and snoring gently in the chair. "She got a little drunk and decided she wanted a tattoo."

Anger returned to Cobalt's face. "I don't take walk-ins. And I don't tattoo intoxicated people, under any circumstances."

"I know. I tried to talk her out of it." He hadn't tried very hard, though. When would he stop letting people walk all over him? Something told him Malik would be in trouble if he mentioned their acquaintance, so he left the kid out of it. "She just barged right in. I followed her."

"I see." Another glance beyond, a shake of his head. "And what about yourself? Are you interested in body art or just humoring your friend?"

He swallowed hard. The thought of Cobalt's hands on his body consumed him, left him semierect. He shuffled in place. Freezing wetness at his crotch reminded him that he was standing there covered in vomit, and his lustful thoughts shriveled.

Cobalt inclined his head, waiting for an answer. Will opened his mouth to say *not really*, but what emerged was, "I didn't know you were into scarification here."

"Of course." A speculative look eased across his features. "If you're considering it, I'll make you a consultation appointment."

He almost said no. But considering the disaster he'd inflicted on the man's business, he decided to at least feign interest. Three months would be plenty of time to call and cancel. No way in hell could he ever show his face here again. "Thanks," he said. "That sounds great."

Cobalt nodded. "Tomorrow. Three p.m. Make a note, Malik."

Tomorrow? Will's eyes bugged after Malik as the kid scurried off to follow orders. "Hold on," he said weakly. "I thought you had a mile-long list…"

A smirk teased those beautiful lips. "I do. But you're a local celebrity, Mr. Ambrose. You'd make a great advertisement for the Grotto. A walking billboard."

The brief idea that Cobalt liked him, even a little, sputtered and died. Of course it was about business—and how could he refuse, after the stunt he and Tess had pulled? "All right." He tried to cover the defeat in his voice. He wasn't sure if it worked. "Tomorrow at three. Thank you."

That gave him around twelve hours to come up with a viable excuse for not going through with it. He didn't think he could stand to let this man touch him for long. And Lyle would kill him if he had it done.

Lyle. Jesus, he was going to be pissed.

"Malik." Cobalt waved the kid over. "Get Mr. Ambrose a bag for his shirt, and hail them a cab. I'll assume you plan to take your friend home?"

It took Will a minute to realize Cobalt had addressed him. "Yes. I'm sorry."

"Stop apologizing." Cobalt's gaze shifted again, and he called, "Trystan. Come with me."

Confusion washed over Will, until a slight figure glided past him from behind and moved to Cobalt's side. The young man was in his twenties, shorter than Will, with a lithe and compact body showcased in tight black vinyl. Pale blue eyes stared apathetically from a cherubic face fringed with corn-silk hair.

Cobalt draped a possessive arm around the vinyl-clad angel. Marking his territory. As if Will needed a sign to know he was taken. "Don't forget," he said. "Tomorrow."

"No. I mean, I won't." Silently, he willed Cobalt to take his beautiful lover away. He couldn't endure another minute of this humiliation—and he couldn't leave without Tess.

Finally, the man steered Trystan toward the back of the room. He paused once to glance over his shoulder. "Good-bye, Will."

Once again a tickle of recognition teased his mind. He knew he hadn't met Cobalt—he damned well would've remembered *him*—but something about him seemed painfully familiar. Had he seen his work before? Heard someone mention his name? His exhausted brain refused to concentrate, and he turned his attention to Tess instead.

It didn't matter, anyway. After he made his excuses tomorrow, he'd never see the man called Cobalt again.

Chapter Three

Trystan stood in the center of the bedroom, silent and still because Cobalt hadn't told him anything yet. His favorite whore knew his preferences and would stand there all night unless he was told otherwise.

But Cobalt couldn't bring himself to take Trystan. Not after meeting Will Ambrose.

His first thought had been that the radio host knew he'd called after all, and had come to torment him with the knowledge. But he'd realized almost instantly that the story of placating his drunken friend was the truth. His presence here had been mere coincidence.

He also realized the photo on the station's Web site didn't begin to do him justice. The image failed to capture his amazing body. More than that, Will in person possessed a kindness and inner strength that made him glow. If humans had visible auras, his would rival the golden summer sun.

Now, Cobalt had compounded his earlier mistake of calling, and invited the delicious Will Ambrose back to the Grotto. For a one-on-one consultation.

He supposed he'd expected the man to refuse. After all, he truly hadn't seemed the type to commission body art. Will didn't even sport a single stud. He was completely clean and unmarked. When he'd mentioned scarification with such casual ease, Cobalt experienced a carnal thrill that eclipsed all previous lust. He would have claimed him then and there, were it not for the company.

But he could never become involved with Will. Perhaps not even as a client. He couldn't bear to douse another spark of human life—particularly one so bright.

Frustration fueled his hunger. He rose from the bed and stripped himself, watching Trystan watch him from the corner of his eye. "Undress," he said.

Trystan complied without a word. He stood there, naked, waiting. His for the taking.

In his mind, Cobalt went to him. He didn't bother with the bed. Just pressed him against the wall and ravished his body, relieved that gnawing beast in his loins. The one that craved Will Ambrose. In his mind, he saw Will's body. Will's face.

In reality, he turned his back on Trystan. "Leave."

"Cobalt, are you sure—"

"Leave me!"

To his credit, Trystan didn't even ask for payment.

* * *

By the time Will dragged himself into his apartment, it was after four in the morning. He wanted nothing more than to strip, crawl into bed—hopefully without waking Lyle— and forget this night had ever happened. He closed the front door, cringing when the click of the lock resounded like a hammer through his head, and got four steps across the floor before he noticed the silhouette sitting on the couch.

"You must've lost your phone." Lyle's voice unfurled in the stillness. He sounded calm, quiet, and composed.

That was not a good sign.

"I'm sorry." In comparison, Will sounded like he'd swallowed gravel. "I tried to call. Check your cell. I went out with Tess, and we lost track—" He cut off with a wince as light flared from the lamp beside the couch.

Lyle stood. He was wearing his uniform.

Will tried to blink the spots away from his eyes. "Are you going to work early?"

"No." His lover offered no explanation. He approached with measured steps, stopped. His face crinkled. "What is that stench? Did you roll around in a gutter?"

A flush scorched his cheeks. "Tess threw up on me," he muttered.

"Jesus Christ, Will. That's disgusting." Lyle stepped back, as though his stink were contagious. "Go take a shower."

Fuck you. I'm going to bed. The retort refused to pass his lips. Despite his exhaustion, it wouldn't be fair to make Lyle sleep next to him like this. If he even planned on going to sleep. He wasn't completely decked out for work yet—no gun or CB or any of his other cop paraphernalia on his belt. Just his cuffs.

"All right," he finally said. "Look, I'm really sorry. I won't forget to tell you next time."

"I know you won't."

Will blinked at him. That almost sounded like a threat. But he still seemed relaxed, like they'd been discussing the weather or the subway instead of Will's sneaking in six hours late, smelling like a used toilet. Maybe he wasn't upset after all. Maybe their relationship really wasn't as bad as he thought.

He considered kissing him on the cheek, a wordless punctuation for the apology, but decided he couldn't take Lyle flinching away from him. Instead, he moved through the living room without a word and stumbled into the bathroom. He closed the door and waited, half expecting a latent explosion from his partner.

Nothing. Not even footsteps or furniture creaking. The other shoe wasn't going to drop.

Relief drew a sigh from him. He stripped as fast as he could with arms that weighed a hundred pounds, and briefly considered burning his soiled jeans. He settled for burying them in the hamper. The smell would fade in time for Lyle to get ready for work, and he'd double wash the whole basket in hot tomorrow. Well, technically today.

The warmth of the shower sloughed most of the fatigue from him. With renewed clarity, his thoughts shifted to Cobalt. He'd just met the most beautiful man in New York— and he'd been drunk, filthy, and gate-crashing. So much for Will Ambrose, radio stud. He moaned and pressed a wet fist to his mouth. The next time Tess had a bright idea, he'd let her immolate herself with it instead of dragging him into the flames.

He'd still have to deal with Cobalt one more time. To cancel the damned appointment. He would look up the number and call. No way in hell was he going to risk being within a block of the Grotto ever again. If the embarrassment didn't kill him, a sober eyeful of the beautiful artist might.

He fumbled for the soap and washed quickly, at once more exhausted than he'd been when he got home. Maybe after a few decent hours of sleep, he could face the rest of his life. He shut the water off, slid the shower curtains aside.

And came face-to-face with Lyle.

"Jesus!" Will lurched back and almost fell in the tub. Lyle stood motionless, expressionless. He was still in uniform. "What are you doing, trying to kill me?"

A small smile appeared on Lyle's face. He reached over and grabbed a towel from the bar near the door. "Just thought I'd help you dry off," he said. "Come on out."

Will shuddered. It was the air on his wet skin, he told himself, not the eeriness of Lyle's creeping into the bathroom to stand in silence until he'd finished showering. Nothing weird about that.

He stepped out. Lyle unfolded the towel, draped it around his shoulders, and started rubbing. Gently. Sensually. "Much better," he murmured near Will's ear.

"Mmm." Will surrendered to his partner's ministrations. Warmth spread through him, made his eyelids heavy. He rested his head on Lyle's shoulder. The towel moved down. Hands cupped his ass through terry cloth and pressed his groin against an arousal. *Not now*, he wanted to say. *Tired.* He could fall asleep right here. Maybe he would. But he had to know something first. "Lyle," he whispered.

"What is it, babe?"

Will hesitated. "Why are you wearing your uniform?"

He didn't answer.

"Lyle…" Will lifted his head. "Please tell me what's going on."

Lyle moved his hands. The towel fell away, and a chill raised gooseflesh on Will's skin. This time he couldn't blame it entirely on temperature. He stiffened and stood straight. Something cold nudged his wrist. A metallic *clink* sounded in the damp air.

Will glanced down. Lyle had snapped one of his cuffs on him.

"What the hell—"

It was all he got out before Lyle seized his arm and hauled him to the empty towel bar. Shock prevented him from reacting immediately. Within seconds Lyle had forced his hands out and cuffed his other wrist, the one that was already injured, securing him to the bar. Dull pain flared through his arm.

Will's lips moved, but no sound emerged. At last he forced his tongue to cooperate. "Is this a joke? Because it's not funny."

"I'm not laughing."

The frigid tone lodged in his gut. Will turned his head and glared at the stone-faced man behind him. "Take them off. I'm going to bed."

"No, you're not."

"Damn it, Lyle!" He jerked back. The short chain clanked against the towel bar, and his wrist screamed.

"Unlock these fucking things," he said through clenched teeth. "Right now."

"Not until I'm done with you."

"Are you stupid? I'm not in the mood. If you need to get off, you've got two hands. Use them." He faced the wall again, unable to look at the bastard anymore. After this little stunt, Lyle would have to jerk off a lot more often. No way he was going to sleep with him for a long time. "Open the goddamned cuffs."

Lyle moved closer. He put both hands on the wall, bracketing Will beneath him, and leaned his head down. "I'm not going to fuck you, Will." His voice simmered with steel-edged malice. "I'm going to punish you."

A wave of sick fear coursed through him. His legs weakened, and he stumbled against the wall. "Jesus," he whispered. "You can't be serious."

In response, Lyle drew back and smacked his ass hard with an open hand. Will yelped. Lyle clamped a palm over his mouth and pushed back, holding his head against his chest. "Shut up," he said in a flat tone. "If you can't be quiet, I'll gag you."

His head throbbed madly. He fought the panic urging him to struggle, forced himself to breathe through his nose. *This is not happening.* Endless seconds dragged, until Lyle finally dropped the hand from his mouth. Will drew a shaking breath and tasted bile. "Let me go, Lyle," he said. "You can't do this."

Another stinging smack left him too stunned to make a sound. "I can, and I will. You asked for this."

Will swallowed against the metallic dryness coating his throat. "You're crazy. I didn't—"

"Shut up!" He swatted again, harder this time. Will's breath hitched. "You've been begging for this, Will. Ever since I met you. Everything you say, everything you *do*"—he slapped the statement home, eliciting a choked sob—"says you need to be punished. So I'm going to give you what you need. And you're going to learn to behave."

"Oh God. Lyle, please..." He was babbling now. He couldn't help it. "I'm not... I don't... Please. Let's just go to bed, okay? I'm sorry about the hand thing. And Tess, even. We can—"

"You're six hours too late to apologize."

"Fucking open the fucking cuffs!" Panic surged over him. He thrashed back, cried out when the chain snapped taut and sent agony flaring through his wrist. He gripped the bar with his good hand and tried to wrench it from the wall. It didn't budge. "Goddamn it, let me go!"

Lyle reached around and shoved something hard in his mouth, mashing his tongue back. He tasted vinyl. A strap tightened around the back of his head. His breath wheezed and stuttered around the obstruction. A ball gag.

"I warned you to be quiet." The hand smacked him again and again in steady rhythm that throbbed progressively worse. He wasn't going to stop. Will twisted and squirmed, trying to escape the punishing blows. The gag muffled a string of cries and curses. "Hold still," Lyle growled. "You're only making this worse for yourself."

Will sobbed. *Stop stop stop stop damn it please stop...* His ass felt like it was on fire. Lyle struck him square in the center, and he choked on a scream, danced aside. *Stop it, sick bastard, just STOP!*

A heavy sigh sounded from behind him. "Fine," Lyle said. "We'll do this the hard way."

Will didn't want to know what the hard way was. He had to make this stop. He stood still, his breath coming in shuddering pants, and looked wildly from side to side. Door to the left. Tub and shower to the right. In front of him, a tiled wall—behind him, a madman. He lunged left, raised a leg, and kicked the door. It shuddered and held shut. He kicked again, ignoring the new pain in his foot. Something splintered, but he couldn't tell whether it was wood or bone.

"Enough." Lyle grabbed him around the waist and lifted him off the floor. He walked back and to the right, toward the shower. The cuffs scraped along the towel bar. Tucking Will under an arm like so much laundry, he sat on the edge of the tub and hauled him over his lap. "I'm going to spank you, Will. You deserve it."

Will bucked and kicked. He pushed at the gag with his tongue. Saliva flooded his mouth and ran down his throat, half choking him. He decided to forget the gag for now and concentrate on kicking.

Lyle shifted beneath him and slung one leg over both of his, pinning him in place. "Anytime you want to stop struggling, let me know, and I'll move my leg."

You fuck. You stupid, stupid fuck. Black spots burst and spread across Will's vision. He wasn't getting any oxygen, because he was panting against the gag. He switched to breathing through his nose and tried to calm his racing heart. *Should've listened to Tess, jackass.* But it didn't matter anymore. He was here; he couldn't escape. All he could do now was take whatever punishment Lyle decided to give him.

A hand came to rest lightly on his burning ass. He flinched. His entire body trembled.

"Are you going to behave?"

Will shook his head fiercely. *Hell no.*

"Fine."

He sensed the arm rise, and closed his eyes just before the first swat landed. There were no pauses between blows this time, no taunts or insults. Lyle spanked methodically— left, right, left, right. Harder and harder. The pain jarred his spine with every smack. He held the bar with his good hand as best he could to keep his weight from pulling on his wrist. After five minutes, tears leaked from his eyes and snot drizzled over his top lip, seeped into his mouth around the gag.

After fifteen, he couldn't even hold up his head.

When Lyle finally stopped, it took Will a minute to realize he wasn't being hit anymore. His ass still throbbed. Sluggish pain pulsed through his groin at regular intervals like a heartbeat. The heat had become an inferno. He'd never known you could *feel* red.

At some point Lyle had unpinned him. He lay spent and shaking across the man's lap, torso angled up and deadened arms stretching to the bar, head hanging. Dried tears and mucus coated his face. The absence of rhythmic, meaty slaps forged a silence that echoed in his skull, punctuated with ragged snorts of air whistling through his nostrils.

Fingers brushed the back of his head. The strap on the gag tightened, then came loose. Will spat the ball out and drew a gasping breath. Fresh tears doubled his vision. He focused on the damned gag. There were teeth marks in its bright red surface, glistening in a layer of saliva flecked with blood.

He concentrated on breathing. In and out, in and out. When the ominous gurgling in the back of his throat eased, he said, "Let me go. Now." He barely recognized the rasping croak that was his voice.

Lyle pushed him to the floor.

He landed hard. A scream wrenched from his throat as pain tore through his arms. Before he could scramble away, Lyle grabbed him by the hair and yanked him to his feet. "You haven't learned anything, have you?"

"Fuck you," Will spat. "I swear to God I'll…"

"You'll what? Are you trying to threaten me?" Before he could react, Lyle brought an arm up and backhanded him.

Will's head bounced off the wall. He tasted blood. Once again, words failed him, and he could only stare at the beast he'd taken for a lover.

"You'll learn." Lyle stepped back with a grim smirk. "I told you before that you were making things worse for yourself. Now you're about to find out why." He bent and retrieved the gag. "You're going to need this again."

The loaded statement drained every ounce of bravado from him. "No," he whispered. "Lyle, please. No more…"

Lyle shook his head in mock sympathy. "Maybe next time you'll listen to me."

"No! Please. Whatever you want—"

The ball smothered the rest of his pleading. Lyle cinched the gag tight, leaned over him. "I want you to learn your lesson," he whispered. And moved away.

Will stiffened. When no blows came, he turned his head slowly, shaking hard enough to rattle the short chain of the handcuffs.

Behind him, Lyle was removing his belt.

Chapter Four

Will couldn't figure out why it was so cold.

Light lay heavy against his closed eyelids. He didn't want to open them. Did he have a hangover? Probably. The bed seemed as hard as cement under him. Nausea filled his pores and clogged his throat. If he moved, he'd puke.

Must've been a wild night. He shuffled back through memories, remembered getting drunk with Tess. And her deciding she wanted a tattoo. She'd dragged him to the Grotto, vomited all over him—

At once the rest of the night flooded back. His body recalled the beating, and pain sank burning claws into him. His eyes stayed closed because they were gummed shut. He was cold because he was still lying on the bathroom floor, naked and covered with bruises and welts from Lyle's hands and Lyle's belt.

The bastard must have unlocked the cuffs so he could take them to work. Will remembered passing out, still chained to the towel bar, sometime during round three. After his first go with the belt, Lyle had decided to fuck him after all. He'd taken him raw and dry. To Will, half-blind with pain and humiliation, it had felt like being raped with a baseball bat.

He risked shifting an arm. The movement sent ripples of pain through him. A startled cry ended when nausea won out, and he ejected half a quart of hot acid from his lips. Tears dissolved some of the crust from his eyes. One of them popped open. When it focused, he stared at the blood and vomit and God knew what other bodily fluids splashed across the floor. Maybe he would just lie here until he died.

But Lyle would come back eventually, and he didn't want to be here when that happened.

He clenched his jaw and tried the arm again. The pain was half a shade lighter this time. At least he didn't have anything left to throw up, but a few dry heaves slowed his progress. He managed to rise as far as hands and knees—then wavered and went back down. A cracked sob left him. This was not good. He had to get up.

From what he could see without lifting his head, the shower was behind him and to his left. He planted his forearms on the floor and slid himself back in short bursts until a foot touched the bathtub. A few more pushes put him alongside the tub. He raised his right arm, propped it on the edge, and levered to his knees.

Better. Still, he could barely move. Maybe a quick shower would loosen enough of his cramped muscles to let him stand. He clambered over the side, careful not to let his ass touch anything, and knelt in the middle of the tub. The tap stuck for a moment and gave him time to study the angry red abrasions circling both wrists.

When the water warmed, he flipped on the shower. Screamed. And slammed it off.

Note to self: don't shower after a beating. The water felt like nails being hammered into his back. Slowly, he regained control of his breathing and scuttled forward. He cupped his hands under the flow from the faucet and washed most of the gunk from his face. The wet warmth soothed his skin and cleared some of the fog from his head. Maybe he could handle a bath.

He flicked the tub plunger down and watched water pool in the porcelain dimple of the drain. He'd have to stay on his stomach. He waited while the tub filled, reminding himself that soap and shampoo were out. When the water level reached his back, pain escalated to a brief screaming pitch and subsided slowly. He drew a shaking breath, turned the faucet off.

After a moment, pale crimson tendrils infiltrated the water. The welts were bleeding.

Will ducked his head under and tried to work out whatever had dried in his hair. He remained submerged as long as he could stand the steady burning against his torn and exposed skin. It wasn't long. Two or three minutes. He let the dirty pink water out, braced his hands on the edge of the tub, and stood.

Lyle had hung the towel back on the bar. How psychoneurotic of him.

He dried his face and arms but couldn't bring himself to touch anywhere else with the rough terry cloth. Instead, he limped to the closet across the hall, dripping everywhere, and found the cotton robe he hadn't worn in months. It would work for now. He slipped it on and tried to ignore the renewed fire in his backside when the material brushed him.

Will headed for the bedroom. He dreaded putting clothes on. Especially underwear. What would hurt his battered ass less—silk or cotton? Silk, he thought, would at least be cool for a few seconds.

He finally settled on silk—boxers and shirt—with an oversize rayon undershirt that hung past his wrists and loose cotton pants. Dressing proved excruciating, but he felt a little better when he was done. Until he remembered that his boyfriend had just beaten the shit out of him...and since said boyfriend was a cop, he couldn't report it to the police. He couldn't go to Tess either. Lyle knew where she lived.

His eye caught the clock, which read 2:25. He'd been passed out on the bathroom floor for at least eight hours. Maybe longer. The vague idea that he was supposed to be somewhere soon prompted another search of his fuzzy memory. It came to him fast: Cobalt and his three-o'clock appointment. The one he planned to cancel.

Because it would keep him from having to make another decision for a few minutes, he shuffled over to the dresser and pulled the phone book from the top drawer. He would call and tell him... What?

Sorry, I can't come in. My partner just tattooed me with his belt, so I don't need your services after all.

He flipped to the yellow pages, found the Grotto. He expected the listing to be bigger, with graphics and slick slogans, but it was just a simple two-line entry. The Grotto and the number. If it weren't listed under *tattoo parlors*, no one would know what the place was. He grabbed the landline phone on the nightstand and dialed. When it started ringing, he glanced in the mirror.

A stranger looked back at him. He wore something that resembled his face—if it had been stripped from his skull and then stapled back on. His cheekbone was bruised where Lyle had backhanded him. Rough patches decorated with flecks of dried blood marked the corners of his mouth, souvenirs from the ball gag. Damp hair had plastered against his skull in stiff, uneven spikes. His eyes were glassed over, empty.

He realized the phone had rung at least twenty times and no one picked up. Damn it. How could he cancel an appointment if no one answered his call? He gave it another five rings and hung up. Forget it, he told himself. He'd just let Cobalt wonder briefly why he didn't show up. It wasn't like the man would remember him for long. Hell, he might even be glad that Will the Uncouth failed to make a return appearance, even without his Amazing Vomiting Friend. But there was his reputation to consider.

What reputation? He couldn't do the show tonight. He sure as hell couldn't sit through it. And he didn't see how he'd ever be able to offer advice to anyone again.

Will opened a drawer and rifled through it until he found a plain black bandanna he'd picked up a while back, before he had changed his mind about buying a motorcycle. He tied it around his head to hide his ruined hair, hesitated, and added mirrored sunglasses. With a stop in the spattered bathroom for his jacket, he headed out with no particular destination. Except maybe throwing himself in front of a subway train.

* * *

Cobalt held his breath until the phone stopped ringing. Ridiculous, he knew, but he didn't want to risk encountering Eoghann again. Without Malik here to screen calls for him, he'd not take the chance. His business wouldn't suffer from a few missed phone calls.

He stood and paced the front room. His gaze strayed to the clock on the wall. Half past two. Will would be here soon—and then what? He still didn't know what he would say to the man. *Excuse me, but I'd like to bend you over my desk and screw you* just didn't seem professional. Nor did confessing that he wanted to use that beautiful body for a canvas and never let another artist touch him.

Perhaps he should simply let Will do the talking and listen to that golden voice of his. It wouldn't be enough to quench the flames he'd ignited, but it might have to suffice. He would not allow himself to get involved. Under any circumstances. Will Ambrose would be safe from this curse.

Cobalt resumed a seat behind the stamping table. The windowless room was not the most cheerful of places during nonbusiness hours. Devoid of life, light, and sound, it became a limbo of sorts. Or a purgatory. The perfect prison for a banished Fae.

Not that he'd minded being banished. There was not much of the Fae realm he missed. Being a lowborn fatherless bastard didn't exactly afford him an easy life, or a happy one. He'd never understood why Eoghann had chosen to take his pleasures with him.

If he concentrated, he could see the luminous outlines of the seal he had placed on the entrance door. It hadn't been necessary—the Law held itself with spoken words—but still, he felt safer for having it there. While the Law prevented any Fae from entering without his permission, the seal had a more specific purpose. It targeted the Unseelie.

As though his reflections had summoned the world he'd left behind, Cobalt felt a whisper of magic penetrate the walls. Another Fae was near. It could have been any of the handful of Seelie he had granted haven to, for whatever reason. He was not the only outcast of the realm. But this magic felt wrong. Darker. *Eoghann.*

A phone rang. His cell this time, instead of the desk phone. He stood and stared at the door. If Eoghann were close enough, the seal should…

Glow. Light pulsed from the lines of the seal, growing stronger, until the room was bathed in blue-white brilliance. The distant ringing stopped.

Someone knocked on the door.

Cobalt froze. He could not face Eoghann in the flesh. Even as a voice on the phone, he'd been tempted to agree, to invite him inside. Face-to-face, he wouldn't stand a chance at refusal. Especially since Eoghann's magic was stronger—he was Unseelie and had lived five centuries longer. He willed the presence outside to leave.

The knocking sounded again. "*Haven.*" A magic-amplified voice penetrated the room. "*Please…help me.*"

That was not Eoghann. But it was also not Seelie. A deep frown etched itself on Cobalt's mouth. Why would an Unseelie seek haven from him? He debated not answering, but curiosity won out. "*Who are you?*" he called, infusing the words with just enough magic to filter outside.

A long hesitation. "*Uriskel.*"

Anger twisted in Cobalt's gut. Uriskel, traitor of traitors. "*There is no haven for you here,*" he said flatly. "*Go and crawl back into your hole.*"

"I beg you, Ciaràn." The voice grew ragged. "He means to kill me."

"Let him, then," he muttered under his breath. He opened the door, planning to explain to Uriskel that since hell had not, in fact, frozen over, he had no intention of granting him haven.

The tall figure outside wore a hooded cloak clutched about his frame with one hand. He wore no shoes. Blood drizzled down his leg from somewhere inside the covering and pooled beside one bare foot. "Knew you'd...see it my way," Uriskel said with a gasp. "Haven?"

"Damn." Cobalt caught his lip with his teeth. He couldn't leave anyone, even an Unseelie snake, to bleed to death. "All right. I'll invite you in, but you're not staying long. Understand?"

The figure nodded within the hood.

He almost felt bad about the caveat. "One more thing. My place is sealed, so when you step through, it's going to hurt."

"Wonderful. Can't wait." Uriskel coughed and wavered on his feet. He twisted to one side, as though he was glancing over his shoulder. "Hurry?"

Cobalt nodded. He moved aside and said, "Come in, Uriskel."

"That's it?" the Unseelie muttered. "No archaic words. Not even Gaelic…"

"Are you coming, or do you plan to feed all of New York's rats with your blood?"

"Coming." Uriskel stumbled forward and hesitated on the threshold. He drew a long breath. The hand holding the cloak shut fell away and the material parted, revealing a glimpse of torn and glistening flesh beneath tattered fabric. He stepped through.

A hoarse cry heaved from his lips. He managed four steps and dropped to his knees.

Cobalt closed the door and crouched beside the stricken Fae. "I am sorry about that," he said, "but you understand why I've done it."

"Ye-es. Gods, Ciaràn." Uriskel shivered. He pitched forward and thrust a hand out to stop himself from hitting the floor. "That's potent. Didn't know you…had it in you."

"It'll wear off in a minute." He almost removed the hood but thought better of it. "By the way, I go by Cobalt here. Call me anything else and I'll not answer."

"Lovely name. Really." Uriskel coughed again. The fit lasted longer, and just when it seemed he'd never stop, he shook himself and straightened. "I'm bleeding."

"How observant of you. Did you just notice?"

"Sympathetic as ever, I see." He pushed the hood back.

Cobalt couldn't help staring. Uriskel's glamour rendered him beautiful—probably to compensate for his horrific natural appearance, which tended to frighten grown men.

Burnished auburn hair framed a tanned and chiseled face. Luminous green eyes glowered at him.

As he watched, the face rippled and distorted. The illusion flickered like bad television reception, and the Unseelie's true face showed in snatches: pale blue skin, angled insectile features. Cold black eyes ringed with gold. Teeth like needles, bared in a grimace. He couldn't hold even a simple spell. No wonder he'd worn a hood.

The glamour solidified again. "Spare some magic?" Uriskel wheezed. "This hurts."

Good. The spiteful thought came and left. "Come on, then." Cobalt eased an arm under him and helped him to his feet. He guided him to the room's sole chair, settled him down. "Let's have a look."

"If you insist." Uriskel spread the cloak apart.

Cobalt sucked a harsh breath. Long, deep slashes scored his chest and stomach beneath the raveled remains of his shirt. There were too many to count, but they formed a recognizable pattern—an intricate Celtic knot that would have been beautiful if not for the manner in which it was made. In every instance, four cuts ran parallel to each other. Like claws. Most of the Unseelie sported claws in their true forms, but this was definitely Eoghann's work.

He'd signed it. Branded the center of Uriskel's mutilated chest with his sigil.

"What did you do?" Cobalt blurted.

"Nothing."

"Lying snake. You've not changed at all."

Uriskel's eyes narrowed. "I did nothing, *Cobalt*. He wants me dead. I don't know why." He glanced down and sighed. "Took his time with this. Hours. And he never even asked me anything."

"I'm sorry." Cobalt shuddered. He'd known Eoghann was cold and unfeeling, but this—he had changed. He'd gotten worse. Cobalt suspected the Unseelie had only lived because of the Law that forbade any Fae from killing another in the human realm. At least in daylight. "I'll do what I can."

He held a hand flat and splay-fingered above the worst of the damage, and called on his magic. He felt the wounds resisting. Eoghann must have enchanted them. He forced harder and was rewarded when Uriskel's skin began to reluctantly knit itself back together. It was slow going. He maintained the spell for five or six minutes before he stopped, gasping for breath. "All I have for now," he said. At least the gashes appeared less angry. The claws of a cat instead of a tiger. "He's hexed you."

"I know." Uriskel drew the cloak around him. "Thank you."

Cobalt arched his brow. "That must've been hard for you."

"What?"

"Thanking me."

"You have no idea." His head dropped back against the chair. "I can stay?"

"For a while. Not long."

"Good. Where can I sleep?"

"Right there."

Uriskel glanced down at the plain wooden chair. "What, on this?"

"Yes." Cobalt consulted the clock again. Five to three. "I'm waiting for someone, and he'll be here any minute. I'll bring you upstairs later."

"Well, aren't you the gracious host. Got a pillow up your ass?"

"Uriskel, shut your mouth."

"Fine." The Unseelie leaned forward and laid his head on folded arms. "Don't mind me. I'll just sit here and bleed."

"You do that."

Cobalt released a pent breath and stared at the door. Any minute now.

Chapter Five

Will wasn't sure how long he'd been walking. He'd passed Central Park a while back, and now he was approaching Harlem. He wanted nothing more than to drag inside the nearest bar and drink himself into oblivion, but he couldn't sit. Hell, he wouldn't be able to stand much longer. And he still hadn't called Tess.

At least he'd managed not to jump in front of a train. The trick, he discovered, was to keep from thinking too far ahead. He had gotten this far by choosing a destination—the next block, the next junk tourist shop, the next Dunkin' Donuts or drugstore or subway entrance—and reaching it, then picking something else. His current goal was the next street that ended in *th.*

He stopped at the corner of 124th. *Where to, Mister?* He stared down the teeming sidewalk, oblivious to the occasional jostler or honking cab. A goal. Something simple. Maybe the next street vendor…

A solid surface crunched against his knees. His breath whooshed out, and white flashed across his vision. He stared dully at the sidewalk, which was suddenly two or three feet closer. His legs had given out.

Now what? No one stopped to help him. He wasn't surprised—dressed like this, he didn't look very approachable. He could just stay here on his knees and wait for something to happen. Maybe he'd get mugged, or shot, or crushed by a curb-jumping taxi.

Will, you need to go to a hospital. The voice in his head was Tess's. And she was right—but he couldn't. Even if he could somehow get past the humiliation of having to explain how his ass had turned a solid shade of maroon, and what made those bruised and bloodied welts on his back and thighs, they'd make him file a report. With the police.

He had a feeling if he did that, Lyle would do everything in his power to get hold of him again. And next time he wouldn't stop with his belt.

Maybe he could check in to a hotel somewhere. A few hours of sleep might let him think in longer terms than five minutes ahead. But first he had to find one. He used the street-sign pole to pull himself to his feet and clung to it until the light changed. One step at a time. He could make another block.

By the time he hit the next curb, his legs vibrated like electric razors.

He marked progress in sidewalk cracks. Made it to one, another, the next. He had to stop twice and catch his breath. When he finally reached the corner, he wasn't sure he had the strength to stay conscious. But he managed.

This block looked exactly the same as the last one. Had he actually moved, or just imagined moving? Nothing resembled a hotel. His vision blurred, doubled, and for a few seconds nothing resembled anything. When his surroundings resolved, he felt cool wetness trickling down his back. It was raining.

No, it wasn't. He was bleeding again.

Forget walking. A cab. He'd hail a cab, and go... Where? A hotel. Right. But he wouldn't be able to stand long enough to check in, much less walk to a room. Tess... She'd be at the studio. He didn't have a key to her place.

A taxi swung to the curb. He didn't remember waving for one. The passenger window hummed down. "You going? Going?" an accented voice called.

"Yeah." Will rattled the back-door handle and popped it open. He climbed in on his knees. Gravity shut the door. He heard it click behind him.

"Where you going?" the cabbie called back.

Hospital. Hotel. Hell in a handbasket. "The Grotto," he said without thinking. "Ninth and...something. Midtown."

The cabbie nodded. And Will blacked out before they hit the first light.

* * *

Cobalt locked Uriskel in an upstairs guest room. The Unseelie wouldn't cause any trouble—for a few hours, at least. By the time he'd given up waiting for Will, Uriskel had all but fainted. He could deal with him in the morning.

Tonight, it would take everything he had not to think about Will Ambrose.

He shouldn't have been surprised that Will never showed up. After all, he knew the man didn't look the type.

But he'd been so animated, for just a moment, when he had asked about scarification. Cobalt had hoped for the chance to convince him to try. Even if he could never have him as anything more than a client.

He headed down to the studio. They'd only been open an hour, but the place was already full. His first appointment wasn't until seven. Two hours to kill.

A familiar couple occupied a table at the back. They were Seelie, frequent guests at the Grotto—and different as night and day. In the Fae realm, it was a rare match made between a Pooka and a Sluagh. Pookas, shape-shifters, were carefree types who spent most of their time communing with nature. The Sluagh preferred the company of the dead. But this odd pairing had come here for freedom and found humans to their liking.

Cobalt made his way to them and waited until the male looked up from the BlackBerry in his hands. "Nix," he said. "How are things in lovely old Eire?"

He flashed a bright smile. "Boring, mate. Lots of sheep. Did we miss anything?"

"Not really." He wouldn't tell them about Eoghann. He regarded his pale companion, who stared toward the back of the room with the expression of someone who'd just caught wind of fresh skunk. "Nice to see you too, Shade," he said.

"Cobalt. Something feels wrong in here." Shade kept her eyes on the stairwell entrance. "You've a new guest."

Nix nudged her. "Stop being so dramatic, love."

"No, she's right." Cobalt held back a sigh. He should have known Shade would sense the Unseelie. Her kind was attuned to dark magic. "I granted haven to Uriskel."

"You didn't!" Nix switched to Fae. "He's Unseelie. Besides, isn't he the one who—"

"I've told you not to talk like that in here," Cobalt admonished. "Don't worry about him. He's injured. And it's temporary." *I hope.*

Shade shifted her gaze. Flat gray eyes stared coolly at him. "I hope you know what you're doing," she said. "Never turn your back on him."

"I won't."

Something behind Cobalt drew the attention of the other Fae. He turned to find Malik in the entrance at the front of the room, gesturing frantically for him. "Excuse me," he said to the couple. "This looks important."

"Later," Nix replied. Shade merely nodded.

Cobalt weaved around tables, returning greetings from the regulars with nods and single words. A ripple of disquiet shivered through his chest. The feeling grew when he reached Malik and took in the boy's wide eyes and set mouth. "What is it?" he asked softly.

"I think you should come out here." Malik went back into the front room without waiting for an acknowledgment.

Cobalt followed and closed the door behind him. Outside, a car horn blared a long, strident note. The sound paused for a few seconds and began again.

"Do you hear that?" Malik moved toward the entrance. "There's a cab sitting at the curb. It's been there at least five minutes. I looked when he started doing that with the horn, and I think he's trying to wake up whoever's in the backseat."

"So?"

For an instant Malik showed his age in a flash of pure teen exasperation. "Whoever it is must have asked to come here. I thought, with all the...er, interesting people you bring in, it might be someone you know."

Cobalt started to dismiss the idea. Another long blast sounded, then a series of rapid and insistent bleats. He shook his head. "It doesn't sound like he's going to leave. I'll deal with this."

He stepped outside. The driver had gotten out of the cab and was leaning in the open front window to blast the horn. The back passenger door stood open. A figure lay slumped in the backseat, forming awkward angles. Something about it looked familiar, but he couldn't make out anything beyond a vague shape.

The driver moved in front of him. "You. You work here?"

"Yes."

"Maybe he's customer of yours. He ask for the Grotto. That's you." The cabbie gestured at the open door. "You take him? Pay fare. He won't wake up. You not take him, I have to call cops."

Cobalt barely heard the cabbie's stream of complaints. He brushed the man aside and crouched at the edge of the curb to peer inside the taxi. Whoever this was, he was in bad shape. The unconscious form's legs were flung against the back, and his upper half hung upside down in the floor well, turned toward the seat—as though he'd crawled in on his knees and passed out. A black bandanna was fastened around his head. Mirrored sunglasses lay on the carpet beside him.

His breath quickened at the familiar sandy brown hair obscuring the face. He brushed it aside. Even in shadowed profile, he recognized him instantly.

"Will!" Was he drunk? Maybe serious drugs. Or both. Cobalt reached out, hesitated. Touched his shoulder.

Will flinched and moaned. But he didn't wake up.

"You know him." The cabbie tapped his arm. "Pay fare. Eleven forty."

Cobalt glared at him. Deciding against causing a scene, he fished a bill from his pocket and held it up. It was a fifty.

The driver snatched it. "I get you change."

"Keep it. Just give me a minute to get him out."

"You got it."

Cobalt shifted to one knee. "Here we go," he murmured. He slid an arm under Will's torso and winced when the unconscious man cried out softly. The sound was pure pain. Maybe he wasn't drunk. He shifted him a few inches away from the seat, and the shirt Will wore slipped down and exposed his lower back.

Cobalt's throat convulsed at the sight of the wide blue-black stripes adorning his bloodied skin. It wasn't hard to tell what had made those marks. Fury roared through his mind at whoever was responsible for hurting him. "Oh, Will," he whispered. "Who's done this to you?"

Will didn't offer an answer. He hadn't expected one.

There was no way to extract him without hurting him. Carefully, he reached his free arm inside and curled it beneath Will's waist. He worked slowly. At last he managed to maneuver him halfway out and lift him in an awkward cradle, with one arm around his shoulders and the other under his knees. Fever heat radiated from his slack body. The back of his shirt was tacky with blood.

Cobalt straightened and backed away from the curb. Will stirred, nuzzling his head against his chest. "Grotto," he mumbled thickly. "Cobalt…"

"Yes." His voice broke on the word. "I'm here, Will."

A soft sigh escaped Will's lips. His body grew heavy. Asleep again.

Cobalt turned and strode back to the building. He kicked at the door. Within seconds, Malik opened up. The boy gaped at them. "What…?"

"Move."

Malik scuttled aside. Cobalt walked in and waited until the boy closed the entrance. "Cancel my appointments tonight," he said.

"All of them?"

"Yes."

"No problem." Malik didn't ask unnecessary questions. "Do you…need help?"

"No. I've got him." His eyes burned briefly. "I'll be taking him through the back. No one here needs to see him like this."

Malik nodded. He moved to the side door and opened it to the hallway leading to the access stairs.

"Thank you." Cobalt didn't wait for the boy to reply.

* * *

A tantalizing scent teased Will's nose, just outside the reach of his awareness. Wood smoke and river water. A country summer breeze. The smell invoked these images, but it wasn't quite that. It was distinctly male, maddeningly sexual. Inviting and delicious.

Consciousness bled into him and brought more sensations. A soft something beneath him. The dull pain permeating every inch of his body. Flickering light dancing beside him.

He'd smelled smoke. *Fire!*

He opened his eyes with a gasp and saw candles. That didn't make sense. Unless he was dead, and they lit hell with candles.

"Will. Don't panic. You're safe."

The low voice came from the gloom beyond the cluster of flames. Will squinted and made out a tall silhouette. "Cobalt?"

"Yes." The silhouette drifted to the right, out of his line of sight. "I hope you don't mind that I brought you inside. I'd not wanted to leave you on the street."

"Inside…where?"

"The Grotto. I live upstairs."

It took him a minute to process what had happened. He remembered trying, and failing, to find a hotel. Then he'd caught a cab. He must've told the driver to take him to the

Grotto—but then what? He didn't remember arriving, or walking inside. "How…?"

"No one's seen you."

A hiss and a flare sounded. He smelled sulfur. The soft light around him brightened a bit, enough to reveal the bed he was lying on. Cobalt's bed. Despite his wretched condition, a shiver of lust raced through him. Then he remembered the man who usually shared this bed—the angelic Trystan—and pushed the feeling away. He was no work of art.

Will closed his eyes and tried to think. He couldn't stay here. Eventually Cobalt would notice the bruise on his face, the sores on his mouth. If he hadn't already. There would be questions he didn't want to answer. He tensed and dragged one outstretched arm toward him, preparing to push up. The sensation of cotton sheet against his skin stopped him cold.

He was naked. Cobalt had seen far more than his bruised face.

A strangled cry wrenched from his throat. He convulsed, tried to curl in on himself, but it hurt too much. Tears formed in his eyes. He squeezed them shut.

"Will…"

Cobalt's unsteady voice poured over him like fire. "My clothes," he croaked. "I need to leave. Now. You… *Why?*"

"I had to."

Should've just let me die. If shame could kill, he would have died right here. "Give me my clothes. I'm leaving."

"Damn it, Will, you can't leave. You can't even walk. If you go out there, you'll just pass out again." He sensed Cobalt moving closer to the bed. "And whoever finds you next won't be as discreet as me."

Jesus. Why did he have to be right?

"I'm sorry. I know how you feel—"

"No. You don't." Will turned his head to the left, where Cobalt's voice had come from. He couldn't make out much in the candlelight. Only dark hair, strong features, and shadows he knew were tattoos. "Just leave me alone, or something."

"Or something?"

"I can handle this." He tried again to rise. Pain slammed his tailbone and shot up his spine. He gasped, focused his gaze on Cobalt. "Look, I…had an accident. With my board. I fell down some steps." Pathetic. But he couldn't stop himself.

Cobalt arched an eyebrow. "Onto a belt?"

"Oh, God." Will's stomach cramped hard. "Please. I can't…"

"Listen to me, Will." Cobalt's voice was unflinchingly tender. "I'll not pass judgment on you. I won't even ask any questions. You can tell me as much or as little as you want— even if what you want to say is nothing. All I want to do is help you." He swallowed, gestured vaguely. "I run a tattoo parlor. My job is cutting and poking people. I'm sure you don't want to go to a hospital, so I'm the next best thing. I know how to treat injuries like this."

Will tried to speak. His tongue refused to cooperate.

"Please let me help you."

The longing in his voice—real or imagined—sent a shudder through Will. "All right," he whispered finally. "Cobalt...thank you."

His gratitude extended beyond the offer to treat his injuries. And Cobalt seemed to understand.

Chapter Six

So much for not getting involved.

Cobalt had to turn away, before those eyes of Will's bored straight into his soul. "I'll need the light," he said. "You may want to close your eyes."

"Okay. Done."

The relief was short-lived. Soon he'd have to put his hands on Will's naked body—and it would hurt both of them. He held in a breath, reached down, and switched on the bedside lamp. At least he'd drawn the sheet over the worst of the damage. Still, the marks visible on his shoulders and around his wrists kindled fresh rage. He wanted to kill whoever had put them there.

Part of the feeling, he realized with self-revulsion, was jealousy. He'd wanted to mark Will, claim him for his own. But not like that.

"I'll have to get a few things," he said. "I won't be a minute."

"Mmm." Will's breathing evened. He was drifting off again.

Cobalt circled the bed and headed for the adjoining bathroom. He shut the door. A frustrated groan formed in his throat, and he shoved a knuckle against his mouth to keep it from escaping. Gods, how could he do this? He'd no hesitation over treating Will's injuries. If he thought it possible without exposing himself, he would heal him completely with magic—assuming he had any left after his earlier session with Uriskel. But what came next? Tend him, heal his wounds...and send him on his way? The beating he'd suffered had to come from someone he knew. Gangs or homosexual haters would not have bound and beaten him so methodically, so *personally*. If he let Will go, chances were good that he'd return to his abuser.

Yet a relationship with him was out of the question. If he stayed, Will was bound to lose his mind or his life. Just like every other human Cobalt had tried to bond with.

He relaxed a bit and moved for the medicine cabinet. There would be time to berate himself later. At the moment, Will needed him—or at least needed the services he could offer. He pulled the mirrored door open and tried to study the shelves with a clinical eye. Lidocaine to ease the irritation of the unbroken skin...

...where he had been battered mercilessly with an open hand, where some of the bruises were finger shaped...

Bacitracin to stave off infection from the cuts...

...where the belt had bitten him, over and over, hard enough to draw blood...

And something general for the pain. Vicodin would be the best choice, but some did not react well to morphine-based medication. He would attempt a small dose and resort to codeine if necessary. Or ibuprofen. Anything that would offer the slightest relief.

He filled a cup with water and gathered everything in a small bowl from under the sink. He expected to find Will unconscious again. But when he returned to the bedroom, Will watched his approach with guarded interest.

Cobalt smiled. "Nervous?"

"Depends. You're not giving me stitches, are you?"

"No stitches." He set the bowl on the nightstand. "Don't tell me. You've a problem with needles."

Will smirked. "Not really. It's more of a thread thing. I just—oh, no. What time is it?"

"Seven thirty, quarter to eight. Something like that."

"Shit!" He winced visibly. "The show. I have to call Tess."

"I assume it's to say you won't be working tonight."

"Uh…yeah. Can't exactly sit in a booth."

The edge in his voice could have sliced solid rock. Cobalt produced his phone. "Here. Call. Unless you'd like me to—"

"No, I'll do it." Will clenched his jaw, propped himself on an elbow, and accepted the phone. "Tess'll shit kittens if she doesn't hear from me. Probably will anyway."

Cobalt turned and walked a few paces away, to give some semblance of privacy and to hide his bemused expression. Shit kittens. He hadn't heard that particular expression before. Perhaps it was unique to Will's vocabulary.

"Hey, Tess." Will sounded resigned already. "Look, you're not gonna like this, but I can't come in—" She must have shouted her response, because a tinny, unintelligible voice reached Cobalt's ears. "I'm at the Grotto... Yes... No, they don't hate you. We're not banned."

His breath caught. After a pause, he said in strained tones, "What did you tell him?"

Another pause. "Okay. Tess...don't antagonize him. Just play dumb. No, I'm—no. I'm fine. Breathe, hon." Fingers drummed lightly on the sheet. "No. I don't need—" He sighed. "Tess, we're through. Yes, really. No! He's just—I'll tell you later. Tomorrow. Lunch at Nick's, okay? Yes. Mother hen. Fussbudget. Drama queen... G'night, darlin'."

When he said nothing further, Cobalt turned back. Don't ask questions, he reminded himself. If Will told him anything, it would have to be volunteered, or he'd resent him forever. "All set?" he said.

Will frowned at the phone. "Tess," he murmured. "If only you were a man. But then..." He stopped, shook his head. "Yes. Thank you."

Cobalt approached him and settled on the edge of the bed, careful not to jostle too much. He returned the phone to his pocket. "Anytime. Now...do you want me to explain what I'm going to do?"

"I guess."

Indifference, then. At least it wasn't fear. "First, I want to have you take some pain medication. Can you swallow pills?"

"Think so."

"All right." He picked up a bottle. "Vicodin. It's the strongest I have, but it's morphine based. Have you taken morphine before?"

"Yes, once. I—yes. At the hospital." The words trailed to a whisper.

"Then you shouldn't react to it." He opened the bottle, shook out two pills, and held them out. When Will took them, he offered the water.

Will blinked at the cup, at the pills. He caught his lower lip with his teeth.

"Here." Cobalt scooped the small white tablets from his palm. "Take the water. I'll put these in your mouth, so you can swallow fast."

Will nodded. Color rose in his cheeks. "That'll work," he said hoarsely.

Cobalt held the tablets, waited until Will opened his mouth. He willed the slight tremble in his hand away and gently placed the pills on his tongue. The pads of his fingers brushed the surface as he withdrew—and his body reacted with a flash of heat. He managed not to moan.

Will raised the cup to his lips. His eyes were closed, his expression unreadable. He swallowed and paused, then drank a bit more. He eased out a breath. "Thank you. Again."

"You don't have to keep thanking me." Cobalt took the cup back. "They should work fast. Now, though, we've come to the hard part. You'll want to lie down."

"Oh, man. Sounds fun already." Will lowered himself onto the bed and propped his chin on folded arms. He stared at the headboard. "What's the hard part?"

"Cream. I've two kinds. One is a topical anesthetic—a numbing agent, for the irritation." His voice threatened to crack. He took a breath, composed himself. "The other is antiseptic, to clean cuts and prevent infection."

Will remained silent for a long moment. At last he said, "Why haven't you asked me about...anything?"

"I promised no questions," he replied as evenly as possible.

Will turned his head. A faint smile lingered on his lips. "I guess I don't really need to explain. It's obvious."

"I'll make no assumptions, Will. You can say, or not say, anything you'd like."

Will's mouth firmed. He hesitated. "It was my partner. Ex-partner," he corrected with a growl. "That bastard is never touching me again."

Cobalt's blood ran hot with the declaration. Gods, but he was strong. Most people in his situation would already be making excuses, saying the monster who hurt them didn't mean it. But not Will Ambrose. "That's good to hear," he said quietly.

"Yeah, well it's...something I should've said a long time ago."

"It matters that you say it now." Cobalt grasped the edge of the sheet. "Ready?"

Will faced the headboard again. "Yes," he whispered.

Cobalt lifted the sheet up so it wouldn't touch his skin while he pulled it back. Despite his care, he still heard Will attempt to stifle a gasp. What emerged was a choked sob. He forced himself to look closely so he could assess the damage and decide where to begin.

He soon realized it didn't matter. Everywhere was bad.

Barely an inch of skin had been left untouched between his neck and his knees. There were even welts on his upper arms. Some of the marks licked around his ribs and his waist like poisonous tails. His backside bore hectic blossoms of deep red set in bruised flesh. Dried blood crusted around his opening.

The beast had raped him too.

Cobalt didn't trust himself to speak. He retrieved the lidocaine and squeezed a generous amount on his fingertips. "I'll have to touch you," he said, his voice hoarse. "I'm sorry. It will hurt."

Will nodded. His body stiffened in anticipation.

He touched the cream to his backside. Will flinched and sucked air through his teeth. "All right," Cobalt whispered. "It's all right. Easy, Will..." He spread the stuff in gentle circles. The heat from Will's tortured skin practically burned his fingers. As he worked, he called on his ebbing magic to enhance the healing process. Just a touch. Depleted as he was, the tap scourged his body through—but he would suffer a few moments of pain to take some of Will's away.

Though it seemed to take aeons, he finished applying both lotions in minutes. He capped the tubes and wiped his hands on his jeans. "There, now. I've stopped," he said softly. "Any better?"

"Actually...yes." Will let out a shuddering breath. "I feel almost human again. You have magic hands."

He cringed at the word *magic*. "I'm afraid I just have better drugs than most." He opened the Vicodin again and deposited two pills beside the rest of the water. "You'll have to wait four hours for these," he said. "The dose you've taken may wear off before then, but I'll not have you poisoning yourself."

"Four hours?" Will shifted on the bed. "I thought…"

"No. Don't try to get up. You need rest."

"But you're done. I thought I should…well, leave."

Cobalt laughed before he could stop himself. "You're staying right here."

"Don't you have people waiting on you? For tattoos, I mean."

"Not tonight. I canceled all my appointments when you turned up."

"Oh." Will bit his lower lip again. The gesture was unbearably sensual. "I'm sorry. You didn't have to do that."

"I don't mind." Cobalt caught his gaze and held it. "You are welcome here, anytime. You're safe." The irony struck him before the words emerged. He had granted haven to Will—yet he could offer no more than that. He could ask for no more, and take nothing.

Will quirked a smile. "I'd thank you, but you told me not to."

"You're welcome." He smiled back. "Do you think you could eat something? You'll need the strength."

"Now that you mention it, I'm starving."

"Wonderful. I'll get you some food." He stood and carefully drew the sheet back over Will's ruined flesh. "Rest, until I return."

The urge to kiss him good-bye nearly overcame him. Here was Will Ambrose, in his bed, and he could do nothing but look at him. It was a torment worse than any death.

At least he'd no need to mourn the loss of his bed. He would not sleep tonight.

* * *

Will decided he had to be dreaming. He'd passed out somewhere, in an alley or a gutter, and his fevered mind invented this to keep him occupied. The Cobalt Fantasy. Wherein the dark and beautiful god took pity on the pathetic and broken mortal.

But the sensations felt real enough. The pain was diminished but present. And what he'd experienced when Cobalt touched him—despite the pain, a rush of pleasure sweeter than honey—was definitely real. He had the erection to prove it.

God. Those long, graceful fingers in his mouth had almost been too much to bear. He'd wanted to suckle them, take them in deep, and be rewarded with the ecstatic moan he knew Cobalt would release.

How he could even think about sex at a time like this was beyond him. But there it was.

Unfortunately, his inappropriately timed lust was the least of his worries. Lyle had called the station looking for him. He could try to avoid him, make sure no one he knew told Lyle anything, but sooner or later he'd have to face him. Lyle never had been the passive type. He wouldn't just forget the whole thing.

He'd have to hope he could find the strength to keep his convictions the next time he encountered Lyle. Preferably without the aid of another beating to remind him why it was over.

His thoughts fled the uncertain future for more stable ground—here, now. He'd expected nothing that happened tonight, so every kindness Cobalt had shown served to shock his system. Making sure no one else saw his shame. Refraining from pointed questions. Tending to his injuries without a hint of disgust or condemnation. Most of all, reacting as though sending him away had never crossed his mind. As though he belonged here with him.

That was the real fantasy...belonging to Cobalt. It'd never happen.

For now, though, he would indulge himself. Cobalt had told him to rest until he returned. That sounded like a good idea. He closed his eyes and drifted, not so much sleeping as floating on the promise of being welcome and safe.

Sometime later, a loud bang startled him back to consciousness. The sound repeated twice. An unfamiliar male voice shouted, "Cobalt! I know you're in there. Open up."

The doorknob rattled. Cobalt must have locked it. Maybe with good reason—whoever was out there sounded pissed. Will debated staying put, but when the banging started again, he decided to look for cover in case the door failed to hold against the assault.

"Blast it, I want a word with you. Open this door!" *Bang, bang, bang.*

Blast it? He'd puzzle that one out later. He struggled to his knees, tried to ignore the sick wave of anguish that shot through him, and studied the room. Three doors—one under siege, another a bathroom. The third was probably a closet. He slid off the bed and managed to stay on his feet, then headed for the probable closet.

It was. A deep blue silk robe hung from a peg on the back of the door. He took it down, slipped it on—

"Fine. I'll do it, then."

There was a brief rattle, a metallic click. "When you said I could stay, I didn't think you meant as a—oh. You're not Cobalt."

"No. Sorry." Will tied the robe shut. His body shook with the effort he'd expended to move so fast. He turned to regard the intruder, half expecting the beautiful blond. Trystan.

But the man in the doorway was a green-eyed redhead. Where Trystan had been alabaster, this man was bronze. Instead of an angel, he was gorgeous as sin.

"How fascinating." Will felt those green eyes taking him in, assessing him. "Any chance you might tell me where he is?"

"I don't know." It was the truth. Cobalt could have gone anywhere to get food.

"Ah, but he'll be back. Won't he?" The redhead moved farther into the room. Closer to Will. "You won't mind if I wait for him."

Will wasn't sure how to respond. It wasn't a question. "Sure. Go ahead," he said.

"Good." The man changed course and took a casual seat on the bed, as though he'd done it a hundred times. "Don't mind me. Go back to whatever you were doing."

"I was sleeping."

The man turned slowly in his direction. A chilling smile surfaced. "Were you, now."

Yes. The thought refused to become a word. All at once, a phantom aroma like the one that had teased him from sleep descended around him, a thick curtain. But this was different. Not wood and water, but earth and fire and incense. Stronger...and darker. Dangerously sensual. Commanding. He blinked, and the redhead stood before him, aiming that smile at his soul.

You, Will thought with helpless abandon. I want you.

"Get out."

Snarled words dispelled the haze. Will shook himself and looked for their source. He found it soon enough.

Cobalt stood in the open door, wearing fury like a glove. And staring straight at him.

Chapter Seven

For one endless moment, Will felt like he'd been shot.

Cobalt deposited the white paper bag he held on a chair by the door. He strode across the room, and Will struggled not to cringe like a dog. He'd never seen anyone this angry. Not even Lyle—and that was saying a lot.

"I swear. If you've—" Cobalt cut himself off with effort. He grabbed the redhead by the arm and frog-marched him to the door. "Speak one word in this room and you're through. Wait there." He propelled him through the entrance. "Don't talk to anyone. Don't touch anything."

If the other man responded, Will didn't hear him. Cobalt's outburst had frozen his senses.

"Will." Cobalt took a step toward him, stopped. "Are you all right?"

IIis voice seemed to come from a hundred miles away. "Yes. I think."

"That arrogant, ungrateful—" He grimaced and ran a hand through his hair. "What did he say to you? Wait, don't tell me. I'll find out." He directed a fierce glare at the doorway.

It finally dawned on Will that he wasn't the cause of Cobalt's fury. For some reason, though, he didn't feel inspired to relax.

"You don't look all right. Why did you... Oh, damn. Will, I'm so sorry." He crossed the room to him. "Come on. You should be in bed." He placed a gentle hand under Will's elbow.

Will jerked away.

The reaction was instinctive, but it had a profound effect on Cobalt. His expression shattered. He stood frozen for a moment before his arm fell limp at his side. He said nothing, only looked at Will as though he'd slapped him.

He had. Metaphorically speaking.

At last, Cobalt drew himself together. "Eat, if you like," he said, gesturing to the bag he'd brought in. "I must deal with him. I'll not be long." He headed for the door but stopped just inside. "Know that you're not being forced into anything. Your will is your own. I'll never take that from you."

The door closed. Will stared at it and tried to make sense of his scattered thoughts. Did Cobalt want him to leave, or was he just reassuring him that he could? Who in the hell was the red-haired man—and if Cobalt hated him so much, why was he here? He could have been another lover. But if that were the case, then Cobalt was his Lyle.

His head pounded with the effort to seize a reasonable explanation. Nothing fit. He shuffled back to the bed, but he couldn't bring himself to lie down. Maybe he'd have to leave after all. He knew nothing about the man who called himself Cobalt. And right now, he wasn't sure he wanted to find out.

* * *

"You disgust me, Uriskel. How could you do this, after the risk I've taken for you?"

Uriskel leaned on the back wall of the guest room and folded his arms. "I've done nothing to your precious Will."

"You know his name! How?"

"You left the door open while you comforted him. Or failed to, depending on the point of view." Uriskel sneered. "You should be pleased. I did exactly what you demanded of me."

"I should not have had need to stop you." Cobalt fought to hold himself in check. "Did you not think the door was locked for a reason?"

"Perhaps the same reason you locked me behind this one."

"Because I knew you'd cause trouble!"

"You might have just said something to me, you know." Though his tone was light, his eyes flashed fire. "There's no need to pen me like an animal. I'll not touch your pretty human."

Cobalt refused to let him force guilt. "You've already done enough damage, you bastard. Now I'll have to explain you to him."

"Well, then. Tell him we're family. Brothers. That should sound about right."

"I can't lie to him."

A strange look flickered across Uriskel's face and disappeared. "Then tell him the truth. Tell him you're not human. Won't that go over well...Cobalt?"

"Damn you, Uriskel."

The Unseelie offered a bitter laugh. "Yes. However, I believe you're also damned at the moment. Tough break."

Cobalt's hands clenched in tight fists. "Since I neglected to mention it before, I'll tell you now," he said. "Stay away from Will. Don't speak to him. Don't look at him. In fact, don't leave this room tonight."

"Fantastic. What am I supposed to do?"

"I don't care what you do, as long as you do it in here."

Uriskel stiffened. After a moment, he gave a mocking bow. "As you wish."

Cobalt turned and left, before his control could desert him.

* * *

Will couldn't bring himself to leave. Not without at least trying for a reasonable explanation. He still wanted one to exist, impossible as that seemed.

He'd gone back to lying down, but with his head pointed toward the door. When it opened, he didn't hesitate. "Who is he?"

Cobalt paused for just a beat. "Skelly. He's from out of town, visiting for a while. Apparently he's acquired some new skills. Lock picking, for instance." He closed the door and picked up the untouched bag. "Not hungry? I suppose I don't blame you."

"Shock does tend to destroy my appetite."

The comment made Cobalt flinch. He set the bag aside. "I'm truly sorry for that. I'd no time to tell you about him. Or him about you," he added under his breath. "He'll not bother you again."

"It's not him I'm worried about."

"What?" Confusion knit his features. After a second, he closed his eyes. "You think I'm... Oh, Will. It's not like that."

Will hauled himself up and slid from the bed to stand beside it. "Who is he, really? To you, I mean. An old customer? A lover?" He almost choked on that one.

"No. Absolutely not." A shade of the anger he'd exhibited earlier darkened his face. "You want the truth. You'll have it—and should you want to leave when you've heard, I'll not stop you."

Chills shivered down his back. Maybe he didn't want to know, after all. But he couldn't stop now. "The truth," he whispered. "Let's hear it."

Cobalt nodded. "Skelly is a fugitive," he said slowly. "He needed a place to hide for a while. He came to me because he doesn't know anyone else here. I let him stay only because he's hurt." He shook his head, touched fingers to his temple. "I shouldn't have. Once he's mended, the bastard's on his own."

Something inside Will shattered. The parallels to his own situation were impossible to miss, but Cobalt didn't seem to notice. Or maybe he did and just didn't care. At least it explained why he'd handled Will showing up the way he did so well. He had experience taking in strays. He'd been nothing special to him.

"Thank you for that." At once, Will felt ridiculous wearing Cobalt's robe. Like a pathetic groupie. "Can I have my clothes?"

"You're leaving." Cobalt looked exquisitely miserable.

"Actually, I wouldn't mind staying tonight, if it's still okay with you. It's cheaper than a hotel." He almost regretted the words when Cobalt winced at them. Almost. "I'd just like to be ready to leave in the morning."

"Of course," Cobalt said stiffly. "Only let me wash them for you. They'll need it. I'll leave them here by the door."

"Fine. Thank you."

Cobalt gave a bare nod. He turned his back, reached for the door. "Good-bye, Will." Without waiting for a reply, he let himself out.

Will managed to wait several minutes, until he was sure Cobalt had gone, before he collapsed on the bed. Silent tears dripped from his eyes and soaked the sheet. Eventually, exhaustion stole him away.

* * *

The city spread around him, a glittering blanket laid beneath a clouded night sky. From the roof, Cobalt could see the river, a black expanse edged with twinkling lights. Such a breathtaking sight.

If only he could drown himself in it.

He'd come as close to the truth as he dared, but it hadn't been enough. Of course it hadn't. If their positions were reversed, he would feel the same. He must have sounded exactly as he felt explaining it—like a shallow cad with a dirty secret. Watching Will's trust vanish in an instant had broken him.

Perhaps it was better this way. A clean break.

"*Tell him the truth. Tell him you're not human.*" He snorted. Excellent idea, Uriskel. Tell him the truth and watch him descend into madness. Or take his own life to escape the knowledge. Yes, that would solve everything.

He shuddered and told himself it was the brisk night air. Will would leave in the morning. He would not come back. So be it. At least he wouldn't return to the beast who'd battered him body and soul.

Cobalt headed for the access door. He'd transfer Will's clothes to the dryer, return them to his room. Then he would begin the process of forgetting, though he knew it was a futile effort. No matter how many centuries passed, he could never erase Will Ambrose from his heart.

He'd gotten three steps when his cell phone rang. Though he hadn't spared the matter a thought since Uriskel stumbled bleeding through his front door, he knew exactly who it was.

He answered.

"Are you harboring spies now, Ciaràn?"

"I told you not to contact me again."

"Send him away. He is mine."

Cobalt didn't want to think about the implications of that statement. "I will. Eventually. But I won't tell you when."

"How sporting of you. However, I have no wish to wait. Give him to me."

"No, Eoghann." For the second time that day, he felt sorry for Uriskel. He hadn't thought it possible. "Whatever is between you, I won't be part of it."

"You are part of it. You offered him haven!"

True. But he wasn't going to let a minor detail get in the way. "I'll not help you. You'll just have to catch him on your own."

Eoghann paused. "I will tell you only once more. Send Uriskel away."

"I won't."

"Very well." Eoghann's voice grew infinitely colder. "Then you will share his fate."

The line went dead.

Cobalt thumbed the phone off. He closed his eyes and rubbed a temple, where his head pounded like a drum. He'd only refused the demand to keep from doing what Eoghann wanted. Now his life was on the same thin line as Uriskel's.

He'd have to let the arrogant bastard stay. He would lose Will and gain the Unseelie who'd forced him away. Perfect.

The black depths of the river seemed more inviting than ever.

Chapter Eight

Will woke to sunlight streaming through unfamiliar curtains. It didn't take long to orient himself. He was in Cobalt's bedroom—but not for long.

He stretched tentatively. The pain was no longer searing. Stiff and sore, throbbing in the worst places, but almost bearable. He blinked the sleep from his eyes and turned his head. The bottle of Vicodin still stood on the nightstand, and there was a note propped against it. *Will—Take these with you. Two every 4 hours.—C.*

Pride—or whatever it was driving him to leave—wouldn't stop him from taking advantage of medication he couldn't get otherwise. He'd bring it.

He maneuvered his legs over the side of the bed and straightened slowly. A wave of dizziness washed over him. When it dissipated, his stomach clenched like a fist. He'd eaten nothing in over twenty-four hours. Walking out of here was going to be a challenge.

He stumbled in the general direction of the door. Cobalt had said he'd leave his clothes there. He found them folded neatly and stacked in a chair with his jacket hung on the back. Beside the chair, a folding table held a tray of food. An oversize Danish. Strawberries and whipped cream cheese.

Cold ham. Orange juice. And a small card with a single word printed on it: *eat.*

This last prescient kindness stung. He wanted to hate Cobalt for it, but his hunger overrode the petty notion. He ate standing there, dimly aware that he looked like a morning-after cliché—wearing Cobalt's too-long robe, hair tousled, stubble shading his cheeks, eating what probably would've been breakfast in bed if he'd been able to sit. It was a scene he might have conjured for the brief fantasies he'd indulged in last night. Only he wouldn't have been alone.

He saved a bit of the juice and used it to wash down two Vicodin, then borrowed Cobalt's bathroom to clean his hands and face. His hair looked terrible. His cheek and mouth matched the theme, but he couldn't do much about that. He wet his hands and finger combed the mess on top of his head. Marginally better. Tess was still going to flip out.

He slipped the robe off, hung it on a hook over the bathroom door, and returned naked to the bedroom. He'd only thought as far ahead as lunch with Tess. Knowing the time would help, but he didn't see a clock anywhere. He'd check his phone. Should be in his jacket pocket. He went to the chair with his clothes and noticed the small off-white card sitting on them. It was a business card for the Grotto. Unbelievable. Did Cobalt actually think he was still interested in getting a tattoo?

He picked up the card and nearly tore it in half before he realized there was something handwritten on the back. He turned it over. A phone number, different from the business phone on the front. Probably a cell. Beneath, he'd written *anytime.*

Will considered ripping it up anyway. He changed his mind and tucked it in his jacket, then consulted his phone for the time. Eleven thirty. He'd never slept this late in his life.

At least he wouldn't be late for lunch. He dressed as quickly as possible, opened the door, and stepped from the room before he could change his mind about leaving. He wasn't sure what to expect outside the door, but the sight he encountered was one of the last.

The bedroom opened to a balcony hallway overlooking a loft. Tall, arched windows with a view of the East River lined the far wall. A striking black furniture set was arranged on the polished wooden floor of the loft—and Cobalt sprawled on the couch, asleep. Wearing tight dark shorts and nothing else. The Celtic star tattoo on the perfect chest Will had seen in the studio book wasn't just Cobalt's work. It was *his* tattoo, his immaculate body.

Will tried not to look at the massive bulge in those shorts and concentrated on sculpted muscle beneath velvet gold skin. The perfection of Cobalt's form was stunning. Not an ounce of fat or an overdeveloped ripple in sight. Even the arches of his feet possessed a seductive quality. Somehow he looked more real, more *there*, than anything else in the room.

The hot weight in Will's groin suggested he should leave before he did something stupid. He tore his gaze from the sleeping vision and followed red EXIT signs down two flights of stairs, through a stark utility corridor, and out a solid metal door that emptied behind the building. He encountered no one. No alarms sounded. True to his word, Cobalt hadn't prevented him from leaving.

That was probably a good thing. If he'd tried, Will wasn't sure he would have resisted.

He made his way to the street and waved for a cab. Yesterday's walk hadn't inspired him to try thirty blocks on foot. After a few false slowdowns, one pulled over. He climbed in and hovered over the seat while he gave the address for Nick's. Convincing himself to sit down wasn't easy. He did, and for a while his ass merely hurt.

It screamed by the time he reached the restaurant. He'd take lunch standing.

He paid the driver and made his way inside. Nick's didn't hop until dinner, so he wasn't surprised to find only a handful of patrons there. One of them was Tess. She sat at their usual table, chewing a thumbnail the way she did whenever she faced impending disaster. When she caught sight of him, she stood and waved. A smile tried to force itself across her face.

Will maneuvered around tables and approached her slowly. He could tell when he got close enough for her to see the bruises, because she gasped and clapped a hand to her mouth. Tears welled in her eyes. She didn't even attempt to hug him in greeting.

"Please don't," he murmured. "Don't make a scene. I need you to stay calm for me, okay? Promise you will."

Tess lowered her hand. She sniffed once. "You look like shit," she said.

"Thanks." He looked at the table with its hard plastic chairs and sighed. "You know, I really don't feel like sitting here today. Let's eat at the counter."

"Oh, God! Will...what's he done to you?"

He shook his head.

"Come on." She grabbed her purse and moved past him. "We're leaving."

"Why?"

"Because I'm going to fall apart, and you don't want me to do it here."

"Good enough." He followed her out. "Where are we going?"

"My place. We'll order in."

Tess lived six blocks away. He could make that. A small inner voice urged him to refuse going, in case Lyle showed up, but he ignored it. Lyle would be at work right now. He just wouldn't stay at her place long.

Trying to decide where he *would* go made his head pound. He'd think about that later.

He didn't try to talk on the way. Stayed silent when they entered her building, rode the elevator to the fourth floor, walked the hall to her apartment. Waited while she keyed them in, waved him through, and shut the door. She stared at him. He tried to smile. "How about a pizza?"

"A pizza. Sure." Her lips firmed, and a tear slid down her face. "With a side of tell-me-what-the-fuck-happened. Right now."

"Can't we eat first?"

"Sit down, Will."

"Jesus Christ." He looked away, ran a hand through his hair. "I can't."

"No. You can't." Tears flowed in earnest now. "Not like I could tell by the way you're walking."

"Come on, Tess. It's not that bad—"

"Damn it, don't lie!" Her voice shrilled like a siren. She caught a breath and swiped at her eyes. "Talk to me, Will. Tell me what happened."

He told her. He left out the gory details, couldn't bring himself to say *he spanked me like a schoolkid*, but he got the idea across. He confessed to the handcuffs, the belt lashing, the bizarreness of Lyle dressed in his uniform, watching him shower. He didn't mention the rape. By the time he finished explaining, Tess had gone from crying to cursing.

"I'll fucking kill him." She crossed the living room to the stand she kept her cordless on and opened a drawer. "Goddamn sick fuck. I swear to God..." She pulled out something black and heavy looking. A handgun. "I'm gonna blow his fucking nuts off."

"Tess!" He walked over to her, more worried she'd blow something off herself. "Put that thing down. When the hell did you get a gun?"

"The Dub gave it to me. For protection. You know how he is." Her breath came in harsh hitches. "That bastard. Sick motherfucking piece of shit. I'll—"

Will laid a hand over hers. The one holding the gun. She was shaking like a subway grate. "Put it down, hon," he said gently. "You know you can't do that."

"Yes I can." Her eyes blazed behind a sheen of tears.

"Okay. Maybe you can, but I won't let you." He pushed down until the gun rested in the open drawer. "You can't shoot a cop. They'll gun you down in the street. Then who would I drink with?"

She stared at him and burst into sobs.

"Oh, babe." He rubbed her back in slow circles, blinking against tears of his own. "It's all right now. I told you, it's over. He can't hurt me anymore."

She shuddered hard, went still. "But he can," she whispered. "He's a goddamn cop, Will. And he's already looking for you." Her throat worked silently. "He left two messages at the station this morning."

Will's stomach shriveled and tried to crawl into his chest. "He did?"

"We have to do something." She glanced down. Her fingers still curled around the gun. She let go fast and snatched her hand back. "Aren't there cops higher than the NYPD? We should call the sheriffs or the state troopers. Get that son of a bitch arrested."

"Hold on." He was beginning to see how the cycle of abuse perpetuated. He'd rather let Lyle beat him again than expose himself to a bunch of cops so they could photograph his black-and-blue ass. Intellectually, he knew that was stupid. But some part of him insisted he could take it and spare himself the humiliation of admission. Trade broken bones for broken pride. "Maybe I should talk to him first," he said. "Officially break it off. He might leave me alone."

"Are you fucking mental?"

Probably. He sighed. "Look, let me just call him. Okay? It won't hurt to call."

"Fine." She picked up the cordless and thrust it at him. "Call."

"Not now. He's at work." Besides, he didn't want to use her phone. If Lyle actually decided to come after him, and knew he was with Tess—he didn't want to think about what might happen to her. "I'll call him tonight."

"Promise?"

"Swear on a stack."

"A stack of what?"

"Abs. Rock-hard ones."

She giggled. "Okay, stud. And if he doesn't sound like he's going to fuck off, we're calling the troopers."

"Yeah. Great." He couldn't summon much conviction. If she'd actually seen what Lyle had done to him, she would've called herself, right now, no matter what lame excuses he gave. "Tess... I have more good news."

"I don't want to hear this, do I?"

"Doubt it. I'm going to need a few more nights off."

She blew out a long breath. "Yeah, I figured that. I've already got Leonard covering your slot for the rest of the week. Think you can pick up on Monday?"

A rush of gratitude filled him. He wanted to hug her, but he wouldn't be able to stand the prolonged contact. He settled for kissing her cheek. "You're the best, babe. Monday it is."

He could sort everything out by Monday. He hoped.

* * *

Cobalt hadn't been asleep when Will left, though he hadn't dared try and talk with him. Even if he'd somehow miraculously changed his mind, convinced him to stay, it would only be that much harder to let him go later. Better to get it over with now.

He was also faced with a more immediate concern. He had to speak with Uriskel about Eoghann. Not something he looked forward to.

He looked inside his bedroom first. Will had eaten, and he'd taken the pills with him. He'd even tried to make the bed. Cobalt swallowed, backed out, and closed the door. It would be hard to sleep in this room for a while.

He moved down the hall to the room he'd left Uriskel in. The knob turned smoothly when he tried the door. He bristled, expecting to find the Unseelie gone, but Uriskel sat cross-legged on the bed with a deck of battered playing cards lain out before him in a traditional Celtic cross tarot spread.

The jack of spades crossed the center card. Uriskel pointed to it without looking up. "A strong male influence in your life forebodes dark times," he said and grinned. He raised his head. "Wonder which one that could be?"

"Uriskel—"

"I know. Shut your mouth, Uriskel." He swept the cards in a neat pile and swung his legs over the side of the bed. "Am I to be released for good behavior?"

"No. You're going to stay awhile."

"Oh, come on. You can't keep me locked in here."

"You don't have to stay in the room."

Uriskel shook his head. "Ah. He left you."

"Because of you!"

"Sure about that, are we?" Uriskel leveled a cold gaze at him. "Humans are fickle creatures, Ciaràn—Cobalt, I mean. Perhaps he just needed an excuse, and I happened to provide one."

"Don't you dare." Part of his anger was fear that Uriskel was right. "I'll not discuss Will with you, snake."

"Fine with me. I've no desire to examine your love life."

"Done enough of that, have you?"

Uriskel's expression hardened. "Did you come to me for a reason, or would you like to blame me for everything else too? Perhaps I'm responsible for global warming and the decline in the blue whale population."

"I've a reason." For once he agreed with the bastard. No need to dredge up ancient history. "Eoghann contacted me last night."

"And?"

"He demanded you. Told me to send you away."

"So you've come to see me off. How touching."

"I refused."

"You did?" Every trace of malice vanished from his voice. "Why?"

"Because I despise you, but I'll not send you knowingly to your death."

"I see." Uriskel stood and crossed his arms. "I'd thank you, but I can't stomach any more grousing. Good-bye." He brushed past, headed for the door.

"And you're going where?"

Uriskel stopped without turning. "Away."

"So you are still a coward."

"Enough!" He whirled around, fury blazing from him. For an instant his glamour evaporated completely. His true form radiated dark light. He morphed back and drew forward, then stopped inches from Cobalt. "I'll not take another insult from you, bastard-born fledgling. Keep your loathing. Gods know I merit that. But don't presume to know me. Ever."

Cobalt managed a faint smile. "You've steel in you yet, Uriskel. I respect that. You have my apologies."

"Keep them," he snarled. "I've no use for platitudes."

"Well, no one's ever accused you of being gracious." Cobalt almost clasped his shoulder in customary farewell but thought better of it. "Go or stay. As you will."

Uriskel closed his eyes and breathed out slowly. "What, exactly, did he say?"

"He told me to send you away, and said you were his." An involuntary shudder slid through him at the recollection. "I told him I would, eventually, but he didn't want to wait. 'Give him to me,' he said. And when I refused him a second time, he promised I would share your fate."

Uriskel uttered a violent curse in Fae. He broke off and looked hard at Cobalt. "He'll come. You know that."

"Yes. But he'll not reach me." Cobalt returned his stare. "Nor you, if you stay."

"Perhaps not," he said, almost to himself. He fell silent for a long moment. At last he said, "I'll stay. But if it seems he's taken the advantage, you must send me away. He'll spare you then. The twisted bastard still cares for you."

"If I do that, he'll kill you."

"He'll try."

"Uriskel. Why would you do such a thing?"

"Because I despise you, but I'll not send you knowingly to your death." His smile was hard, brittle. "You'll not be a martyr for the likes of me."

Cobalt nodded and tried to banish the idea that Uriskel had changed after all. A single selfless, if backhanded, declaration did not erase decades of treachery. Still, he could probably stop antagonizing the Unseelie for a while. "Well then," he said. "We may as well despise each other over breakfast. I assume you've not eaten."

Uriskel arched an eyebrow. "Perhaps I have. Be sure that you count your humans carefully, Cobalt. I'm partial to white meat."

Cobalt surprised himself by laughing. "You'll have to settle for pig. I'm fresh out of human."

"Pity." He cracked a smile. "Another time, then. Bring on the pig."

Cobalt led him from the room. Uriskel had to be kidding—but just in case, he'd watch him closely around humans. Shade's warning had lodged in his gut and refused to abate. "*Never turn your back on him.*"

He didn't intend to. Not for a moment.

Chapter Nine

Tess made him take the gun.

Will had finally decided to check in to a hotel. Just for the night. That way, if Lyle reacted badly when he called, he wouldn't be accessible. But Tess wouldn't let him leave her place without the goddamn gun. He'd relented to calm her down and packed the thing in a borrowed backpack, along with the change of clothes she kept there for him in case of emergencies. He didn't plan to use it.

He rode the subway uptown. Easier to stand in a train than a cab. He exited at Forty-second and walked the two blocks to the Econo Lodge he'd stayed in a few times before, when he'd been too drunk to even consider going home. Even then he'd been avoiding Lyle's temper. Or Yvan's, or Adrian's, or whoever might have been waiting for him. How did he always manage to get involved with closet sadists?

It didn't matter now. Once he disentangled himself from Lyle, there'd be no more relationships for him. Problem solved.

He checked in with his credit card and plodded to the room he'd been given. It was a single-bed unit, clean, a little too warm. Someone had left the heater on. He took a minute to hang the DO NOT DISTURB tag on the outside door handle, then dropped the backpack on the floor and turned the heater down. He left it running low for the noise. The last thing he wanted right now was complete silence.

He shrugged carefully from his jacket. Despite the painful warning his body provided with the action, he came close to sitting down on the bed. Habits died hard. He decided to stay on his feet long enough to call Lyle, get it over with. If things didn't go well, it would take him a long time to fall asleep.

His phone was still in his coat pocket. He pulled it out and discovered a blank screen. Dead battery? He usually kept the charger in a pocket too. But a quick search of them turned up nothing. It might have fallen out in the bathroom at home. He held the On button, and the phone flashed to life. Must have accidentally turned it off. When the screen resolved, he stared in disbelief at the message it offered him.

(10) Missed Calls

Ten? There weren't even ten people who had his cell number. He checked the incoming-calls log, and a chill swept through his veins.

Lyle. All ten calls had been from Lyle.

"Persistent son of a bitch, aren't you?" he muttered. A spate of anger suspended his worry, long enough for him to punch in the number.

Lyle answered on the first ring. "Will! I've been trying to call you all day."

"I know." The normal tone of his own voice surprised him. He hadn't expected to be able to hold a lucid conversation with his soon-to-be ex-partner.

"Where are you?" The question was gentle. Concerned.

"Never mind that."

Lyle gave a deep sigh. "You're angry."

"How'd you guess?" Congratulations, you've just won the Understatement of the Year Award. He kept his snide comments to himself. "Lyle, I need to tell you—"

"Wait. Will... I'm sorry. I went a little overboard."

"A little!" Make that Understatement of the Century. "My ass looks like ground beef, Lyle. I've got more stripes than a goddamned zebra. And *I told you to stop*. You didn't. So we're through."

"Oh, babe. Don't say that."

"Say what? That we're through?" He closed his eyes. "How could you think we're not?"

"I made a mistake, Will. Let me make it up to you."

The bastard sounded as sincere as a funeral. "You can't," Will said flatly.

"Come on, babe." There was a pregnant pause. "You liked it."

"What?" He was too stunned to say anything more.

"Your cock says you liked it. You were hard as a rock."

Will's stomach gave a funny little twist. He didn't recall having an erection—but then, he really didn't recall much of anything, except pain. And humiliation. "I..."

"Maybe that was the wrong thing to say. You're not ready yet." His voice emerged smooth and reasonable. Tender with care. "Give me another chance, Will. Please. I'm so sorry."

"No." Will found his tongue at last. "Damn it, Lyle, we're through. Don't come near me."

Another pause. "Are you sure that's what you want?"

"Yes!" *No.* Christ…had he really gotten off on that? It wasn't possible. But Lyle sounded so sure. So convincing. Things had been good once, and Lyle always managed to make it seem like they could be again.

"All right. I'll leave you alone." Still gentle. Like he was humoring a child. "If you change your mind, though…you know where to find me."

"I won't."

He disconnected before Lyle could feed him any more smooth-talking bullshit. Somehow he managed not to throw the phone across the room, but he turned it off in case the bastard called back.

At least he wouldn't have to call the state cops. He would've been grateful to Lyle for that, if he didn't want to see him burn in hell.

* * *

Cobalt turned the radio off when it became apparent Will would not grace the airways tonight. He'd suspected as much, but he had hoped to hear his voice. Perhaps another night.

He left his office and made his way into the busy studio, where Poets of the Fall flowed through the speaker system and floated above the chatter. His first impulse was to seek out Uriskel and ensure the Unseelie was keeping his promise to behave. As "Sleep" gave way to the Indigo Girls, he spotted him sitting alone at a table. A studio book lay open and pushed back to the opposite side. On the empty space before him, Uriskel shuffled the playing cards he'd used earlier. His hands moved blur fast, with the fluid grace of long practice.

Cobalt approached slowly. Uriskel seemed to pay no attention to him, or anyone else. He placed the deck facedown on the table and passed a hand over it, to the right. The cards fanned obediently in a perfectly spaced line. The last one appeared to jump into his hand. Just as quickly, he passed over them to the left and flipped them all faceup. The line remained ruler straight. His performance exhibited all the dexterity of a human illusionist. Cobalt suspected actual magic, but he sensed nothing emanating from Uriskel—save for perhaps faint disdain that bordered on loathing.

One card near the center of the line had remained facedown. Uriskel teased it free with a barely perceptible flick and flipped it. The jack of spades. He scowled at it, dropped it back with its mates. At last he looked up and noticed Cobalt watching him. The cards vanished almost instantly.

"Fascinating trick." Cobalt glanced down at the studio book. It lay open to a scarification piece, a Celtic knot that bore a striking resemblance to his own chest piece—and the marks scoring Uriskel's. The notion that Eoghann may have copied his work in order to torture someone sickened him. Even if that someone was Uriskel. "Have you considered dinner performances?"

"Absolutely. I plan to tour Vegas." Uriskel leaned back in the chair. He stretched his arms behind his head and grimaced briefly. Still hurting, then. "So. What have I done now?"

"Nothing, outside of a few fashion offenses."

"These are your clothes. What's wrong with them?"

"They don't suit you." Cobalt stifled a smirk. Out of everything he owned, the Unseelie had chosen the outfit he'd worn last Halloween—a navy blue sailor suit. At least he hadn't put on the hat. "We'll get you something better tomorrow."

"Sounds delightful."

Cobalt pulled out a chair and sat down. "I may have neglected to mention this, but while you're here, you can't use your name."

"You did." Uriskel gave him a dry look. "And I suppose now you'll tell me what I'm to call myself."

"Skelly."

"Given it a lot of thought, have you?" He sighed and lowered his arms. "Anything else you neglected to mention?"

"Nothing comes to mind."

"Well, be sure to—" He bolted upright. His gaze fixed on the entrance door and narrowed. "Who is that?"

Cobalt followed his stare and saw only Malik. "My shop assistant," he said. "Why?"

"I sensed… Oh. That explains it." He turned away and slouched in the chair. "Really, Cobalt. You'll let anyone in this place, won't you?"

Before he could demand an explanation, Nix and Shade wandered inside. Cobalt smiled and lifted a hand in greeting.

"Don't call them over here," Uriskel muttered. "Especially the Sluagh."

"Mind your manners." Cobalt stood. He waited until the Seelie couple reached them, and said, "I don't think you've met Skelly."

"No. But when you've seen one rat..." Shade left the words hanging in the air.

Uriskel faced her with an arid expression. "You've a need for rabies testing?"

"Oh, I like him." Nix laughed. Ignoring the black look from his mate, he circled Uriskel and stuck a hand out. "I'm Nix. That's Shade."

"And I'm a rat, apparently." He stared at the outstretched hand. "You'll excuse me for being rude, but certain kinds don't react well to my touch. You're one of them, cat-man."

Shade snorted. "Lies."

"Care for a demonstration?"

Nix snatched his hand away. "You're excused."

"All right, children." Cobalt sighed and glanced at the clock. He had a center-stage appointment in five minutes. "Anyone want to offer a definition for haven?"

Shade settled her gray eyes on him. "Point taken. No more offending our gracious, if somewhat gullible, host." A half smile lifted her mouth. "Nix. We should get to know Cobalt's new friend. It may take all night."

"Fantastic," Uriskel said with a barely concealed groan. "Perhaps the Sluagh would care for some refreshment. Like a nice, steaming bowl of my blood."

Shade's smile grew a fraction. "I don't drink foreign brands. Such a nasty aftertaste. But I'll let you buy me a local brew…sailor."

Nix doubled over with a howl of laughter. "This is going to be fun." He pulled out the chair next to Uriskel. "Go on, Cobalt. We'll be fine here."

"I'll bet you will." He shook his head, turned away, and headed for the center booth. The first day, he told himself, would be the hardest. Tomorrow the empty ache inside him would diminish a bit. Tomorrow he wouldn't see Will's tortured flesh every time he closed his eyes, or the look on Will's face for the moment he trusted him—like the sun breaking through clouds.

Tomorrow. But not today.

Chapter Ten

He'd only meant to grab a quick nap. But when Will woke, it was to sluggish sun behind the thick curtains of the hotel-room window.

"Damn it!" He rolled over instinctively. Pain slapped him and brought tears to his eyes. His back arched and fell. Cursing again, he bolted upright—and his ass reminded him that was a bad idea. He jolted sideways. And fell off the bed.

He landed on his knees with a bone-jarring thud. For a moment he didn't move. Shock gradually gave way to incredulity...and then he laughed, and laughed, and laughed some more. Every time he thought he'd stop, a mental image of himself flopping around on the bed like a beached fish set him off again.

When he finally got himself under control, he felt okay. Not great—he still throbbed in places he'd never even realized had nerves before—but better. Actually healing. Maybe there had been some kind of magic in Cobalt's treatment.

No. Cobalt was off-limits. The man already had enough wounded strays and beautiful lovers. Will wasn't interested in the role of fawning fanboy.

"Phone," he muttered aloud. "Where's the goddamn phone?" He flung an arm on the bed and prospected through twisted blankets and disheveled pillows. His fingers brushed plastic. He grabbed the phone and turned it on.

Two missed calls. Both Tess.

He dialed her number, feeling strangely relieved that Lyle hadn't tried to call back. Maybe he really would leave him alone. The phone rang too many times, and Tess finally picked up with a sleep-slurred "this'd better be Will."

"What if it's not?"

She groaned. "Don't mess with me. 'S too early. You didn't call last night."

"I know." He shifted to take some of the pressure off his knees. "I fell asleep. Sorry, hon."

"Thought you might have. Only reason I didn't call the cops."

Will smiled. "There you go again, being psychic."

"Yeah." Bedsprings creaked in the background. "Hold on, 'kay?"

She didn't wait for him to affirm. A muffled thump said she'd put the phone down. He waited and after a minute, he caught himself humming. Providing his own Muzak. He didn't recognize the tune. Must have heard it somewhere recently.

"You there?" Tess sounded marginally awake now.

"No. I'm headed to Florida. This is a recording."

"Things must've gone well last night, wiseass. Unless— hold on." Her voice slid to a warning cant. "You did call that slimy bastard, didn't you?"

"Yes, Mother." He chuckled at her annoyed growl. "I did. And he's going to leave me alone. I told him we were through, and he accepted it." That was the important part. He didn't need to tell her the rest.

"You better be sure about that. He didn't threaten you? Say anything stupid?"

Oh yeah. Lyle had said a lot of stupid things. But they weren't threats. "Nope," he said. "No yelling. No vows for revenge. Actually, he apologized."

"Not fucking good enough," Tess said through her teeth.

"That's pretty much what I said." "*You liked it.*" Will shivered and pushed the phantom thought away. Regardless of his body's reaction—and he still wasn't convinced of that—Lyle was an asshole. And permanently gone from his life. "So, I'll definitely be back on Monday."

"Good, because I'm starting to like Leonard in your spot."

"Ha-ha."

"I'm serious." He could almost hear her teasing grin. "No gallons of fan e-mail to delete, no phones ringing off the walls, no underwear in the mail. It's nice and peaceful at the station."

"Must be exciting."

"Terribly." She paused. "Is it Monday yet?"

"Tess, I think I love you."

"You'd better." She cleared her throat, and her tone grew serious. "What are you going to do now?"

Good question. He knew what he had to do but didn't want to think about it. Time to pick up the pieces and move on. Again. "I guess I'll head home and...clean up." He managed not to choke on the last words. He'd have to face the mess in the bathroom.

"Want some help?"

He wanted to scream. The last thing he wanted was to walk into his apartment alone, much less spend a few hours scrubbing caked blood and vomit from the floor, the tub, the wall behind the towel bar. But he couldn't let Tess see how bad things had gotten. She might do something stupid—like try to shoot Lyle after all. "No, it's cool," he said in what he hoped was a normal voice. "I just need to relax for a while."

"All right. You up for going out tonight? I'll buy you a drink. Or five."

He laughed. "You're on. By tonight, I'll need it."

"I'll call you after wrap-up."

They hung up, and he stared at the phone for a minute. One bar left. Another reason to get home—his charger had to be there.

Will got to his feet and padded into the bathroom. While he relieved himself, he looked longingly at the shower. No way he could stand it. The showers in this place had jet-intensity pressure. Good for sobering up or soothing a hangover, bad for massive bruising. He settled for running his head under the tap.

On his way back to the room, another unpleasant thought occurred to him. The clothes in the bathroom hamper would stink beyond salvation by now. He'd lose his favorite jeans and two of his best shirts, at least. He decided to stop at the Asylum on the way home and pick up a few things. He hadn't been there in a while. They probably had new stock.

Besides, he didn't really want to go back home yet. The ghosts were waiting.

* * *

The Alternative Asylum carried everything from Levi's and Raw Vibes to slave collars and vampire teeth. They kept the place dark at all hours and pumped heavy synth music through the speakers. An occasional dramatic hiss from the back of the store announced a fog machine going off in front of the Romper Room. Will edged past a display of multiflavored condoms and headed for the jeans.

Halfway there, the smell hit him. Smoke and water and sultry summer air. *Cobalt.*

He stumbled in place. The scent was real enough to taste. For a moment he didn't understand why it was hitting him now—and then he saw the two men standing by the shirt racks. Their backs were to him, but there was no mistaking either the tall, dark-haired one or the barely shorter redhead. Cobalt and his reluctant refugee.

Some part of him insisted on getting out of there before he was noticed, but he couldn't make himself move. Just being near the man sent him into heat. Not good for his determination to refuse to join the legion of Cobalt worshippers.

Two men don't make a legion.

Will told himself to shut up. He wouldn't be a third. Hell, he wouldn't even be an only—not for a long time. Not after Lyle. What he would do was get the jeans he'd come for and get out. Before he took a single step, Cobalt froze in the act of shunting a shirt aside. He turned slowly. Shock registered on his face and slid into controlled blankness.

"Will?"

"Yeah. Hi." *Busted.* "I didn't know you shopped here."

"Not often."

The redhead, Skelly, glanced over at Will and smirked. "You know, I've a need for a new coat," he said. "Think I'll go and have a look at them. Have fun with your little friend." With a bare nod to Cobalt, he cleared the rack and walked toward the back of the shop.

Cobalt glared after him for a moment, then lapsed back to polite neutrality. "You're better, then."

"Getting there." Will hooked a thumb in his pocket. "Thanks. For…you know. Everything."

"It wasn't a problem."

"Yeah. Well. See you around."

Cobalt simply nodded. As though Will were a passing acquaintance who hadn't been naked in his bed two nights ago.

It was an effort to start moving, but he managed. Damned if he would stand there and pretend nothing had happened. If Cobalt wanted to forget it, that was fine with him. Save him the trouble of getting over it.

"Will…wait."

He almost didn't. "What?"

"I have something at the studio that I think belongs to you. A cell phone charger."

Damn. Of course it'd be something he needed. "Yes, it's mine," he said. "Mind if I come by and pick it up? My phone's just about dead." He tried to sound casual about it. He hadn't wanted to go back to the Grotto at all.

"I could bring it to you, if you'd like."

At first he thought maybe mind reading was one of Cobalt's many talents. But it was just as likely the man didn't want him at his place. He could take him up on it—but did he really want Cobalt to know where he lived? It probably didn't matter. Wasn't like he'd actually drop by sometime. He just wouldn't invite him inside.

"Fine. Thank you." He gave his address and added, "I'm going home after this, so if you could…"

"Yes. I'll bring it directly."

At once, Will couldn't stand playing the forced-distance game anymore. He wanted to scream, throw something, slap Cobalt right in the face. Anything to erase that awful blank expression. But since he didn't want to cause a scene, he just nodded and walked away.

He would not let that son of a bitch see how much he'd hurt him.

* * *

Being around Will Ambrose was bad for Cobalt's reasoning—because he lost it every time. What was he thinking, offering to bring the damned charger to him?

He knew, of course. He couldn't bear to have Will return to the Grotto. It would undo every resolution he'd made to let the man go and therefore spare his life. Still, he could have simply mailed the thing or paid a courier to deliver it. Asked Malik to bring it, even. But no. He'd chosen to torment himself further.

"Any chance you might do something about that seal of yours?"

Uriskel's voice pulled him from his thoughts, and he realized they'd almost reached the building. "You know I can't remove it," he said. "I am sorry, but—"

"Yes, fine. Just suffer, Uriskel. Nothing I'm not used to." He sighed and stared at the door. "I don't suppose there's a back way in."

"It's sealed. The windows too."

"Marvelous." Uriskel glanced at the bag in his hands. "Would you take this, then? I'll need my hands free to break my fall."

Cobalt nodded, took the bag. "I'm sorry—"

"Save it." There was no anger in his tone, only a weary resignation.

"All right." He unlocked the door, walked inside, and waited. Uriskel only paused an instant before he crossed the threshold. He managed five steps this time and collapsed predictably on hands and knees. He made no sound, but it was a full minute before he moved again.

Cobalt tried to ignore a stab of guilt. At least Uriskel could come and go as he pleased—once invited, the invitation held unless Cobalt chose to revoke it. But he could do nothing for the pain. He'd not risk allowing Eoghann to find a way around the Law and inside his sanctuary.

"I'll need to leave for a while," Cobalt said after the Unseelie got to his feet.

Uriskel smirked. "Plans with your pretty human?"

"I've told you, I'll not discuss him with you." Cobalt thrust the bag at him. "Feel free to amuse yourself as you see fit. I'll not be long."

"You should not—" Uriskel cut himself off. "I assume you'll return before dark, then."

"Yes." With Eoghann's threat hanging over them, it was no longer safe to venture out at night. The Laws prevented the Fae from killing one another in the human realm— though it did not stop them from cutting and torturing, as Uriskel had demonstrated when he arrived at the Grotto. But when the moon showed its face, this death protection was negated. More than one Fae had been murdered by moonlight here. Now, with the lunar cycle approaching its zenith, he could not risk straying from the security of the Grotto for long.

"Very well. I'd wish you good fortune, but it wouldn't seem sincere."

"And the same to you."

Cobalt entered the studio, vaguely aware of Uriskel trailing behind him. Once inside, the Unseelie headed for the stairs at a weary plod. Drained, no doubt, from fighting the effects of the seal. He tried to ignore a twinge of empathy.

He retrieved the charger from his office and headed back outside to hail a cab, locking up again behind him. Before long, a taxi pulled over. Cobalt climbed in and gave the address Will had told him.

Damn. He'd managed not to think about their encounter until now. Will had seemed reserved, and more than a little angry. Not that he could blame the man. Cobalt had deliberately kept his distance, hoping to reinforce the idea that he could never involve himself with Will. It had almost worked—until he'd foolishly invited himself to see him again.

A brief ride brought him to a walk-up brownstone in decent condition. Spare but well-maintained bushes lined the front of the building, fenced by a wooden border, and a few worn spots near ground level marked places where graffiti had been patiently sanded away. Fire stairs with minimal rust zigzagged the exterior on the left side.

He followed the sidewalk to the entrance. The recessed door sported a dull brass push-button combination lock. To the left, labeled buzzers lay in a row beneath a speaker. He took a breath and pressed 3-C. He waited a full minute. No response.

He tried again, held the button a bit longer this time. Still nothing. Either Will hadn't gotten here yet, or he'd decided not to let him in. As he stood there debating whether to wait a while, risk unlocking the door, or simply leave, a voice behind him muttered, "'Scuse me."

He turned. Not Will. The man on the sidewalk was pale skinned, gaunt to the point of sickliness. His clothing fluttered loosely on his frame. A knit cap clung to his head like a second skin. He clutched a bag from a video-rental store in one hand, and his eyes fixed on the ground while he waited for Cobalt to move.

"Sorry." Cobalt stepped aside.

The man gave him a hesitant glance. "No prob—hey. You're that tattoo guy. Cobalt, right? From the Grotto."

"Yes."

"Right, I been to your place before. Got this done there." He pushed up a baggy sleeve to show an elaborate cross entwined with snakes. Inked, but only partially colored. "Always meant to get it finished, but it's too late now."

A strange thing to say. "Why's that?" Cobalt asked.

He looked away. "I've got HIV, man." His lips barely moved. "Can't be getting my blood all over people."

Cobalt's heart wrenched. A litany of typical sympathetic phrases danced across the tip of his tongue, but he didn't doubt this man had already heard them in spades. Instead, he smiled and said, "Have you considered airbrushing?"

The man blinked at him a few times—then threw back his head and laughed. "Damn, you're good," he said. "Most people'd be backing up like I just spit on them and running for the next train." He held out a hand. "Name's Jared."

Cobalt took it without hesitation. "And you know mine," he said. "A pleasure."

"Most people wouldn't say that either." Jared dropped his hand and watched him warily. When Cobalt didn't wipe his palm on anything or stammer a hasty excuse and leave, he said, "So. What brings you to this pretty little urban oasis?"

"I'm supposed to meet someone here."

"Customer or friend? Don't answer that. Not my business." Jared smiled. The expression banished some of the sickness from him and revealed a hauntingly attractive face. "Not having any luck with the buzzers?"

"Not really."

"They don't work half the time anyway. Who're you here to see?"

He hesitated. "Will Ambrose."

"Ah, the radio boy. Our most famous resident." Jared stepped back and studied him for a minute. "If you want, you can come in with me and try knocking."

"You don't mind? I'd rather not get you into trouble."

"Don't need you for that." He gave a light laugh and punched a code into the lock. "Besides, you won't rob anybody or anything. Right?"

"Right." Cobalt waited while the man opened the door. "By the way, I'm serious about the airbrushing. If you'd like to get that finished, stop by anytime. I'll make sure you get in."

Jared stepped through, waved him inside. "You don't have to do that, man," he said to the floor. "But thanks. I might take you up on that."

"It's not sympathy," Cobalt said. "I just hate to see a fine piece like that go to waste."

Jared smiled, though the motion seemed weary now. "Yeah. Hey, listen…thanks for treating me like a human. I don't get that much anymore."

"Thank *you*. For believing I'll not rob anyone."

"Sure." He nodded toward the stairs. "I'm on the first floor. There's no elevator, so have fun climbing two flights."

Jared waved and made his way down the hall. Cobalt watched him for a moment, heavy with sorrow. Ten years among humans and he still mourned the frailty of life—and marveled at the strength of those who faced death with such courage and acceptance.

At last he mounted the stairs, his thoughts turning to Will. He should not have come. He'd simply hand him the charger, wish him well, and leave.

It would be easy, he told himself. Easy as plucking his own eye from his head.

Chapter Eleven

The third-floor hallway was not empty. Near the end, a figure crouched awkwardly by the wall—swaying on the balls of his feet, his head bent.

Cobalt didn't need to see his face to know who it was. He strode the length of the hall and knelt beside him. "Will," he said gently. "What's wrong?"

The swaying stopped. Will raised his head and stared with red-rimmed eyes. "Can't do it," he said, his voice broken and rasping. "Can't go in there."

"All right. Okay." Cobalt's heart ached for him. "Is your...anyone else inside?"

Will shook his head. "B-bathroom," he stammered. "I can't..." He closed his eyes, and a long breath stuttered from him. "Jesus. I'm sorry. Can you help me up?"

Cobalt straightened and held a hand down. Will took it with both of his. He levered himself to his feet, kept his gaze averted. "Thanks," he murmured. A pause. Then: "I'm all right. You can just leave the charger."

"You're not all right." Despite his best intentions, he couldn't just leave Will like this. "What's happened? Let me help you."

Will stared at him for a long moment. At last he seemed to reach some decision, and his features grew resolute. "This is not an offer, but I could use a friend." He nodded at the door across the hall. "It won't be pretty in there."

At first Cobalt wasn't sure what he meant, but understanding hit him soon enough. Here was where his partner had beaten him. Will had struggled—of course he'd struggled. He hadn't yet cleaned up the mess, and now he fought the memories that would surge against him when he laid eyes on the aftermath.

"I'll come with you, if you'd like," he said.

Will sighed and raked his hair. "Yeah. I think I would." He produced a key from his pocket, crossed the hall, and unlocked the door. He stood with a hand on the knob for a moment. Something dark flickered in his face, and he held his breath while he opened the door.

Hot, sour air poured into the hall. Will recoiled and plunged inside. When he didn't look back, Cobalt followed him and found him headed across the living room at a determined gait. He stopped before a window and switched on the box fan mounted there. "Sorry," he muttered. "Stinks in here."

"It's not bad." But it was—and not just the rank odor of sickness that had settled into everything. Cobalt could practically smell the spent emotions. Fear, desperation, and shame had forged a dark signature, underscored with old salt and metal. Sweat and blood.

Nothing appeared disturbed in the main room. To the right lay a shadowed alcove, a hallway, and beyond that an open area marking the border of a narrow kitchen. He would have thought the bedroom would be hardest to face; but outside, Will had said *bathroom*. He had to assume the beating had taken place there. Which was even worse.

Will hadn't moved from the window. He reached up and idly twitched a curtain, stared outside. "Did I mention it won't be pretty?" he said without turning.

"You did." Cobalt let himself study the room and waited for Will to choose his actions at his own pace. Nearly everything was shades of blue, with black or silver accents. Though the place could have been painfully neat, showroom perfect, the occasional spot of casual disarray suggested that Will lived alone. Thank the gods for small favors.

At last, Will moved away from the fan and headed uncertainly across the room. He stopped by the hall. "Down here," he said, his voice barely carrying the few feet to where Cobalt stood. "Can you...?"

"Of course." Cobalt went to him and followed him to the first door on the right. It was ajar, and the smell emanating from the opening curdled his stomach. Like part of Will had died in there and lay decaying for as long as he'd been gone.

Will closed his eyes, reached in, and turned on the light. When he opened them, he studied Cobalt's face. "Is it as bad as I think?" he whispered.

Cobalt looked—and immediately wished he hadn't.

Outside of the blood, it was impossible to tell what had been spilled, though he doubted any of it was toothpaste or shampoo. Dried splatters and droplets formed a grotesque pattern on cold gray tile. Long, wavering tracks smeared through the unspeakable mess suggested that something—

someone—had been dragged across the floor. Dark handprints clung to the rim of the tub like dead spiders.

"Oh, Will," he said. "It's worse than you think."

Will nodded. The color drained from him, but he pivoted to face the room and stood motionless for a long moment. He walked inside with careful steps, turned a slow circle. His features appeared serene. With calm precision, he approached the toilet, lifted the lid, knelt. And abruptly vomited.

Cobalt hurried in and dropped beside him. He dared not touch his heaving shoulders, but he rested a hand on the back of Will's head and stroked his sweat-damped hair. When the retching subsided to choked gasps, he folded a hand over Will's trembling one. "All right, then," he said gently. "You've seen. Now go and rest, and let me take care of this for you."

Will turned his head and fixed him with a glittering gaze. "No. I can't ask you to do that."

"You're not asking. I'm offering."

"But—"

"Let me help you." He reached out, smoothed Will's hair back from his brow—and instantly regretted the unconscious gesture when an ache settled in his groin. Gods, how he wanted to kiss the torment from those drawn lips. "You shouldn't have to do this."

Will closed his eyes with a sigh. "I'm going to hate myself for this...but okay. I'll take you up on it. And thank you."

"You're welcome." Cobalt helped him to his feet and guided him to the door. "Go on, then. I'll assume you have something in here to clean with?"

"Under the sink." Will shuffled into the hall, turned, and made a tired gesture. "My clothes, in the hamper. They're hopeless. I was just going to throw them away."

"Yes. I'll take care of it."

"Mm-hm." Will stared dully beyond the doorway. He blinked a few times, caught a breath. "He's a cop. Lyle, I mean," he said. "I took a shower when I got home, and he...he came in here, waited for me. I didn't even hear him. He handcuffed me to the towel bar..." His words ground to a hoarse stop. "I'm sorry. I can't." He lurched away, stumbled around the corner. A moment later, a thump sounded from the vicinity of the kitchen, a fist pounding a flat surface. On its heels came a single, wrenching sob.

Cobalt fought the urge to go out now and hunt down this Lyle, to snap his fragile human neck with his bare hands. Instead he opened the cabinet under the sink and gathered what he would need. This was the least, and perhaps the most, he could do for Will.

In that moment, though, he would have done anything to ease that devastated look in his eyes. Anything at all.

* * *

Will gripped the edge of the sink and glared at the drain as though it were to blame for all his troubles. He would not throw up again. Would not. No.

His stomach hitched, settled. The greasy slick in his throat slithered away and left a dull sour-metallic taste. He spat and triggered a gag reflex that threatened to bring on another round of heaves. *Jesus, no more.* He stood perfectly still, breathing through his nose until the feeling passed. It took forever.

He grabbed a glass, filled it with water, and tried to rinse the awful taste from his mouth. It helped a little. He stood there a minute longer, willing the ghoulish replay to leave his head. He'd known it would be bad—but Christ, he didn't think it would look like someone had slaughtered a pig in there. The floor looked awful, but it was the wall that had thrown his guts into reverse overdrive. His blood on the wall. And the damned towel bar. He'd take the thing down and get rid of it, when he could stand looking at it.

Focusing on Cobalt seemed to help drive away the demons. The man had uncanny timing. Three times now, he'd been there just when Will couldn't refuse his assistance. The truth was, he probably wouldn't have been able to come back inside his apartment alone, and Cobalt was the only one he could deal with to accompany him. He'd already seen what Lyle had done. That was why he'd taken him up on the offer. Not because he was attracted to him. Anyone with more than two brain cells drooled over Cobalt. No surprise there. It was like having a crush on a rock star.

A rock star who was currently on his knees, scrubbing blood and puke from his bathroom floor. Who'd held his head unflinchingly while he emptied his guts in the toilet. No one had ever done that for him. Not a single one of his lovers, not Tess. Not even his own mother.

However, also like a rock star, Cobalt already had plenty of groupies.

Will shook himself and moved away from the sink. He looked through cabinets until he found a fat, vanilla-scented candle. Maybe it would help to cut some of the stink in here. He set it on the short counter closest to the living room and found a lighter in his jacket. Once the candle was lit, he eased the jacket off, thought about a smoke, and decided against it. He'd take Cobalt's suggestion and rest for a while.

First, though, he made sure the front door was locked and chained. Just in case.

He lay on the couch, on his side, and found it didn't hurt as much as he'd expected. He might even manage to sit for a while tonight, when he went out with Tess. Had to remember to call her so she wouldn't freak out. With that thought in mind, he drifted without dreams.

When he opened his eyes again, Cobalt sat on the chair across from the couch, watching him. Will stole a moment to watch him back. Once again he was struck by the artist's pure sensuality. Dark hair and flawless skin. Fierce, fluid tattoos. Even his piercings blended with the curves of his face, part of him rather than tacked on. He wanted to lick the lower-lip stud and find out whether it was hot or cold.

Cobalt shifted and leaned forward in the chair. "It's done," he said. There was a rawness in his voice, a pained look in his eyes. He made them both vanish and said, "I've left your charger on that table there, by the door."

"Thank you." Will pushed up and settled cautiously in a seated position. Tolerable, for now. "I can't repay you the same way, but would you like a drink? Unless you want me to come over and clean your bathroom sometime."

Cobalt smiled. He glanced at the watch on his wrist and said, "A drink would be fine. Unfortunately, I can't have anything alcoholic. I'll have to work in a few hours."

"I was thinking coffee." Will tried to ignore the suggestion that he was a drunk. He probably would've assumed the same thing.

"Of course. Thank you, yes."

Will levered himself to his feet and walked to the kitchen. Maybe if he wasn't looking at Cobalt, he could think a little more clearly. The man overloaded his senses. He had to keep in mind that any relationship right now, even a fling, was a bad idea—especially when it involved someone who was already attached.

Then again, what the hell made him think Cobalt would *want* a relationship with him? He had to stop fantasizing. Make coffee, exchange pleasantries, and put this interlude behind them both. Cobalt was probably anxious to get back to his studio, anyway. He stuffed a fresh filter in the machine, scooped grounds, and brought the pot to the sink.

"How are you feeling, Will?"

He almost dropped the pot. Cobalt's voice, soft with concern, came from a few feet behind him. "Don't sneak up on me," he muttered and turned the water on. "All right, I guess. Considering." He filled the pot halfway, moved to the coffee machine, and got it started.

"That's good. I'd just been thinking that perhaps I should have given you more supplies. You need to take care of your—Well, you'll want to at least use the antibiotic. To prevent infection."

Will turned to face him and smirked. "You just want to get my shirt off again."

"Perhaps I do."

An answering laugh died in his throat when he realized there was no trace of amusement in Cobalt's face. Only desire. Will swallowed, licked his lips. He opened his mouth but couldn't think of a thing to say.

Cobalt closed the distance between them. At once, the scent Will had come to associate with him filled the room, filled his being. It was everything cleansing and purifying— water, fire, wind. Sweet and dangerous. Cobalt's hand rose, and those long fingers brushed the side of his face, settled under his chin, and lifted. Jesus, he was going to kiss him.

And Will wasn't going to stop him.

Cobalt lowered his head. "Will." He moaned, his mouth inches away. Apparent indecision froze him there, and Will tried to come to his senses. He couldn't let this happen. He had to say no, move away, before—

Then Cobalt's lips were on his, and pure lust washed the thoughts from his head. The contact was electric hot, jolting him all the way down. A bare taste of the man reminded Will of his scent...clean, raw power. He wanted more. Tongue and teeth and naked flesh.

No. Logic finally penetrated his hormones. This was a bad idea. Will pulled back firmly and turned aside. His body cried foul, but he ignored it. "I'm sorry," he said, and made himself look back.

Confusion and hurt played across Cobalt's face. He blinked, straightened, and the neutral stare he'd displayed earlier returned. "I'm the one to apologize," he said. "I was inappropriate. You're hurt."

"It's not that." Will eased out from between Cobalt and the counter, and approached the fridge with no particular intention outside of putting some distance between them. "Mostly it's because you're involved. I don't do multiple partners." He tried to sound angry, or at least firm, but only managed a pathetic whine. At least he'd said it now. Subject closed.

But Cobalt didn't seem inclined to drop it. "I've told you, Skelly and I are not lovers. I am doing a favor—"

"Yeah, I know. You're letting him heal. Just like you did for me, right?" This time he couldn't keep the frustration from his voice. "So why should there be any difference between him and me? I'll bet we're not the only strays you've taken in."

"Please. He is nothing like you."

"Besides," Will said. "I wasn't even talking about him. I meant Trystan."

"Trystan?" Cobalt repeated, as if he'd never heard the name.

"Yes. Trystan. Pretty little blond dressed in black. The guy you were hanging all over when I brought Tess to your place. Remember?"

Cobalt flinched. Seconds ticked by in silence. He crossed his arms tightly in front of him, and his gaze dropped to the floor. "No. That is, I do remember, but…" He let out a sigh, looked up. "Trystan is not my partner. He's a prostitute."

"Oh my God." Memories of that night filtered back through the obliteration Lyle's beating had imposed. He knew he'd recognized something about Cobalt. It was in the way he'd said his name—the same way the troubled caller had addressed him at the end. The one who'd said "*I pay men for sex.*"

A bitter smile stretched Cobalt's lips. "What you must think of me now," he said. "I'll be going, then. I won't trouble you again."

"It was you," Will blurted.

Cobalt raised an eyebrow. "What was?"

"You called my show. The night I went to your place."

For an instant Will thought he would deny it. But his gaze unfocused, and he said, "Yes. I did."

"Shit. Cobalt, I'm sorry. I'm not supposed to know—I *didn't* know, until just now."

"And this knowledge changes things for you?"

The pain he'd heard on the call came flooding back, and once again Will found himself desperate to comfort him. "Not really. Like I said, it's the multiple-partner thing that concerned me. I don't like swingers."

"Well, it should. I meant what I said, Will." He shook his head and backed toward the living room. "I have driven men to insanity. To death. I am cursed."

"I don't believe that."

"No? Perhaps you should visit the Kerner Clinic in Lower Manhattan. Or the Heywood Cemetery. You will believe."

"It has to be something else. Not you. There's no such thing as a curse."

"I should not have—" Cobalt stopped himself, turned away. "Good-bye, Will."

"Wait!" Will caught his lower lip in his teeth. This wasn't working the way he wanted. "Please, listen to me for a minute. Don't leave."

Cobalt stood rigid and motionless. At last, he said in a rasping voice, "I must."

He walked around the corner and headed for the door.

Chapter Twelve

Cobalt got as far as putting a hand on the doorknob. But he couldn't make himself leave.

What a fool he was. Had he really thought Will would never know he'd called? He should not have confessed—it would have been easier for both of them if he'd simply let Will assume he and Trystan were lovers. Then he could have walked away.

And he definitely should not have kissed him.

Yet it was done, and to leave now would be cruel. Somehow, he had to explain why things had to end here, without revealing his true nature.

"Thought you had to go."

If there had been any trace of hostility in Will's voice, he would have gone then. But there was only concern and a touch of sadness. His hand fell away from the door. "I'd like to stay a bit, if you'll have me." He turned, managed a smile. "I was promised coffee."

"Yeah, you were. Come on."

He followed Will back to the kitchen and took the seat he was offered. The table rested against the wall beneath a window, though the view was not much. Just the back of a stacked parking service. Cars in cages. Still, it was better staring at a window than a wall.

Will opened a cabinet and extracted two mugs. "How do you like it?" he said. "I've got sugar, milk, and powdered shit."

Cobalt smirked. "As appetizing as powdered shit sounds, milk and sugar will suffice."

"You got it." Will poured and prepared both coffees the same, and set a cup on the table in front of him. "One shit-free coffee."

"Thank you." Cobalt wrapped both hands around the warm mug. "I believe I owe you an explanation."

Will moved closer to the table. He glanced at the other wooden chair but didn't sit down. "I don't know if you do," he said. "But I think you could use an ear, and maybe some advice."

"So you'll want to hear my troubles now." He ran a finger along the rim of the mug, an absent motion. "Shall I bore you with my sordid affairs?"

"That's what I do. People talk, and I listen."

People, indeed. But he was not one of them. "Very well, then." He pushed up his right sleeve to reveal the Gaelic names he'd had tattooed there. "In ten years, I've had three lovers. Each of them lost his mind and attempted to end the relationship by committing suicide. The third succeeded. That was four years ago, and I've not taken another since."

Will stared at him. After a minute, he said, "Is that it?"

"Is that not enough?"

"I'm sorry. It's just—well, I guess I expected a common theme or something. If it's supposed to be a curse."

Cobalt closed his eyes. "*I* am the common theme."

"Cobalt. Look at me."

He looked. Will held an arm out to reveal a long, jagged scar on the underside of his forearm. "This was Yvan," he said. "When I told him I'd gotten my own show, he came after me with a knife. He thought I planned to get famous and sleep around. After him was Adrian, who had six or seven lovers on the side and broke my leg when he decided I'd given him syphilis. Then came Brett. He knew how to hit without leaving marks. And you know about Lyle. Do you think I'm cursed?"

Cobalt shuddered at the wave of empathy Will's litany brought on. How could one man endure so much? He wasn't sure how to respond, so he simply answered the question. "Of course not. You could not have been at fault. They were."

"But it's your fault that your lovers were suicidal?"

Damn it, yes. "My circumstances were different."

"How? I see plenty of similarities." Will set his mug down on the table and crossed his arms. "People tend to attract, or be attracted to, certain types. I'm a magnet for closet psychos with violent streaks. You end up with guys who're severely depressed."

"You don't understand." Frustration brought Cobalt to his feet. The theory made sense—for a human. How could he explain that they only descended into madness after they discovered he was Fae? He'd have to lie. But Will would know if he did. Gods, he should have left when he had the opportunity.

A light touch on his arm brought his focus back. Will stood before him, practically glowing with concern. "It can't be your fault," he said. "It's the way you are that attracts men like that. The needy ones. You anticipate needs, even little things. Like leaving food out for starving strays." A smile tugged at his mouth. "You were good for them. And you didn't destroy them. They destroyed themselves."

Everything inside him drew taut. He'd never desired any man more than this, and that should have been the greatest reason to leave him alone. He wanted to protect Will from those who would harm him—including himself. It took every bit of control he had to keep from touching him, claiming his mouth once more.

"Cobalt? You didn't hear a word I said." Will frowned and caught his lip with his teeth.

The sensual gesture spurred flames in Cobalt's groin. "Ah, Will," he groaned. "I did. But must you do that?"

"Do what?"

"This." He stood, reached out, and brushed a finger along his lower lip. "You bite it, and it maddens me. I'll not be able to stop myself."

"From…"

Cobalt fisted his free hand. The nails dug hard into his palm. "From kissing you again."

"Then don't stop."

An invitation was more than he could bear.

He tried to move slowly, but raw passion swept tenderness aside. His hand slipped to the back of Will's head and held him in place while he pressed his mouth to his. The taste of him was divine, intoxicating. *More.* The word reverberated through his mind and overruled all thoughts of stopping. He probed with his tongue, and Will parted for him.

He deepened the kiss. Hands settled on his waist and sent a jolt to his throbbing cock. He moaned, felt Will shiver against him. Were it not for the injuries, he would have crushed the man to him, touched him everywhere. But he had to see where his hands fell. He drew back to catch a breath and to navigate better.

Will's eyes blazed at him. He leaned forward until they were nearly pressed together. His tongue darted out and caressed the stud in Cobalt's lip. "It's warm," he whispered. "Not cold."

"You leave nothing cold in me." His voice emerged ragged. "Will. I want you against me. Your back, though... I'll not hurt you. But I need your touch. I need to feel you."

"Allow me, then." Will's hands slid lower to frame his ass and draw his hips forward. His erection rubbed Will's hard cock. "Shit," Will hissed. "You feel that. Right?"

Cobalt made a low, animal growl. "More. Please..."

"God, Cobalt." Will pushed against him and forced him back until he met the wall. Fingers brushed his crotch, made him gasp. "Let me touch you. All of you."

"Yes." He could barely get the word out.

Will fumbled with the catch on his jeans. A frustrated sound escaped him. "How does this thing work?" he said through his teeth.

"Let me." Cobalt unfastened them, drew the zipper open.

Will tugged everything down at once and wrapped a hand around his shaft the instant it sprang free. His touch burned. The heat sank into Cobalt's flesh and shot to his core. He wondered idly why smoke failed to pour from his mouth.

As the heated grip began to stroke, he braced one hand against the wall and used the other to draw Will's face to his. He nipped lightly at his lower lip, then kissed it. "Will," he whispered. "So sweet."

Will moaned, pumped faster. With his free hand he reached up and grabbed Cobalt's wrist. He drew the arm forward, squeezed once, and slid a finger into his mouth.

Cobalt's breath exploded from him. His sac tightened and convulsed, vibrating at the edge of release. He arched his hips, and his palm beat an erratic rhythm on the wall.

Will drew back. His tongue trailed along the underside of Cobalt's finger. Then he took two in his mouth and sucked hard.

An inarticulate cry fell from Cobalt's lips. His seed spurted, splashing Will's shirt, his hand, the floor. Will closed his eyes and groaned deep in his throat—with Cobalt's fingers still in his mouth. The vibration sent aftershocks of pleasure through him, and his cock twinged in Will's hand. He fell back panting against the wall. "You should let go now, love," he whispered. "Unless you'll be wanting another go."

Will released him slowly, fingers and shaft. He glanced down and smiled. "I guess you are getting my shirt off again."

"Yes. And perhaps a bit more." Cobalt covered himself again with a swift tug. He entwined his fingers with Will's, pulled him forward gently, and cupped the bulge in his pants. "You'll let me return the favor...won't you?"

Will bit his lip. "Oh, God. Cobalt..."

"I thought you might."

He had no trouble unfastening Will's jeans.

Will didn't even realize he hadn't expected reciprocation until Cobalt pulled his zipper down, notch by notch, with aching slowness. Damn, he was really going to touch him. Part of him wanted to stop now, while he still had a chance to end this before he went off the emotional deep end.

The rest of him didn't give a shit what his sensibilities thought.

Cobalt ran a thumb along the inside of his waistband and stopped at his hip. "I don't want to hurt you," he rasped.

"You'll only hurt me if you stop." His cock strained against the fabric. The ache there eclipsed his sore ass, drove away every other sensation except Cobalt's thumb on his flesh—and that intoxicating scent of his, which seemed to grow stronger when he was aroused, like some kind of pheromone. How could any man smell like that?

Cobalt slid the fingers of both hands between fabric and flesh and bent to Will's mouth again. His tongue demanded entrance. Will took him in with a soft moan and held his head in place while Cobalt worked the jeans down. He gasped when cool air flowed around his inflamed cock. Jesus, he'd never been this hard in his life.

A finger rubbed his opening and trailed the throbbing vein on the underside of his shaft, spreading his thin, leaking fluid. Will's body clenched and shuddered. He thrust his hips forward, a silent plea for the full contact he craved.

"Will," Cobalt murmured against his lips. "Let me taste you. I want you in my mouth."

"Yes," he breathed before his brain could process the demand. "Christ, yes."

Cobalt smiled. He reached up and caught Will's wrists, held them as he sank down and knelt on the floor. "Look at you," he said hoarsely. "So swollen. Fit to burst."

"Tease," Will ground out. He was practically vibrating, and Cobalt had barely touched him. His balls were drawn tighter than Fort Knox. He was going to come just thinking about Cobalt's mouth on him.

The grip on his wrists loosened. Cobalt ran his hands down Will's arms and settled them on his hips. His tongue flicked the engorged head, lapped a glistening bead from the slit like a bird tasting nectar.

Will groaned at the fire spreading through his groin. "Please..."

"Yes, love. Now." Cobalt dipped his head and swallowed him in a single thrust, all the way to the base.

Will cried out. He braced his hands on Cobalt's shoulders and drew breath through gritted teeth. His mind insisted this was a new level in the fantasy—the dark god on his knees in front of him, sucking him off. Calling him *love*.

But the sensations were too powerful to be imagined. A hot mouth and a silk tongue clamped around his cock, hard muscles rippling beneath his palms, strong hands bracketing his hips. Ecstasy spiraling through him, driving him with dizzying speed toward release.

Cobalt drew back slowly, slid forward. Fucking him with his mouth. His blazing-hot, wet mouth. The pace increased, and the hands on his hips squeezed harder. Fingers dug into his bruised flesh. Pain entwined itself with pleasure, a sensual dance like nothing Will had ever felt before. It left him breathless and aching for more.

But he had no time to be disgusted at his apparent welcome of pain.

"Cobalt." He plunged a hand into the dark, silken hair. "Gonna come. Ease back…"

Cobalt made a delicious little sound of expectation and thrust his head forward, taking Will's cock completely in his mouth. He sucked hard, indicating with the pressure of his hands that he wanted Will to finish right where he was.

"Shit!" The word was torn from his lips. He cradled Cobalt's head, and his hips jerked once, twice. His body went rigid for what seemed like an eternity, poised on the brink of release. At last he climaxed with an explosive cry. He felt the convulsions in Cobalt's throat as the man swallowed his cum.

Will's legs weakened. He struggled to stay on his feet until Cobalt released him, and then sank to his knees with a shuddering breath. "You. Damn," he gasped. "That was… Thank you."

Cobalt smiled and brushed a thumb across Will's mouth. "You've no need to thank me, love. I wanted it just as much—and the sounds you make are thanks enough."

Will nodded, too spent to say more. His head still spun. He finally understood the term *mind-blowing orgasm*. And he also understood something else, something he'd never realized before. His reaction to Cobalt wasn't purely physical.

None of his partners had ever wanted to pleasure him after they'd gotten what they wanted. When Cobalt asked permission to touch him, he'd fallen in love a little.

Okay. Maybe a lot.

Chapter Thirteen

Cobalt helped him stand, and Will nodded toward the table while he clothed himself again. "Coffee's probably cold now," he said. "Sorry about that."

Cobalt gave his hand a brief squeeze. "I find I've no appetite for coffee anymore."

"Good. Me neither." Will broke away and wandered toward the living room. *Now what?* Generally, there were two ways this could go. One: acknowledge that sex had happened and explore the possibility of a relationship. Two: make awkward small talk until Cobalt excused himself for work, which would probably happen quickly if they went the small-talk route.

He had no idea which one he wanted to happen. What if Cobalt didn't want a relationship? What if he did—would that make him the rebound guy? The only thing he knew for sure was that he wanted more of Cobalt. His tongue, his hands, his body. Everything.

"You know, I've yet to get your shirt off again."

Will turned so fast, he almost tripped himself. Cobalt had come up directly behind him and stood staring at him with an expression that reflected the desire he still felt. Will swallowed hard. "Yeah. Guess I should change."

"Will...have you been treating your injuries?"

Will blinked a few times. Not the conversational direction he'd expected. "Uh, not really. I was going to try for a shower later."

"A shower." Cobalt shook his head. "You must take better care. You'll not enjoy an infection, believe me. May I?" He fingered the hem of Will's shirt.

Will nodded, self-conscious all over again. He turned away and held his breath while Cobalt lifted his shirt. He could still feel the shape of the welts, could recall instantly and completely the sensation of the belt drilling his flesh while he stood there, bound and helpless. *You liked it.* Christ, had he? Even now the memory stirred something deep in his gut—the whisper of a thrill. Utterly outside anything he felt toward Lyle. He'd experienced it on a deeper scale when Cobalt had pressed on his ass.

Did he actually enjoy pain?

"Relax, love," Cobalt said quietly. "You've no need to be ashamed."

For an instant Will was terrified he'd voiced his thoughts. Then he realized he'd tucked himself into a stiff, defensive posture and had tried to move away. He stepped back, straightened, and forced his muscles to unclench. "I'm sorry."

"Stop apologizing." The anger in Cobalt's voice made him flinch, but the man's next words reassured him. "It's the beast who did this to you who'll be sorry."

Will tried to ignore the idea that Cobalt might attempt to exact revenge. "Is it bad?"

"Bad enough." His tone gentled. "There's no infection, but it needs cleaning. Can we get this off?"

"All right. I'll just—"

"I'll help you." Cobalt eased the shirt up and over his head and slid it down his arms, leaving Will cradled loosely in front of him. "What do you have here for medical supplies?"

Will laughed. "A bottle of Advil and half a box of Band-Aids. With pirates on them."

"Pirates."

"Yep. Tess got them for me, when I...had blisters on my feet." Christ, he'd forgotten about that. A while back, he'd spent an entire night walking around the city, half-drunk and terrified to come home, in case Lyle was there waiting. Because he'd done a live-event broadcast, and there had been fans, and more than one had kissed him quite publicly. For some reason he'd convinced himself Lyle had seen or known about it. But he must not have—because if he had, the beating would have come then.

If Cobalt noticed the hesitation in his statement, he didn't ask about it. "I'm afraid pirate bandages won't be sufficient, much as I'd love to see them on you." The amusement in his voice reflected in his face as he came around and placed the bunched shirt on a chair. "Warm water for now. But I'll be sure you have antibiotic ointment, for the next few days at least. Do you have a clean cloth?"

Will half turned and gestured at the sink. "There's a package of dishcloths in the drawer there. I haven't opened it yet." Strange, he thought, that Cobalt was ordering him around like Tess, and he wasn't bothered in the least.

Anyone else would've gotten a dose of fuck you and there's the door. Maybe the mind-blowing orgasm had shorted something vital, like his self-preservation instincts or his common sense. Probably both.

Cobalt crossed the floor and pulled out a slim, plastic-wrapped package of light blue terry cloth. "This should do," he said. He opened it, shook one free. "It'll be a bit rough, but... Oh. Will, I apologize." A deep frown settled into his mouth. "I'll not tell you what to do. But I'd like to help you, if you'll let me."

Will smiled. Apparently Cobalt could also read his mind like Tess. "I'd like you to help me," he said. "Very much."

"Mmm. Yes. Well." Cobalt closed his eyes, and Will could practically feel him dislodging an image from his mind. "Come over here, please. Closer to the sink."

Will approached him, and Cobalt directed him to lean on the counter, his back facing him. The position was sensual enough to kindle fresh lust. He forced himself to think non-sex thoughts, like laundry and moldy take-out food. It didn't help.

Water ran in the sink. After it stopped, there was a gentle sloshing and a fast patter of drips. Will tensed without thought, anticipating the touch of the cloth.

"Breathe, Will."

He nodded and let out the breath he'd been holding. Drawing another eluded him for an instant, but he managed to settle into a shallow rhythm. Damn. What was wrong with him?

"Ready?"

"Yes," he whispered.

There was a pause. The fabric touched unbroken skin first, wet and wonderfully warm. Water drizzled down his side and pooled in his waistband. A shiver worked its way up from his toes to end in his throat. The cloth slid sideways and rubbed along one of the welts with slow, steady pressure. Once again, the pain enhanced his pleasure. He let out a soft whimper.

Cobalt froze. "Too much?"

"No." *Jesus.* This was nuts. He knew he hadn't enjoyed what Lyle did to him, and he sure as hell didn't want Cobalt to beat him with a belt. But he couldn't deny that something was happening here. "Keep going. Please."

Cobalt obliged, wiping to the other side of his back. The faucet ran briefly. He came back and moved down to the next welt, applied the same steady pressure—and Will felt himself growing hard again.

I'm a freak.

He closed his eyes and tried to force the idea from his mind. All of it. He did not enjoy pain, would not seek it out. This wasn't the reason he'd been consistently attracted to men who hurt him time and again.

Damn it. Maybe it was.

"May I ask you something odd?"

Cobalt's voice sounded thick and unsteady. Just like Will felt. If he asked whether he was a masochist, Will was going to scream. And throw something heavy. Like the coffeepot. *No no no.* "Sure," he heard himself say.

Cobalt hesitated. "Have you given any more thought to scarification?"

The breath he let out was part relief, part confusion. "Why?"

"I...suspected you were interested. Once. When we first met." He paused, wrung the cloth out again. "I'll understand if you no longer are."

Something in his tone tore at Will's heart. "Before I answer, can I ask you something?"

"Of course."

"What's it to you?" Shit. That sounded harsher than he meant. "I mean, it seems important to you, and I'd like to know why."

Cobalt paused for so long, Will thought he wouldn't reply. At last he said, "Curiosity, I suppose. You hadn't seemed the type."

"I didn't know there was a type." Will held his breath while Cobalt made another pass with the cloth. "What makes me seem like I wouldn't want it?"

"You're clean."

"And people who get scarified don't shower?"

Cobalt laughed softly. "What I mean is, you've no tattoos, no piercings. Typically, scarification is a next-level process. You are a virgin."

"Wow. I don't think anyone's accused me of that in...ever."

"Ah, Will." Cobalt's hand rested on his waist for an instant and left. "You are a blank. A beautiful, empty canvas begging to be filled. An artist's dream."

"Every artist?"

"Mine."

Had Will imagined the possessive note in his voice? It was still too much, believing that Cobalt might want him and him alone. "Well," he managed to say after he banished a searing memory of Cobalt's mouth on him. "In that case, I might still be interested."

"How about tonight?"

Yes. Now. He shivered against the counter. "I can't," he said. "I promised Tess I'd drink with her tonight. She's worried." Before he could think through the consequences, he added, "Want to join us? Tess won't mind."

Cobalt hesitated, sponged a few errant dribbles from his lower back. "Unfortunately I'll be needed at the Grotto tonight. I've neglected my duties there too long. Not that I regret for a moment what took me away from them," he said in hoarse tones. "I would do it again, without hesitation."

Will decided he would too. Only he'd rather have skipped the beating that brought him to Cobalt's bedroom.

"Well, then. Tomorrow night?"

The question took Will aback, and he realized he hadn't been taking Cobalt's interest seriously. Consciously or not, he'd filed it away under *small talk after sex.* "You want me to come to the Grotto?"

"Of course I do." The cloth rubbed over the last of the welts. "We'll not be able to begin right away, but I'd like to discuss the process with you. Design, placement. Timing."

"Oh." A small flicker of disappointment kindled in his gut. Cobalt was talking scarification, not sex. "Sure. I can do that. What time?"

"Eleven. I always finish early on Saturday nights." Cobalt wrung the cloth out and hung it over the divider between the sinks. "You may have your shirt back now."

Nodding, Will turned to find an intense expression on Cobalt's face. A touch of anger, a heavy dose of heat and desire. The dark god returning in full glory. The sight arrested his tongue.

"Will. This man who hurt you. If you want me to, I'll…"

"No." He shook his head for emphasis. "It's dangerous to fuck with Lyle. He's a cop. Besides, he promised to leave me alone. I told him we were through."

"And you're certain he'll keep this promise?"

"Yes. For the same reason—he's a cop. And he's in the closet." As the words left his mouth, he almost managed to convince himself. "He won't risk being outed, especially with me. I'm a shit-heap celebrity."

"A what?"

Will laughed. "That's a Tess term. King of the shit heap. The best of the worst." He smiled and shrugged. "She doesn't mean it in a bad way. It's kind of a radio joke. Deejays don't hit the same level as film stars. I'll never be Tom Cruise—and honestly, I'm glad for that. Too much attention, if you ask me."

He was babbling again. He made himself stop, and his teeth found his lower lip.

Cobalt groaned. "Gods, Will. You'll be my undoing yet."

Gods?

Cobalt lowered his head, claimed his mouth, and the odd thought was driven from his mind on a fresh wave of heat. A few seconds, an eternity, and the full, firm lips drew back with reluctance. "I must go," Cobalt whispered. "You're all right, then?"

He nodded, his ability to speak having fled with the kiss.

"Tomorrow night."

"Yes. See you then."

A quick smile and the dark god left.

Will didn't move until he heard the front door open and close. It took him a few minutes to realize he still held the shirt crumpled in his hands. He slipped it on and barely winced when it slid down his back. Cobalt's ministrations seemed to heal him far faster than they should.

Maybe it was psychological. He'd never felt anything as amazing as Cobalt's touch.

He drifted toward the bathroom without realizing his intended destination. Once there, he pushed the door open and stared. Sparkling floor. Pristine tub. No trace of his brutalization remained.

"I'm not going to fuck you. I'm going to punish you."

He shuddered and stepped back. Walls and floors could be washed—but who was going to scrub his mind?

The notion of setting so much as a foot in that room brought back his nausea. Good thing he didn't have to piss or anything. At this point he'd rather relieve himself in the sink than enter the bathroom. This didn't bode well for future toileting needs. He couldn't exactly shower or dump in the kitchen. He supposed eventually he'd lose the urge to purge every time he looked in there. Maybe. Hopefully.

Will headed back for the kitchen and shifted his mental gears to the Cobalt position. Not a hard thing to do. The man had barely left his mind since he'd met him. Now they'd been intimate, and he had no clue where to go from here. Another relationship—assuming Cobalt even wanted one—was just a bad idea, no matter how desperately he tried to justify it. He'd been smacked around by love enough for several lifetimes. And all his other partners had seemed normal and sane in the beginning, so who was to say Cobalt would be any different?

But damn, he wanted more. More of those hot lips, that firm flesh, that impossible, delicious scent. He wanted it all—Cobalt inside him, filling him, rocking that timeless rhythm until they both exploded with pleasure.

He carried the untouched mugs to the sink and dumped the cold coffee, rinsed and set them in the drainer. The cloth Cobalt had used to wash him lay over the divider. A few faint red-brown smudges showed on the surface, and his stomach twisted a bit. On impulse, he grabbed the cloth and dropped it in the trash.

Just as it hit bottom, the door buzzer cut through the apartment like an angry hornet trapped in a window.

Will jerked. His heart gave a few rapid thuds and settled back. *Cobalt?* Maybe he'd forgotten something. He made his way to the intercom and pressed in. "Yeah?"

"Will Ambrose." A bored monotone, male, the voice unfamiliar.

"Yes."

"FTD. Delivery for you."

He blinked. FTD... Wasn't that a flower-delivery service? Maybe Tess had sent him something as a joke. Congratulations-on-ditching-the-bastard flowers. Or maybe it was some other FTD. Federal tax department, freakish turtledoves. "I'll come down," he said into the speaker, not wanting to give a stranger access to his apartment. Just in case.

A look through the spy hole in the front building door revealed that it was, in fact, flowers. A huge bunch. Yellow and black tea roses, white orchids, lacy sprigs of baby's breath. The black roses made his brow furrow. If this was Tess's idea of a joke, he'd tell her exactly how amused he was with a hilarious dose of salt in one of her drinks tonight.

He opened the door.

"Ambrose?" The bouquet, arranged in a fat black vase, was big enough to hide the delivery person, so it looked like the flowers were talking.

"That's me."

The flowers lurched toward him, almost hungrily. "Here you go."

Will accepted the vase in slow motion and got a glimpse of the FTD guy, a slab of a specimen who looked like he'd be more at home repossessing cars than delivering flowers. "Terrific," he muttered. "Who sent them?"

"Read the card, buddy. I just drop 'em off."

"Mm-hm." He cradled the vase in one arm and dug in a pocket, producing a few crumpled bills. "Thanks."

The delivery guy took the cash and lumbered off without another word.

Will barely noticed. He kicked the door shut behind him and started up the stairs, shifting stems in search of a card. He found a small envelope with *Will* across the front in neat cursive writing—the florist's hand, most likely. Still frowning, he teased the flap open and extracted a small cream-colored card.

Babe, sorry if I hurt you. Thinking of you. I'll be waiting. Love, L.

He dropped the vase like it was full of snakes. It thumped and rolled back down the stairs, spilling petals and stems and whole flowers in a colorful spray that looked more macabre than cheerful.

Before he went out with Tess tonight, he was getting the lock changed. Lyle still had a key. And he wasn't going to risk coming back here drunk to unwanted company.

Chapter Fourteen

It was six o'clock when Cobalt returned to the Grotto. An hour before opening. Forever until he'd see Will again.

The man was addictive. One taste of him and Cobalt wanted more. *Needed* more. He should have left Will's apartment when he'd gotten as far as the door. The longer he allowed himself to believe he and Will could be together, the harder it would be to let him go.

He'd no choice in letting him go. He could not destroy Will the way he had the others.

The main room was deserted save for Malik, who was cleaning the tables with a soft rag. Cobalt watched him for a moment, admiring his attention to detail. The boy actually lifted the sample catalogs and cleaned under them rather than going around the massive books. He also wiped down the antitheft chains and ensured the books were returned to the centers of the tables. A hard worker who didn't ask questions and never pried into his personal life. How had he gotten so lucky?

Whistling, Malik adjusted one of the chairs at the table he'd just finished and headed for the next one. He caught sight of Cobalt on the way and let out a slight gasp. "I didn't even hear you come in," he said when he recovered. "When did you get back?"

"Just now." Cobalt smiled and grabbed the broom leaning on the wall, where the boy normally placed it for use after he finished the tables. "I'll help you."

"That's all right. I'll get the floor in a minute."

"I insist. I've nothing better to do."

"You're the boss." Malik flashed a crooked smile and started another table.

Cobalt made a few passes with the broom but turned up little in the way of dirt. He kept going anyway, working toward the display booths at the back of the room. "This is likely the cleanest tattoo parlor in New York, thanks to you," he said. "I should give you a raise."

Malik laughed. "Just doing my job," he said. "I want your place to look great."

"Our place."

"What?"

Cobalt leaned on the broom. "The Grotto is as much yours as mine, Malik," he said. "You've earned your keep. As far as I'm concerned, we can start your apprenticeship anytime."

"Oh, Cobalt. Really?" His eyes glittered, and a broad grin broke on his face. "That is so…sweet!"

"Not at all. You've proven yourself. There's nothing sweet about it."

"No, not *that* sweet. It means cool. Awesome. I think." A flush crept up the back of his neck. "My roommate says it all the time. I'm trying to be more American."

"I see." Cobalt smirked. He would have teased a bit, but Malik was already uncomfortable. No need to embarrass the boy further.

They returned to work in companionable silence. Cobalt forced himself not to watch the clock, to count the hours until tomorrow night. He could still feel the heat of Will's lips against his and taste the salty sweetness of his seed in his throat. Gods, what bliss.

"Cobalt."

The hesitant summons ripped him from images of Will. He glanced across the room. Malik had stopped wiping and stared at him with a concerned expression. "What's wrong?" he said.

"There's something you should know. Something... weird."

Frowning, he leaned the broom against the wall. "That'd be what, then?"

"Well, earlier—" Malik swallowed and breathed out hard. "After I came in, I forgot to lock up behind me. So I went back, and the front door was...glowing."

His heart seized. "Glowing?" he echoed stupidly, fumbling for a lie. None came to mind.

"Yes. It looked like graffiti or something, made out of light."

"Interesting." Damn. He half hoped Uriskel had gone out and was skulking around outside, waiting to be let in. It was better than the alternative.

Malik raised an eyebrow. "You're not concerned?"

"Not yet." He tried a smile, though it didn't quite take. "I suppose if—"

"I've been here all day. If that's what you're thinking."

The sound of Uriskel's voice skewered his hope. "Skelly," he said in forced casual tones. "Have you met Malik?"

"Haven't had the pleasure." Uriskel oozed from the shadows around the stairs, a cold smile on his features. In dark belted jeans and a formfitting black shirt adorned with straps and buckles, the Unseelie looked every inch the sensual predator he was. The silver Celtic pendant was a nice touch. "So you're the shop boy," he said. "Charmed."

Malik's eyes narrowed and sizzled with instant dislike.

"Enough," Cobalt hissed at Uriskel. To Malik, he said, "I apologize for my guest. Skelly isn't from around here. I'm beginning to think they don't believe in manners back home."

"There's a lot we don't believe in back home," Uriskel said. "Taxes. Organized sports. Betrayal." His green gaze settled on Malik for an instant, then moved lazily to Cobalt. "So. What will we do tonight? Perhaps you're up for a round of cards. I've brought my deck."

"I'll be working. I've a business to run." He grabbed the broom and thrust it toward the Unseelie. "Make yourself useful."

"You've got to be kidding."

"You'd know if I were."

Uriskel's lip curled in a snarl, but he relaxed it instantly and let out a mock sigh. "Very well. I'll be sure you can eat from your floor, then." He strolled over and took the handle.

"Anything else I can do for you, Master Cobalt? Shine your shoes, kiss your—"

"Skelly." He made the name a warning.

Muttering under his breath, Uriskel moved as far from Malik as possible and started sweeping.

Cobalt shook his head. "I need to make some calls," he said. "Can you handle things in here, Malik?"

"Of course." The boy smiled, but a glance in Uriskel's direction had him scowling again.

Cobalt left them to their uneasy peace. He had more pressing problems—because if Uriskel hadn't been the one to activate the seal, it must have been Eoghann.

* * *

The K Factor wasn't a bad place to have a few drinks with a friend. They kept the music balanced enough to be loud on the dance floor and just below conversation level at the bar. The drinks were priced fairly, the stools were padded thickly, and the bouncers would only break one arm instead of both legs if you caused enough trouble.

Unfortunately, the K attracted mostly straight clientele. A lot of college kids. And another drunk sorority single had decided Will looked lonely. And eligible.

The brunette and her knockers—they were so big, they needed a separate zip code—slid onto the stool next to Will and propped an arm on the counter. "So," she said, as though he'd been waiting for her. "Do you do it?"

He smirked. "Probably not."

"Then why're you sitting at the bar?" She gave him a sloppy smile full of gleaming white teeth. "C'mon. You do it."

"Okay." He raised a hand in surrender. "I'll bite. Do what?"

"Drink!" She straightened and slapped a hand on the bar top. "I'll buy. You get plowed and take advantage of me."

Will shook his head slowly. "I don't swing your way, sweetheart."

"Everybody swings my way. I mean, look at these." She cupped her pendulous breasts and pushed up until they almost spilled from her plunging neckline. "How can you say no to these? They're perfect."

"Sissa!" A male voice parted the crowd, and a flushed, thick-necked college boy dressed in laundry-day casual made his way over. "Come on, babe. It was a joke."

The girl tossed her head. "Get away from me, Tyler. I'm talking to... What's your name again, swinger?"

"I didn't tell you." Will grimaced. He had no desire to throw down with Tyler the Tank.

Apparently Tyler felt the same way. He rolled his eyes and glanced at Will. "Sorry, man. She gets like this. Thinks everybody talks to her chest instead of her face, you know?"

"Asshole," Sissa said, with heavy slippage on the sibilants. "I'm drunk, not deaf."

"I know. I'm sorry." Tyler grabbed her hand. "Come back out and dance."

She pulled away. "Why'd you wanna dance with me? I'm freakish. Ronie has *normal* tits. Ask her."

The boyfriend flashed Will another apologetic look. "You're not freakish. You're great, okay?"

"Just great?"

"Sissa, *please.*"

"Say it."

Tyler's face darkened. Finally, he sighed and said, "You have the best boobs in Uptown."

"Uptown!"

"In the city. In the whole damn world, okay?"

One corner of her mouth lifted. "You mean it?"

"Hold up." He stepped away, cupped his hands to his mouth, and shouted, "'Scuse me, people! I have an announcement." The bar noise dialed back a few degrees, and he spun her on the stool to face the crowds. "This is my girl. Doesn't she have the most amazing boobs?"

Whistles and catcalls erupted from the male portion of the patrons—and a few of the females too. "Hell, yeah!" one guy shouted. "You wanna trade her?"

Will cringed. Somebody was sleeping on the couch tonight.

Grinning, Sissa gave her tit-praising man a sloppy kiss. Then she stood on the stool and flashed the entire bar.

The resultant cheer was louder than a Yankee Stadium home game.

Will dropped his head in his hands and waited for the drama to subside. And they said gays were exhibitionists. Still, he had to admit that couple would probably work out. There weren't many guys confident enough to let their significant others flirt openly with strangers—or caring enough to recognize and deal with their body-image issues.

Eventually the place settled down to a normal roar. Will heard someone take the stool next to him, and smelled female. He didn't bother looking up. "I'm gay."

"This is a news flash?"

"Tess." Relief accompanied his smile. He leaned over, kissed her cheek, and whispered in her ear, "Don't ever leave me alone here again."

She laughed. "Poor baby. Have we been hit on by the fairer sex?"

"Fair, my ass." He groaned and tried to dislodge the image of Sissa's tits hovering above him like fleshy blimps. "Drink. Now."

"Deal." Tess got a bartender's attention and ordered them both shooters and draft chasers.

"So," Will said. "Has Leonard ruined my slot and killed my audience yet?"

"Oh my God, Will. You wouldn't believe how many calls I'm getting." She screwed her face and mock whined, "When's Will coming back? I miss Will. Will is the sexiest man alive. I hump my radio every night when Will comes on."

"Seriously?"

"Would I lie to you?" Tess grinned and watched the bartender set the drinks out. She picked up a shooter. "Here's to radio-humping fans."

"Crazy is the new black." Will grabbed his shot, clinked the glass with hers, and tossed back. Damn, that felt good. He almost ordered another one but decided it'd be better to pace tonight. If he got too drunk, he might do something stupid.

Like wander into the Grotto and beg Cobalt to fuck him.

He started on the beer. "How's Tess tonight?"

"Peachy." Her features went somber. "What about you? Are you...?"

"I'm fine." It came out sharp, and he smiled to try and soften things. "Really. I'm a lot better. Cobalt—" Damn. He hadn't meant to bring up that subject. No point speculating about it with Tess when he didn't even know what was going on there. Besides the fact that he couldn't go five minutes without longing for the man's touch again. "I'm all right."

Unfortunately, Tess never missed a thing. "By Cobalt, you mean that smoking-hot, why-are-all-the-sexy-ones-gay tattoo artist at the Grotto?"

"No. I was gonna dye my hair blue. You didn't let me finish. Cobalt or azure?"

"Will!" She tapped his shoulder. "What's going on with you and Cobalt?"

"Nothing. I'm thinking about getting a piece done, that's all."

"Uh-huh."

He sighed into his beer. "Drop it, Tess. I'm still getting over the last love of my life."

"Damn. I'm sorry." A frown creased her brow. "Speaking of the world's biggest asshat, he's still leaving you alone. Right?"

He hesitated too long, and she pounced.

"I knew it! What's he doing now? I swear to God, if you don't call the sheriffs, I will."

"He sent me flowers," Will mumbled reluctantly. "I don't think the sheriffs are going to arrest him for that."

"Flowers? Jesus. He really is psychotic."

"More like deluded. He says he's waiting for me to come back to him."

"You are *not* going to—"

"Hell no." *You liked it.* A shiver whispered up his spine, and he squirmed on the stool. "If I ever suggest otherwise, you have permission to blow my brains out with the Dub's gun."

She put a hand on his arm. "You want to keep the gun? Just in case."

He shook his head. "It's not going to come to that. I'll bring it to the studio on Monday."

"All right. If you're sure…"

"Positive."

"Okay. But you tell me immediately if he does anything stupid. Or I'll start giving out your cell number to your biggest fans."

"Oh shit." A male voice sounded behind Will. "Tessie's pulling out the big guns."

Will turned to find the Dub himself grinning at them around an unlit cigarette, and shot a mildly surprised glance at Tess. Her cheeks went pink, and she offered a guilty little oops shrug. The he's-forgiven-for-the-moment signal. "Hey, Dub," he said. "How's it hanging?"

"Long and loose." He put an arm around Tess and squeezed, almost lifting her off the stool. "How'd you piss her off this time? Leave the toilet seat up at work?"

"It's Friday." Tess tried to pout, but it didn't quite erase her smile. "I said we'd go out Saturday, Dub. Me and Will are talking shop."

"You mean like radio shop or girlie shop?"

"Girlie," Will said. "We're comparing nail salons."

The Dub laughed, with only a little extraneous force. Will knew the man wasn't exactly homophobic. Just misinformed. Sometimes he tried too hard to prove that he didn't have a problem with gays—but at least he tried. It was more than a lot of people bothered to do.

Tess rolled her eyes and mouthed, *Sorry.* "Seriously, what are you doing here?" she said. "I told you I was hanging out with Will tonight."

"I scored tickets to the Pit show." He flourished two rumpled squares of paper. "Thought you might want to go. Take Will if you want. Get some shopping done." His smile insisted he really didn't mind, despite the edge of disappointment in his voice.

"Oh, man." The brief sparkle in Tess's eyes went out. "Gonna have to pass. But thanks."

"No, you're not." Will slid down from the stool. The relief of pressure on his still-sore ass confirmed this was the right decision. He grinned and patted Tess's hand. "It's a bitch getting Pit passes. You guys go have fun. I'm…exhausted, anyway." He'd almost said, *I'm beat.* That wouldn't have gone over well with Tess.

"You sure, dude?" The Dub got his socially expected protest out first. "I don't wanna break up the fun here."

Will nodded. "Really. I need to crash. It's been a long week."

"You definitely need rest." Tess gave him a grateful smile. "I expect you at the top of your game come Monday. You have to save Manhattan from Leonard."

"Yeah. Everybody but the radiophile. Leonard can have him." He pecked her cheek. "Night, babe." Then, unable to resist, he turned to the Dub and said, "You want one too?"

Another almost-forced laugh. "Nah. I'll let Tessie pass it on for you. Later, man."

"You kids behave yourselves." Will lifted a wave and headed through the crowd for the exit. Definitely a cab kind of night. He couldn't take sitting on a plastic train seat yet. He'd go home and straight to bed. He wouldn't think about Cobalt.

Yeah, right. Might as well vow to give up that pesky breathing addiction.

Chapter Fifteen

Saturday could not have come slower if the gods had halted the rotation of the planet.

Thirty minutes before opening, Cobalt headed downstairs to ensure things were ready. Thus far he'd refrained from mooning about like a love-struck fledgling— if only to keep Uriskel from making harsh comments about the situation. The Unseelie had a knack for ruining relationships.

He reached the main room. And what he found there stunned him so thoroughly, he could not move or speak for a full minute.

Uriskel and Malik stood by the wall, locked in an embrace. Uriskel's back faced the stairs, and his head bent to the boy's neck in a tender nuzzle, then moved to his ear. He whispered something. Malik sighed softly and rested his head on Uriskel's bent shoulder.

The boy's eyes shone with the glossy blankness of a seduction spell.

"Bastard!" Cobalt ran to them and ripped Uriskel away. He dug his fingers into the snake's neck and shook hard. "Release him. Now."

Uriskel raised his arms, palms spread in surrender—or warning. "Take your hand from me, breedling. I'll not stand for this." His voice simmered with dark promise.

Cobalt snarled and let go. "Release him."

"Fine." Uriskel waved a hand.

Malik shuddered and blinked rapidly. "What... *You.*" He shot Uriskel a poisoned glare. "I don't want your help. Leave me alone."

"You'll not have it, boy. You—"

"Skelly," Cobalt said through his teeth. "We must talk. Now." He grabbed the Unseelie's arm and pulled him toward the stairs.

Uriskel twisted from his grasp. "I've not forgotten how to walk." He turned on a heel and stalked up the stairs.

Cobalt watched him, then turned to Malik. "He'll not bother you again," he said.

"I can handle him." Malik shuddered again. "I don't know what happened. All of a sudden, I just felt like...being near him."

"Yes. He has that effect on people." Cobalt glared into the shadows. "I'll be back soon."

Leaving Malik to finish his preparations, he took the stairs fast. Uriskel stood by the loft windows, staring out at the glittering night. He made no acknowledgment of Cobalt's arrival.

"Disgusting rat," Cobalt snapped. "What in the name of the gods were you doing?"

The Unseelie shrugged. "Having a bit of fun."

"He's practically a child. And my employee." Cobalt crossed the loft in four strides and stopped just behind the motionless figure. "I'm tempted to deliver you personally to Eoghann, traitor."

"Do it, then."

"Damn you, Uriskel!" He gripped a shoulder and spun him around.

The rage burning in Uriskel's eyes forced him back a step.

"I'll save you the trouble." His tone was barely restrained. He moved around Cobalt and walked across the loft.

"Uriskel."

The Unseelie stopped by the rail. "Don't."

"Why were you seducing Malik?"

He turned slowly. "My reasons are not for you to know."

"I see." Cobalt glared at him. "Much like your reasons for turning me in to the Seelie Court."

"Yes. Much like those." He measured his words with care, as though he had a limited supply and could not use too many. "I'm leaving, Ciaràn. I should not have stayed."

"Coward."

His eyes flared. "Watch yourself, fledgling."

"Why?" Cobalt couldn't stop himself. For a decade he'd wondered why this snake had not only spied on his affair with Eoghann but gathered the evidence of it and presented it to the court. He'd already ended things himself when he was summoned and sentenced. "You are Unseelie. Why did you betray Eoghann—your own kind?"

"Is that what he told you?"

"Even if he hadn't, I could have surmised that much on my own."

"You know nothing," Uriskel spat. "Particularly if you believe Eoghann above lying—to you, to the Unseelie queen, to anyone if it suits his purposes."

"I'd not believe Eoghann incapable of lying," he said. "But you are still Unseelie. Why should the dalliance of a lowborn Seelie have mattered to you?"

"Fool! It was not you I sought to expose."

"Really. You—a bottom-crawling, castaway Unseelie—were attempting to bring the queen's consort to justice in the high court? Forgive me while I decline to believe you."

"Believe what you will." Uriskel quivered in place, and his flesh rippled as though his true form was fighting its way out. "I'll not explain this to you. Fortunate bastard that you are, you'll not suffer under the weight of truth."

Something in his tone pierced Cobalt's heart. A weary note of surrender shot through with bitterness. Without understanding his sudden empathy, he said, "Uriskel, please. Help me understand. We've a common enemy, and I truly have no wish to see you killed."

Uriskel snorted. "If that's so, you are among scant company. Most beings wish my death on a regular basis."

"I want the truth," he said. "Please."

Instead of answering, Uriskel moved to a chair and dropped into it. His fingers clenched the arms hard enough to dent the leather. "Blast you," he whispered. And then, as if the words were ripped from him, he said, "I am not Unseelie."

The lie was so bold, Cobalt couldn't deliver a response. But Uriskel wasn't finished.

"My mother is. Was," he said. His gaze fastened to the floor and stayed there. "But my father is Seelie. I'm certain you know the Law."

Cobalt's jaw loosened. "Halfling," he said. "You should be…"

"Dead. Killed at birth, by Seelie Law." He closed his eyes. "I was spared in exchange for my life in service to the high court. I am the perfect spy. The perfect assassin. I can move freely among the Unseelie."

A cold weight settled in Cobalt's chest. What hell Uriskel must have been through—playing one side to serve the other, never belonging to either. "Why do you not leave the realm? There are many Fae here who stay to escape the Laws."

"It's not permitted. There are penalties for my disobedience." Uriskel shuddered, suggesting that he'd already experienced these penalties firsthand. "The Seelie Court enjoys their games. They'd not be amenable to losing their favorite pawn."

Cobalt frowned. "The court sent you to expose Eoghann, then. Why?"

"Because you were not the only Seelie to have fallen into his web."

"I see." Anger kindled in him, and he tried not to direct it at Uriskel. Not yet. "These other Seelie. I suppose they were highborn. They must have been, to garner the Court's interest."

"Yes."

"You bastard."

Uriskel raised an eyebrow but said nothing.

"You gave me to them because I was lowborn." Cobalt's fingers dug his palms. "They'd not have punished a highborn for such an affair. You threw me to the wolves to save your own hide."

In a blink, Uriskel shot from the chair. He grabbed a handful of shirt and jerked Cobalt forward, nearly lifting him from the floor. "Wretch! I saved your miserable life!"

"Put me down."

Uriskel relaxed his grip with an animal grunt and turned his back.

"Explain this to me," Cobalt said. His stomach gave an odd little twist. "How, exactly, did you save my life?"

"Never mind that. I lied. You'd best continue blaming me for everything."

"Uriskel…"

"No." He moved away. "I'll not take your pity or your feigned concern."

Cobalt touched his shoulder. He flinched and whirled on him, burning with rage.

"Sheltered whelp! You've no idea what goes on in the court. What games they play with the lives of Faekyn." His teeth ground audibly, and a vein throbbed in his temple. "The Seelie king ordered me to testify against you. You, Ciaràn of the glen, and no one else. Not even Eoghann."

The twist became a vise clamping his gut. "Why?"

"Perhaps your face displeased him. Or his ale had soured, or the sky was gray that day. Who knows why the nobles act as they do?" Uriskel let out a rush of air through his teeth. "He called for your execution. I asked that you be banished instead. The rest of the court agreed. So here you are, and here you'll stay."

For a long moment, Cobalt couldn't speak. Finally he said, "What have I done to merit such kindness from you?"

"Do not accuse me of being kind." A slight smirk lifted his lips. "I've a reputation to uphold. And don't thank me."

"Thank you."

"You're deaf as you are thick, Cobalt."

"I am that." He glanced at the clock on the wall. Thirty minutes before opening. "You mentioned cards. How about a round before work?"

Uriskel shot him a narrow-eyed stare. "So now you're attempting to befriend me?"

"No. I simply want to humiliate you at nine-card don."

Uriskel almost laughed. "Sure you'd not rather play fish, breedling? It's more your speed."

"You'll eat those words. Come on." Cobalt led the way to the stairs and wondered how he could have been so wrong. Guilt over his shabby treatment of Uriskel gnawed at him, but he could not help feeling there was more to the situation that had not been confessed.

He pushed it aside for the moment. Work awaited. And then, at last, Will Ambrose.

Chapter Sixteen

The cab dropped Will off twenty minutes before eleven, a block away from the Grotto. He'd spent most of the day sleeping, and the rest shopping for something to wear—and feeling like the stereotypical gay man the Dub thought he was. For Christ's sake, he'd actually considered getting a manicure. He'd talked himself out of that before some overzealous nail jockey could convince him that real men wore pink nail polish or some such bullshit.

This is not a date, he reminded himself firmly. Cobalt wanted to talk body art and nothing more. He would not make a fool of himself.

At least he hadn't gotten drunk before he came here.

There weren't many people out on this block. A couple holding hands passed him without a glance, headed in the opposite direction. A late-night jogger overtook him and left whispers of music from her iPod in her wake. Just ahead, a lone man leaned against a utility pole, staring at his feet, hands stuffed in his pockets. He appeared to be talking to himself. And there was something wrong with his skin. A rash of some kind on his face and arms.

Homeless, Will thought. He patted his pockets automatically, expecting to be propositioned for change.

The leaning man looked up when he passed. "Excuse me," he said. "Do you have the time?"

Will was already digging quarters loose when his brain processed the man's words. "Oh. Sure," he said. "It's about quarter to eleven."

"Thank you."

He nodded. "No prob—" A quick, sharp breath cut him off. What he'd taken for a rash was actually tattoos. Scarified tattoos. The raised lines appeared on every bit of his exposed flesh, and the patterns suggested they continued elsewhere. The man's appearance should have been repulsive, but the markings had been made with obvious skill and care. They weren't monochromatic either. The artist had somehow elicited a range of colors. Shades of red, from deep maroon to pale scar pink. Browns. Dark blues. Even some black.

Breathtaking as it was, though, Will had to wonder what kind of man would submit to being cut this much.

He finally realized he was staring. "Sorry," he blurted. "Um. Nice work you have."

The man smiled. "Will you be getting your own, then?"

"Huh?"

"You look to be headed there." He pointed toward the Grotto. His hands, even his fingers, were marked with scars.

"Oh. Yes. That's where I'm going." Will shook his head. His mind felt foggy, and for a moment he forgot why he was out. "I…"

"Cobalt."

The name brought his focus back. "How do you—wait. Did Cobalt do your pieces?"

"Some of them." Another smile. "He's quite talented."

"Yeah." The guy was starting to creep him out. "Look, I'd better go," he said. "Don't want to miss my appointment."

"Of course you don't."

Will resisted a strange urge to thank the man and hurried the rest of the way to the Grotto. He'd heard of tattoo addicts—people who craved the experience, and sometimes even the pain, of the tattoo process. So much that once they ran out of skin to mark, they'd go back and start getting cover-ups, or have the older tats removed to make room for new ones. If that was the case with the guy back there, he'd taken addiction to a whole new level.

He felt better once the door of the Grotto was between him and the scarred creep.

The kid Tess had introduced him to the first time here, her brother's roommate, sat behind the table in the entrance room, reading a paperback book. He looked up with a smile that faltered when Will slammed the door shut a little too hard. "Mr. Ambrose," he said. "Are you all right?"

"Sure." Will pulled himself together and smiled. "Nice to see you again, uh…"

"Malik."

"That's it. Sorry. I'm bad with names."

"It isn't an easy one to remember." Malik closed the book, stood, and opened the inner door. Music rolled out— mellow indie rock, vaguely familiar. "Go right in. You're expected."

"Thanks."

Will entered the darkened room. For a business that was a few minutes from closing, there were still plenty of people hanging around. Most of the tables were occupied. A few stragglers stood alone or in small groups. No one looked ready to leave.

He looked toward the glass booths at the other end of the room and spotted Cobalt in the center one, talking to a shirtless woman with a fresh tattoo on her chest. Cobalt appeared to be holding gauze bandages in one hand and a tube of ointment in the other.

Will grinned. Apparently the man couldn't help spreading the Gospel of Wound Care.

He headed for an empty table to wait. On the way, someone called his name. He looked around. Didn't see anyone familiar.

"Your name is Will, isn't it?"

This time he saw the speaker. The redheaded fugitive. Skelly.

He moved toward the table where Skelly sat with two others, a Goth girl and a guy in a cable-knit wool sweater and Dockers. Skelly grinned at him. "Cat got your tongue?"

"Funny," the sweater guy said. The girl silenced him with a look.

"Hey." Will put his hands in his pockets. "I'm just waiting for Cobalt. Planning a piece. You know." He had no idea what to say to any of them. Cobalt never mentioned why this guy was a fugitive. Hopefully not because he was a mass murderer. And he'd never seen the other two—though they seemed odd. The three of them together didn't quite fit the scene, but Will couldn't put a finger on the problem.

"Wait with us, then," Skelly said. "We'll not bite...though I'd watch the girl."

The girl in question narrowed her eyes at him, then favored Will with a disinterested stare. "I'm Shade," she said. "That's Nix."

"And you're Will." Nix patted the empty seat between him and Skelly. The gesture should have looked prissy and ridiculous, but it put Will instantly at ease. "Have a seat. We were about to ask Skelly to show off his card tricks."

"Were we, now." Shade frowned. "I could think of more interesting activities. Watching paint dry, for example."

Nix gave her a brilliant smile. "Want some help with that stick in your ass, love?"

"No. It's quite comfortable, thank you."

"It should be. It's been in there for years." Nix winked at Will. "I hope you'll forgive my wife. She's a bit antisocial."

"And water's a bit wet." Skelly produced a rumpled deck of playing cards and shuffled them with the rapid perfection of a Vegas dealer. He fanned them facedown on the table. "Choose a card, Will."

"Okay." He teased one out, pulled it toward him, and picked it up. The jack of hearts.

Skelly collected the cards with a practiced flick and split the deck one-handed. "Drop it in there," he said. "Don't let me see it, now."

Will obliged, curious in spite of lingering reservations about the man. Skelly closed in the card with a snap and shuffled the deck so many times, Will expected the spots to fall off them. He spread them across the table again. Lifted the last card by a corner and ran a finger along the fanned deck to flip the cards faceup in a graceful ripple. When he reached the end, he reversed direction and turned them back over.

A single card remained faceup in the line. Skelly slid it free. The jack of hearts.

Will couldn't hide his amazement. He smiled. "That's the one."

"Well done!" Nix clapped a few times. "You must tell me where you've learned this."

A dark, pained expression shadowed Skelly's face. He gathered the cards and made them vanish. If he'd put them in a pocket, the motion had been too fast to follow. "I'll not reveal my secrets." He spoke lightly enough, but his eyes held a warning that Nix seemed to understand.

"If I'm not mistaken," Shade said, "our host approaches."

Will looked toward the back of the room and spotted a tall figure, unmistakably Cobalt, making his way to them. But Shade sat facing the front, and she hadn't turned around before she made the announcement. A disquieting shiver licked at his spine. How the hell did she know that?

Shade smirked. "Woman's intuition," she said, as though she'd read his mind. "Eyes in the back of my head."

The unsolicited explanation didn't exactly make him feel better.

Before he could drive himself crazy with speculation, Cobalt was there. His blue eyes fastened on Will, and his sexy smile seemed meant for no one else. "I hope my friends haven't put you out much," he said. "They've a knack for frightening my customers."

"Hello, Cobalt. Nice to see you, Cobalt." Nix grinned and winked at Will again. "I think that's our cue to exit, love." He stood and stretched. "Skelly, we're off to catch that new horror flick. Join us?"

Skelly groaned and slouched in his chair. "Fabulous," he said. "Is there likely to be much drying paint?"

"To be sure, we'll drop you in an alley. You can watch the graffiti." Shade rose to her feet like a ghost drifting from a grave. Worry rippled her slack features for an instant. "There's a foul wind out."

Cobalt frowned. "Perhaps you should stay in tonight."

"No need. We're three, and the cloud cover is thick."

"Very well." He glanced at Skelly. "Stay with them."

"Oh, I wouldn't dream of leaving their side for a moment."

"How fortunate we are," Shade said drily.

Will followed the bizarre exchange in silence. It was like being stuck in some low-budget experimental sitcom. *Conversations Overheard in the Mental Institution.*

Cobalt banished his unease with a grin. "I've set things out upstairs," he said. "If you're ready? Malik will close up down here."

The lights came up as if Cobalt had given a signal. The remaining customers came to life, standing from tables, collecting jackets and cell phones and personal items.

Conversation levels rose and fell, and a general sprawling shuffle toward the exit began.

Will roused himself from the chair, intending to make the appropriate social noises. *Good-bye, nice to meet you, see you around.* He breathed in—and Cobalt's scent filled him, overpowered his senses. He locked gazes with the artist and refused to look away. God, those lips. That tongue. The memory of where they'd been yesterday throbbed in his stiffening cock.

"Will?" Cobalt sounded as breathless as he felt. "We should…"

"Upstairs. Right." *Way to not make a fool of yourself, Ambrose.* He blinked to clear the spell and turned to the table with good-bye on his lips.

Skelly and the odd couple were gone.

"Good-bye," he said anyway.

Cobalt smiled. "Come. I've looked forward to this."

Trying not to read anything into that suggestive statement, Will followed him.

* * *

A leather-bound book, thicker and more battered than the sample catalogs downstairs, rested on the coffee table in the upstairs loft. Will stared at it and wondered if he'd have the guts to go through with scarification. The idea that he might enjoy the pain worried him. More than that, though, he'd be under observation while Cobalt put his hands on him—and he wasn't sure he could control himself.

Cobalt came around the couch, bearing a tray with two long-stemmed glasses and a corked blue bottle in an ice bucket. He set it next to the book. "I'm not working now, so I hoped we could have that drink we missed yesterday." He cut his gaze away, pulled the bottle out. "Interested?"

"Sounds great." Will struggled to keep his voice even and watched him pour. The bottle had no label, no markings at all, and the liquid it contained was a dark, velvet red. "Shiraz?" he guessed.

Cobalt corked the bottle and handed him a glass. "Elderberry wine," he said. "It's...imported."

"Alcohol I've never heard of. I'm impressed." He sipped and damn near moaned in pleasure. It was silky and sweet with a smooth bite, like sugared raspberries blended with a dash of exotic spice and a hint of chocolate. His tongue wanted to run off and marry the stuff. "Where have you been all my life?" he said with a grin. "I need to hook up with your supplier. This is amazing."

"I've a full case. You're welcome to a bottle or three." Cobalt sat beside him and pulled the book closer. "So. How much thought have you given to your piece?"

"Uh..." Damn. He hadn't gotten further than Cobalt touching him in front of a live audience. Things were blurry after that.

Cobalt laughed. "Much, I see. It's perfectly fine. This decision should not be rushed." He opened the book to the first page, a photo of a woman's arm marked with a trinity eye. "These first few are smaller pieces. Stock designs. You may want to start there."

"What's a stock design?"

"Preset images made for multiple reproduction. Most stock are simple, unobjectionable, and popular in appeal. A single rose, a star, a fish, or a snake. The Superman shield. You'd not believe how many adults still want to be Superman."

"Oh, I think I would." Smiling, Will turned the page. Man's arm with star. Woman's ankle with flower. Nicely done but unimaginative. "What's the alternative to stock?"

"There are a few. I can render from photos, though that's usually ink work. Tribal and Celtic patterns are commonly done. And then there's custom design."

"And custom is original stuff?"

Cobalt nodded and flipped to the center of the book. Here was a dragon wrapped around a man's thigh. A line of scorpions snaking down a spine. "Custom involves more extensive work. An artist creates the design from scratch, and there are multiple rendering sessions. It calls for a greater commitment."

Will decided he'd imagined Cobalt's voice catching on the last word. "I think I'd like a custom piece," he said. "If I'm going to have something permanent on my body, I don't want the same thing a hundred other people have."

"Now we're getting somewhere." Cobalt leaned back, raised his glass in the air, and took a sip. "All right. You'll need to work with someone on the design. I've had clients who've sketched their own ideas or worked with freelance artists. I can recommend one if you like."

Will bit his lip without realizing it. "Can you design one for me?"

Cobalt went still. "Me?"

"Yes. I don't know any artists, and I'd rather work with…well, someone I know."

"Oh, Will." Cobalt closed his eyes. "I've not created designs in a very long time. I render them, but…"

"It's all right." Disappointment soured the sweet aftertaste of the wine in his mouth. "I should probably hold off on this anyway. I don't know if I'm ready."

"Will."

He definitely hadn't imagined the catch this time. "No, really," he said. "It's fine. I'm not upset or anything."

"I want to." Cobalt's voice barely rose above a whisper. "You must understand something, though." A breath shuddered from him. "I've created designs only for a few. Those I cared for in deeper ways. And the last one broke my heart." He smiled, but it wasn't a happy expression. "For me, creation is commitment. I'd be giving you part of myself. So I'll offer it—if you truly want to take it."

For a moment Will forgot how to breathe. But before he could think through the stupid mistake he was about to make, he heard himself say, "I do."

Chapter Seventeen

If ever there were a moment Cobalt wished himself dead, this was it.

Commitment was the last thing he should have with Will. He'd come as close to the truth as he could with his explanation, hoping—expecting—to be turned down. He could not design a piece for anyone without bonding with them. All Fae bonded with marks of their own design, from simple cuts to elaborate patterns and images. He'd done so with Eoghann. And of course, the three humans he'd condemned to nonlife, and death.

He'd not add Will's name to that list. Somehow he would have to take this promise back.

Will watched him. Waiting for a response. He knew it would be wicked of him to continue this charade. But just now, he couldn't bear to disappoint Will again. He would work things out. Find a way to change the situation. Some other time, when Will was not sitting beside him catching that luscious lower lip and driving his blood to boil.

He reached over and closed the book, aware of Will's gaze on him. "We'll not need this, then," he said, trying to sound casual. "It will take some time to decide. And there'll be other concerns outside of the design itself."

"Such as?"

"Placement, for one." He managed not to ravish Will with his eyes, envisioning the body beneath the clothes. "Sensitivity is a consideration there. Certain areas are more tender than others and will cause more pain."

Will blanched and looked away. "I can imagine which ones," he muttered.

The words were hammer blows. Cobalt forced all thoughts of bonding and claiming Will's body from his mind. "How rude I've been," he said. "Forgive me, Will. Your injuries have yet to heal, and I've blathered on about cutting you."

Will hitched a smile. "I wouldn't be here if I didn't want to have you cut me."

"Yes. Of course." He swallowed a moan and shifted against the stirring in his groin. Having Will ask so directly to be marked nearly unhinged him. "But we're a ways from that yet. I'll not begin the actual process until you're healed."

"Well, you're helping that along nicely."

"How do you mean?"

"Healing me." Will drank the last of the wine in his glass with obvious pleasure. "Whatever you're doing with your cleaning and your tubes of gunk, it's working. I mean, I'm sitting down and hardly gritting my teeth."

"You're hurting? You should have told me. I'll—"

"Relax. It was a joke." He smiled, showing all his teeth. "See? No gritting."

Cobalt shook his head and returned the expression, amazed once again at his strength. Not many could joke about such monstrous abuse in so short a time. "At the least, your emotions have healed a bit," he said. "But the physical side of things still needs tending. Have you applied anything today?"

"I, uh, forgot to get the stuff." Will ducked his head a bit. "Actually, I forgot what it's called. So...I guess the answer's no there."

"Well, then. We'll remedy that now."

"We will?"

"Yes. You'll not suffer a moment longer than you have to because of that monster." Cobalt stood and extended a hand.

When Will took it, lightning struck and traveled through his arm, straight to his cock.

He overcompensated and pulled Will to his feet harder than necessary. Their bodies impacted. Will bounced back and stumbled. Without thinking, Cobalt threw his free arm around his shoulders to catch him. A quick hiss escaped Will's lips.

"Oh, Will, I'm sorry." He moved his arm away. "I didn't mean to hurt you."

"You didn't." Hoarse words. Lust in his gaze.

You'll not take advantage of him. Letting go, stepping back, was a physical pain. "Come with me. Please. My room... It'll be easier. You can lie down."

Will nodded. The fire in his eyes banked but didn't go out.

At last Cobalt had to look away. He led him into the bedroom, turned on a light, and gestured. "I'll get what I need. Just be a minute." His throat tried to close as he added, "You'll need your clothes off."

"All right."

Damn. Why did he have to agree so readily? It would be impossible to leave him alone.

Cobalt slipped into the bathroom and closed the door, afraid Will could hear the pounding of his heart. He gripped the sink, listened to the rustling from the next room. Will disrobing—slowly, as though it pained him. Of course it did. He'd been beaten like a mangy cur, less than a week ago.

He opened the medicine cabinet, grabbed the bacitracin and lidocaine. And waited until the bed creaked under Will's weight to return to the bedroom. He tried to steel himself for the sight he knew awaited him.

He failed.

His eyes burned, and he shoved a knuckle in his mouth. It was healing. He knew that. But it looked so much worse. The bloody welts were puckered and stiff. The fading bruises had spread and blossomed with awful colors. A gruesome kaleidoscope patchwork covered him from shoulders to thighs—red and orange, yellow and green, black and blue.

Will stirred and looked over his shoulder. "Pretty, isn't it?"

"No." Cobalt swallowed bile. "Say the word, Will. Police officer or not, I'll be glad to snap his neck like a twig."

"Please don't. They don't give gays conjugal visits in prison."

Cobalt stared at him. And laughed.

"All right. But should you change your mind…" He crossed to the bed and sat down. "I'll be quick about this."

"Thank you."

He applied the antibiotic first. Will's muscles fluttered and clenched beneath his fingers, but he didn't make a sound. The lidocaine took longer. There was more ground to cover. The bruised flesh was hot, taut. Firm. Cobalt forced his hands not to linger on Will's ass.

"Done?" Will nearly choked out the word.

"Yes. I'm sorry. I know it stings."

"Mmm."

Cobalt twisted the caps back on the ointments. "I'll put these back so you can get dressed." He walked into the bathroom without looking back and closed the door. Waited.

The bed creaked.

Gods help him. He wanted Will more every moment. But he couldn't touch him now, and he shouldn't touch him ever. It would surely destroy them both. Yet part of him insisted it could work. Will had so much more strength than the others—than any human he'd met. Perhaps he was strong enough to face the truth and keep his sanity.

No. He'd not risk Will's life for a possibility.

He waited another minute and came out. "Would you like…more…wine…?"

Will hadn't dressed. He sat on the bed, the sheet pulled to his waist. "It's not fair," he said.

"No. It's… What?"

"This is the third time you've gotten my shirt off." A slow smile worked its way across his face. "I haven't even gotten yours off once."

"Will." He wanted to say that he couldn't. He mustn't. He wanted to warn him again what would happen. What *had* happened. But none of these things came out. "Will..."

"Cobalt." Half tease, half longing.

He came to the bed. Climbed up and knelt beside Will. "Shall I make it fair, then?"

"Yes. Please."

Cobalt obliged, tugging his shirt over his head and down his arms. He let it fall between them. "Fair now?"

"No." Will reached out and brushed the bulge in his jeans. Heat flowered in his groin. "I'm naked. You're not."

Groaning, he unfastened them, slid them and his underwear down. Kicked his shoes free. Yanked the rest off. "Now?" he breathed.

"Yes. God, yes."

He could wait no longer. He bent to Will, cupped his hands around his face. Brushed his mouth with his lips, then his tongue. Sweet elderberry wine and sweeter flesh. Gods, the heat.

"Cobalt." Will's whisper tickled his lips. "Why do you smell like that?"

"Like what?"

"Wood smoke. Wind and water." He swallowed. "It's the sexiest damn thing."

Something deep inside him writhed and strained, struggling for the surface. Will could pick up his mating scent. It was nearly impossible for a human. He'd heard of it only among the strongest empaths—those who felt the emotions of others as truly as their own.

Strength. Will had such strength.

"Does it matter why?" he finally managed to say.

Will shivered against him. "No."

"Good." He kissed him again, deeper. "Let me touch you," he murmured.

"Wait." Will pulled back. "Fuck me."

The demand drew a gasp from him. "I can't," he grated. "I'll hurt you."

"You won't. It's not as bad as it looks." Desire threaded his voice. "I need all of you. Please fuck me."

"No."

"Cobalt…"

He tipped his chin with a finger. "I'll not fuck you. You deserve better. You deserve to be loved, worshipped." He placed a kiss on his forehead. "Let me worship you."

Will decided he'd died. Lyle must have killed him. And heaven was Cobalt.

For a moment he couldn't do anything but stare. Here was the most incredible body he'd ever seen, naked and in bed with him. Refusing to fuck him because he wanted to worship him instead. Gods didn't bow to acolytes. And Cobalt was a god—dark and wild and perfect.

"You've not answered me, Will."

The husky voice dragged him from his visual feast. "Answer what?"

"May I worship you?"

"Um. I guess."

A low laugh. "Stay here. I'll be just a moment."

Will watched him climb down and walk naked to the bathroom. What an ass. There should be poems written about Cobalt's ass. Beautiful, from the stylized ankh tattooed just above his split to the chiseled muscle that flexed when he moved.

Second thoughts tried to cool him down when Cobalt was out of his sight. He wasn't supposed to get involved with anyone. It was a Very Bad Idea. And there wasn't a chance in hell he'd be able to write this off as a one-night stand. He should stop now before the worship started, before he fell more in love than he already was.

Not happening. He could no more say *don't have sex with me* to Cobalt now than he could go find Lyle and say *please beat the shit out of me again.*

Cobalt returned. He had a tube.

Will failed to suppress a laugh. "You've got gunk for every occasion, don't you?"

"Of course." Smiling, he reached aside and turned a dial set on the wall. The lights dimmed. He approached and held the tube out for inspection. Astroglide.

"Good idea," Will murmured through a rush of heat. That thick cock of his was going to be a tight fit. One he looked forward to immensely.

Cobalt mounted the bed. "You're sure I'll not hurt you?"

"Yes." Will took a breath, slid the sheet down, and rolled on his side. He rose to hands and knees, waited. Warm, firm hands bracketed his hips.

"No, love," Cobalt whispered. "Not like this."

"Huh?"

Cobalt guided him back to the mattress, directing him with his hands to lie on his back. "That would be fucking you." He smoothed Will's hair back, trailed a finger down his jaw. "There'll be time and place for that. It won't be tonight."

At once, Will understood the meaning of the word *swoon.*

Cobalt leaned down, stopped with his mouth a few hairs from Will's. "I'll not be able to turn back from you," he said.

Did he mean now? Never? Will didn't care anymore. If Cobalt didn't touch him soon, he would shatter. Damn the consequences. "Please…"

Cobalt completed the circuit. Electric heat surged through his mouth. Cobalt's tongue opened him, probed him. Will thrust back, and his tongue found the back of the stud through his lip. An answering gasp had him reaching, threading fingers through dark hair, holding on while he drowned in the kiss.

Cobalt broke away slowly. He positioned himself over Will and pressed his lips to the hollow of his throat. Will shuddered. He closed his eyes and gave over to pure sensation—the heat of Cobalt's body, his scent filling everything. Firm lips on his flesh, trailing kisses down his chest. A tongue flicked his nipple, and he cried out. His eyes flew open.

"So sensitive." Smiling, Cobalt licked again and gave him a gentle nip, eliciting a gasp. He tickled the hardened nipple for a few seconds, then shifted and gave his attentions to the other one. He scraped his teeth on the soft skin, circled the peak with his tongue. A hand came to rest on one knee and trailed slowly up his thigh.

Will's breath left on a moan. His cock was so hard, every time his heart beat he thought it would split. "Touch me," he begged in a ragged whisper. "Christ, Cobalt. I need…"

Smoldering blue eyes lifted to meet his. "Yes, love. As do I." Cobalt moved down, kissed his stomach. Worked himself back until he straddled Will's legs. Bent to Will's engorged cock.

Will tensed in anticipation. He felt hot breath just before Cobalt's tongue lapped his head and slid down the underside of his shaft, leaving a line of liquid fire. His groin arched in response. He clutched handfuls of sheet and groaned through clenched teeth when Cobalt drew his balls into his mouth and sucked.

The silk tongue retraced the path up his cock. Will panted like an asthmatic. Cobalt reached the top and opened up, sending him sliding into the heated sheath of his throat.

"Uhnn." Will's eyes fluttered back in their sockets. He raised his head to watch, his cock delighting equally in the sight and sensation of Cobalt's mouth clamped on it, sucking, moving up and down with short, firm strokes. Cobalt hummed his pleasure, and the vibration ripped a gasp from Will's lips.

Jesus. He was going to come already. He didn't want to end it yet. "Wait..."

Cobalt released his cock, looked up at him. Naked desire burned in his gaze. "Ah, Will," he breathed. "I'm afraid I can't wait much longer."

"Then don't. I want you in me."

He made a strangled sound and fumbled for the lube. Dropped it beside him. Grabbed a pillow and slid a hand under Will's ass. "Lift," he whispered.

Will obliged with a moan. Cobalt positioned the pillow under his hips, pushed his legs gently apart. Fingers smoothed cool, thick wetness on his opening. Will's cock twitched and throbbed in time with his heart. "Oh-God-please-Cobalt-now."

"Yes, love. Now."

On his knees between Will's legs, Cobalt held his hips and placed his swollen head against him. He pushed in slowly. Will felt every inch of flesh glide through. The pain was there, as he knew it would be, but sheer pleasure eclipsed it. Finally, Cobalt buried himself completely and let out a trembling breath. "Tight," he gasped.

"More." Will bucked against him, wiggled his ass. "Need you."

"Yes."

Cobalt rocked back, eased in, repeated. A languid pace, like the opening measures of a love song. His head nudged the sweet spot with every thrust. Sensations swirled and spiraled through Will's body, building in waves that crested higher, broke harder. The hands on his hips convulsed. Fingers dug into his flesh, demanding, desperate.

"Faster," Will urged. "Harder."

"Mmm…" Cobalt drew out farther, shifted from rocking to pumping.

The waves became hurricanes. Will's breath came in snatches and gasps, small breathless noises torn from his lips. His cock tapped Cobalt's stomach in time with the increasing frenzy of thrusts. His balls were tighter than a virgin's ass. "Ah, *Christ*," he groaned. "Cobalt. I'm gonna come."

A fiercely sensual growl ripped from Cobalt's throat. He plunged deep inside, curled his body down. Will's hands sought his back and clung there. At his touch, Cobalt cried out and shuddered, pumping his ass full with hot, wet bursts.

The sensation brought Will to hoarse, screaming climax. He arched up, his cum spurting with jet intensity to spray Cobalt's chest.

Still inside him, Cobalt lowered himself onto Will and held him tightly, until his breathing settled to a ragged crawl. He kissed him once. Again. "Will. You'll be the death of me."

The words penetrated from somewhere inside a hazy cocoon of ecstasy. "Not if you kill me first," he murmured. "Damn. You're amazing."

A small smile. "You are divine. And I did warn you, love."

"About what?"

"That I'll not be able to turn back." He shifted his hips, and Will felt his cock stir inside him, growing hard again.

Renewed lust kindled him like lightning. "I'll not tire of having you. As long as you'll have me still."

"Oh, God…"

"Is that a yes, then?"

Will shivered and gave an eager thrust. "Yes."

Cobalt didn't bother going slow this time.

Chapter Eighteen

The warm weight against his side made Cobalt loath to leave his bed. But sleep would not come, and soon his restlessness would disturb Will.

Sighing, he inched away and rose as evenly as he could. Will didn't stir. He was likely exhausted—their lovemaking had lasted hours, and Will hadn't yet recovered physically from his trauma. Toward the end, Cobalt sensed his strength flagging even as his words insisted he could go on. He'd eventually plead exhaustion himself to save Will from having to admit defeat.

And what hours they had been. What pure bliss.

But he'd damned himself now. He could no longer imagine life without Will, and he could not continue lying to him. Something would have to give.

He slipped a robe on and left the bedroom, leaving the door ajar in case Will awoke and wondered where he'd gone. He walked down the few steps to the loft and turned up the lights.

A low snarl drifted from the vicinity of the couch.

"Who's there?" he demanded. "Uriskel?"

"No. It's Santa Claus. Merry Christmas." His voice sounded muffled and thick. "Do you need the damned light?"

Cobalt frowned and moved around the front. Uriskel lay facedown on the couch, his face buried in a cushion. One hand trailed on the floor, and the wine bottle—empty now— lay a few inches away. The back of his black shirt glistened with moisture. Perhaps it had rained. But the rest of him didn't appear wet.

"Drowning your sorrows, are you?"

"Didn't think you'd mind much. You seemed through with it." He turned his head until one eye surfaced, and squinted through it. "You don't intend to put the light out, then."

"No." Cobalt picked up the bottle and carried it back to the case. "How went the evening? Shade's intuitions are unfortunate but sometimes true. I worried."

No response.

"Uriskel?"

A heavy thump shook the floor.

Cobalt whirled. Uriskel had fallen and landed in an awkward sprawl with one leg still resting on the couch. "Blast," he said. "That hurts."

"Sure you've only had the one bottle?" He crossed the room and knelt next to him. "Come on. I'll help you to bed."

"Don't touch me." A breathless grunt.

Cobalt's brow furrowed. "What's the matter?"

"Nothing." He closed his eyes. "I'll sleep here."

"No, you'll not." Cobalt slid a hand under his shoulder.

Uriskel hissed and jerked away—but not before Cobalt felt the wetness on his shirt and pulled his hand out streaked with blood.

"Fool," Uriskel muttered. "Told you not to touch me."

Ice crept through Cobalt's veins, even as his heart ached for the halfling. "It was him, wasn't it?"

"'Course it was." He strained to move, winced. "Fetch me a blanket, Cobalt, will you? I'll just bleed on your floor."

"Take my hand."

"You've a death wish. Truly." His gaze slid from the outstretched hand to Cobalt's face. "Why do you not turn me out? You understand he'll kill you for it."

"Take my hand," he repeated.

"Stubborn ass." Uriskel took it and let Cobalt help him up. "Perhaps I'll go to bed after all."

"Why did you not tell me?"

"I'd no wish to interrupt your tryst." He smirked. "Besides, I've not been here long."

"Let me heal you."

"Isn't your human still here? You'll risk him finding out."

"He's asleep."

"Wore him out, did you?"

"Uriskel."

"Yes, yes. Shutting my mouth." He turned away. "The clouds never cleared, so he couldn't kill me. At least the bastard didn't draw it out this time." He peeled off his shirt, flinching when it cleared his shoulders.

Seven-point stars were carved into his back. One inside another, over and over. It was sloppy work, the lines jagged, the depth varying from scratches to heavy gouges. Two separate symbols scored each shoulder—septagrams inside circles.

"By the gods," Cobalt whispered. "He's lost his mind."

"You don't say."

Shivering, Cobalt held a hand near his back and summoned his magic. There was resistance. Not as bad as the first time Uriskel had stumbled through his door, but hexed enough so that he couldn't heal the wounds completely. He sent healing into them until his spark was nearly gone. "All right," he gasped. "Better?"

Uriskel nodded without turning. "Shame," he said. "I rather liked this shirt."

Cobalt waited while he put the bloodied clothing back on. "How did you escape him?"

"He underestimates my capacities." Uriskel straightened the shirt, stiffened. "He'll not do so again, though. Unfortunately, he's no fool."

"Do you know yet what he wants from you?"

"Information." Uriskel faced him but wouldn't meet his eyes. "I've not told him anything. But..."

The ice returned to his blood. "What?"

"He knows things." He looked up, and there was true regret in his face. "Cobalt, he knows about your Will."

"No." He shook his head, as though the reinforcement would render it a lie. "He can't... How could he? If you've not told him, how could he know?"

196 S. W. Vaughn

"He knows." Uriskel reached out briefly, then changed his mind and lowered his arm. "And you must let him go. I'll survive Eoghann's torments. Your human won't."

Cobalt's eyes burned. For once in his life, Uriskel was right.

* * *

Will woke sated, drowsy. And alone.

He stretched and smiled in the lowered light of Cobalt's room. Sore in all the right places. Damn. Phenomenal sex might not cure bruises, but it went a hell of a long way toward healing other things. Like his battered emotions.

He sat up slowly. The bathroom door stood open, and so did the door to the bedroom. Cobalt might have gone out to his loft or something. What time was it? He remembered looking for and not finding a clock the last time he was in this room. And there were no windows to help with a guess either.

Will climbed out of bed and got dressed. He couldn't have been asleep too long—it didn't feel like morning yet. So maybe Cobalt was a light sleeper. The Grotto usually stayed open until two a.m., so he was probably used to being up through the small hours.

He should have been exhausted, though. He'd certainly claimed to be.

Despite the open door, Will knocked at the bathroom. No one answered. He went in, relieved himself, washed his hands and face. The continued silence bothered him. Where was Cobalt? He might've considered the possibility that it really had been a dream, if it weren't for the impossible-to-mistake physical sensation of having been fucked for hours.

Worshipped, he silently corrected himself. That's what Cobalt called it. And it had seemed like more than a fuck. Will could count the number of partners he'd had who paid that much attention to his needs in bed on one hand. With five fingers left over.

He headed for the loft. Cobalt had to be there. The lights were on low, just enough to reveal shadows and shapes, and at first he thought it was empty too. The view from the windows confirmed it was still late—or early, depending on which end of the day the approach took. City lights glittered and stretched to the shores of the river, but a smudged gray band across the dark horizon proclaimed the approach of the sun. It was raining. Drops and spatters of water decorated the outside of the glass.

Finally, Will noticed the tall figure to the left of the windows, watching the rain. He took a step forward. "Cobalt?"

"Not exactly." The figure turned.

"Skelly." A whisper of discomfort chased his disappointment. "Er. Have you seen Cobalt?"

"Yes."

Will waited. When the redhead offered nothing further, he said, "Where is he?"

A wicked grin surfaced. "He's busy."

"Come on. Don't mess with me." Will ran a hand through his hair and tried to feel as confident as he sounded. "If he went out, that's cool. I'll just wait."

"Why would he go out, when everything he needs is here?"

"Funny."

"I don't mean you, Will."

The warning note in his words made Will's skin crawl. "Knock it off."

"Really. You can't be that stupid." Skelly started across the room, a languid stroll that screamed self-possession and dismissal. "Do you think you mean something to him? That you're special?"

Yes. No. I don't know. "Maybe," he said, hating the quaver in his voice.

Skelly shook his head. "Poor fool. They all believe that at some point."

"They?" He couldn't seem to spit out more than one word at a time. His stomach twisted and churned like he'd swallowed a washing machine.

"The distractions. The ones he uses to try and make me jealous." Unforgiving green eyes glared at him. "But he always comes to his senses eventually. He's already apologized. And he has no desire to see you again."

His teeth practically chattered. "You...you're lying."

"Am I, now?"

"I want to hear this from Cobalt."

Skelly arched an eyebrow. "Do you need proof? Here, then." He lifted his shirt. His chest bore an elaborate scarified Celtic knot, with a striking resemblance to the one Cobalt had in the same place. The redhead flashed another condescending, territorial smile. "We're a matched set, you see. Destiny and fate and all that."

Images raced through Will's head. The way Skelly had entered Cobalt's bedroom the first time he'd met, when the man made himself right at home. The impression of a lover's spat when Cobalt dragged him out. The indulgent dismissal exhibited at the Asylum when Skelly left him to his "little friend." The familiarity with Cobalt's other friends, and Cobalt's obvious concern for Skelly's welfare when he'd left. *Jesus.* The churning in his stomach intensified, and it was all he could do to keep from puking right there.

A strong wave of scent plowed over him. Earth, fire, and incense. His gaze was drawn to Skelly, and relentless thoughts battered him. Skelly was gorgeous and exotic. Sensual. Exciting and perfect. A hundred times more man than he could ever be.

"Honestly, Will." No one could disagree with that voice. It contained nothing but the cold truth. "Why would Cobalt want you, when he has me?"

"I…" Dimly, Will realized he was crying. The tears deepened his shame. "I have to go."

"Good-bye, then." So cold. Ice in his words.

Will turned and stumbled for the stairs, half blind and hurting more with every step. He'd thought no one could ever cause him more pain than Lyle. He knew better now.

Chapter Nineteen

Sunday passed in a slow, agonizing blur.

Will kept the door locked and barely moved from his couch. Tess called twice. He begged off talking, claiming a cold. She didn't buy it. He didn't care.

Lyle called once. He didn't answer the phone. Didn't check for a message.

Cobalt didn't call at all.

Stupid. How stupid he'd been, to think a man as beautiful and perfect as Cobalt would want to be with him. And why hadn't he seen through that lame-ass fugitive story? As if Skelly could have been anything but the perfect lover for the perfect man.

The sun rose. The sun set. Will stayed on the couch.

He slept late on Monday. Only a cramped reminder from his stomach that he hadn't eaten a damned thing the day before got him moving. He managed to stand and shuffle out to the kitchen, despite every stiff, sore muscle in his body protesting movement. In the fridge, he found half a quart of expired milk, a head of wilted lettuce, and an open box of baking soda. He opened cabinets with just about the same success rate. Finally, he grabbed a can of mandarin oranges he'd intended to use for a salad. He opened it and drank everything inside straight from the can. Oranges, juice, a couple of seeds. Who gave a shit?

With his snarling stomach settled to a dull ache, he headed for the bathroom. He felt no residual fear or haunting memories when he walked inside. The new pain had eclipsed the old one so thoroughly, he barely registered what had happened in here. In fact, if he'd been forced to choose between Lyle and Cobalt, he'd take Lyle and let him beat his ass every day. Provided suicide wasn't an option. Maybe Cobalt hadn't been completely lying when he claimed he'd driven other men to insanity and death. They'd gone suicidal when they found out the truth.

He showered. The water carried his tears away almost before he realized he was shedding them. Almost.

Dried and dressed, marginally less sore, he returned to the kitchen and heated water in the microwave for a cup of instant-cappuccino-like substance. Two sips in, he gave up. He found half a pack of cigarettes in a drawer and smoked three in a row. They were stale. He barely tasted them anyway.

He had several hours before the show. Spending them here, sitting alone and torturing himself with his thoughts, didn't appeal to him. He could see what Tess was doing, but the certainty that she'd make him spill his guts left him cold. He didn't want to talk about anything. Especially Cobalt.

Well, damn it, he lived in New York. He'd just go out and walk around. Even if he didn't find anything to do, at least there'd be plenty of people around to distract him. People he didn't know, who wouldn't remind him of anything. Who wouldn't give a flying fuck if he looked like someone had murdered a puppy in front of him and then forced him to eat it raw.

He started out, stopped. He'd promised Tess he would bring her gun back tonight. He didn't want the damned thing, and he wouldn't feel like coming back here before the show. It took him a minute to puzzle out the logistics of carrying it around. Since he was neither a woman nor flaming, he wasn't about to carry a purse. Finally, he decided on a light windbreaker with big zippered pockets.

Outside, the world remained maddeningly normal and unchanged. The sun had evaporated all evidence of yesterday's rain. People walked, hailed cabs, talked on cell phones. Horns blared. Sirens wailed. Street vendors sold pretzels, hot dogs, roasted nuts, cheap jewelry and books and women's accessories. Life went on without Will's participation.

He picked a random direction and walked. For a while he noticed nothing, allowed no thought to form in his mind. Eventually he decided a cup of decent coffee might bring him closer to feeling human again. At the next corner, he checked the street sign. He was in Midtown. Starbucks every couple of blocks. He turned on Seventh, headed east, and spotted a familiar green sign on the next block.

Inside the shop, he glanced around, and his heart skipped when he caught sight of two men in beat-cop black at the side counter. But neither of them were Lyle, and he settled back to who-cares mode. Cops in a Starbucks. Big shocker. He got in line behind a rail-thin woman with acrylic nails and a bad bleach job, and waited while she ordered a mile-long drink with half this and double that and light foam but not too light and could you make that extra roasted and put it in two cups? Will rolled his eyes.

The young male barista caught him and gave him a thanks-for-the-sympathy grimace. Will nodded, and a smile tried to surface. It almost made it.

Finally, the bottle blonde was shuffled aside to wait for her faux-pretentious coffee, and Will stepped up. "Venti caramel macchiato, please," he said. "Hold the snobbery."

The barista laughed and hit buttons on his register. "You sure? We're having a sale on social mobility. The longer your coffee order takes to place, the more you have to pay."

"Perfect. Reverse consumerism." Will fished out a five and a single. He paid with the five, got back a few coins, and dropped them and the single in the tip jar. "Go to college. Avoid human-relations fields."

"With that extra dollar, I can afford Juilliard now." His easy smile conveyed the joke. "You look familiar. Have you been here before?"

"Probably."

The barista frowned slightly, then snapped his fingers. "Got it. You're Will Ambrose."

Will managed not to snarl at him. He was going to make Tess take his picture off the Web site. "That's me."

"Your show is great. Have you been sick or something? The station never said why you were off the air last week."

"Sick. Yeah." *Please get my coffee and shut up.* "Think I caught the flu."

"That's rough." Concern edged into the barista's face. "You do look pale too. Hope you feel better soon."

"Thanks," he murmured.

At last, a girl called out his order, and he moved along to pick it up. The bottle blonde still stood at the other end of the counter, pointing at one of her cups and complaining loudly. Will snorted annoyance. He grabbed his coffee just as the woman whirled with indignation—and plowed straight into him at full speed.

He went down. She shrieked and wobbled, spilling the scalding contents of both cups on his chest. His own coffee hit the floor just before he did, and hot liquid drenched his back when he landed hard. Somehow he managed not to scream. But his legs convulsed and caught the blonde at the ankles while she tried to teeter away on spiky, I'm-so-fashionable heels.

She shrieked again and fell right toward him.

He got an arm up, trying to break her fall—or at least keep her from breaking his ribs. As though the god of fuck you had choreographed the entire incident, she managed to insert one of her tits right into the palm of his hand and pin his arm between them.

An earsplitting scream erupted in his face. "Let go of me, you perv!" she shouted, spitting and jerking like a wet cat. One of her flailing hands gripped the pocket of his windbreaker as she tried to right herself. "Oh my God! Is that a gun? He's got a gun! He's got—"

The cops were already there. They'd probably started moving with the perv comment. One of them hauled her up and maneuvered her back. The other stood over Will, one hand on the butt of his piece. "Keep your arms out, pal. Get up slow."

"Jesus." Will closed his eyes. This was so not happening. "Hey, she ran into me. I didn't do anything except fall and get burned."

"I said get up. Now." A thumb unsnapped the holster. Fingers wrapped around the handle of the gun. The bastard was actually going to draw on him.

Will stifled a groan and staggered to his feet. He kept his arms as far out as he could without falling back down. "Look, she—"

"Shut up." The cop reached his free hand out and patted down the side with the lumpy pocket. It didn't take long to find the gun. "Take your jacket off and put it on the floor."

Son of a bitch. Will complied. Slowly, so he couldn't be accused of refusing to cooperate later when they figured out he was gay. When he finished, the cop slammed him against the counter and cuffed his hands behind his back.

The friendly barista stood far back from the counter, white-faced and staring. Will could see the headline now: GAY RADIO HOST ARRESTED IN STARBUCKS FOR ASSAULTING WOMAN. BARISTA REVEALS ALL.

Tess was gonna kill him.

* * *

At least they didn't strip-search him.

They found out fast who he was. In fact, it seemed like the arresting officer already knew—like he and his partner had been listening in on his conversation with the barista and waiting for him to do something even slightly illegal.

Which was ridiculous. He'd never been arrested for anything before.

But they hadn't even given him a phone call. What they had done was bring him to an interrogation room, knock him around a bit, and tell him to wait while they checked the gun. Knowing the Dub, it was definitely unlicensed and unregistered. And of course Will didn't have a permit to carry. He'd be fined up the ass if they didn't throw him in jail for assault.

They'd left his hands cuffed. After all, he was a dangerous criminal. Who probably needed medical attention. He could feel raw patches on his chest and back where his skin had blistered and peeled off. *Thank you, Starbucks, for making your coffee so hot.* Cobalt would've probably had some gunk for the burns.

Damn. Cobalt was the last thing he wanted to think about right now.

He concentrated on the sweat dripping from his temples and the fact that his nose itched unbearably. Of course. Didn't something always itch when you couldn't move? He tried to will the sensation away. When that didn't work, he attempted to rub his nose on his chest. No dice. The human body wasn't constructed to let that happen.

He'd just decided to scratch it on the edge of the table in front of him when the door opened. And Lyle walked in.

Will felt sick all over again. Lyle shouldn't have been here. This wasn't his precinct. He stared, shuddered. "What the hell are you doing here?"

"Your name came over the wire." Lyle shut the door with a frown. "What were you doing with a stolen gun?"

He opened his mouth, shut it. Spikes stabbed his gut. "It's not mine," he said.

"Then whose is it?"

Will shrugged. He didn't want to drag Tess into this. God knew where the Dub got the damned thing from.

"Let me guess. This has something to do with Tess."

Will hesitated too long. "No."

"I should've known." Lyle shook his head and sat down across the table from him. He leaned forward with a concerned-father expression. "When are you going to learn that she's no good for you?"

"She's my friend." Christ, that sounded pathetic. "And it's not hers."

"Friends don't give friends stolen weapons."

Will looked down at his lap. *Go away, Lyle.*

When he didn't respond, Lyle sighed. "Look. I can get you out of here, but it's going to be a pain in the ass for me, okay?"

"Yeah? And what do you think you're getting for this favor?"

"Nothing. Jesus, Will." Lyle actually looked hurt. "I just don't want to see you do time."

"Why don't I believe that?"

"Come on." He lowered his voice. "I said I was sorry."

Will suppressed a scream. "There's not enough sorry in the world, Lyle."

Lyle closed his eyes. An ugly flush crept over his face. After a minute and a few deep breaths, the color faded and he looked at Will. "Got any idea what's going to happen to you if you end up in jail?"

"I can guess."

"Do you want that?" He leaned forward again, teeth gritted. "You're attractive. They'll know you're famous and gay. And they'll never leave you alone. You'll be competed for, fought over. Raped. I don't want to see you get hurt."

"Unless it's you hurting me. Right, Lyle?"

"No. I never meant to hurt you."

Bullshit. It was on the tip of his tongue, but he didn't say it.

"Just let me get you out of here, all right? I'll drop you off wherever you want." He lowered his gaze. "And you'll never see me again."

"Promise?"

Lyle flinched. "Yes. I promise."

"All right." It wasn't the best option, but Lyle was right about one thing. He didn't want to go to jail. Not even for a night. He was through being anyone's bitch.

Lyle pushed back in the chair and stood. "Only thing is, we're going to have to leave the cuffs on. Just until we clear the building."

"Why?"

"I have to make it look like I'm transferring you. Once I get you into my district, I can make you disappear—well, your arrest record, anyway."

Will definitely didn't like the idea of going anywhere with Lyle in handcuffs. But it wasn't like Lyle could sneak off with him. They were in the middle of Manhattan. There was no such thing as a deserted street here.

He stood. Burns and bruises belted out a few bars of renewed ache. "Okay," he said. "Lead the way."

Chapter Twenty

Will hadn't counted on an alley. Or an unmarked car. Or being put in the back of the car with the cuffs still on.

"It's just for show," Lyle told him in a low voice. "I've got to make sure this looks convincing. The cons are a lot harder on cops in jail, you know."

"Yeah." He did feel a little guilty about Lyle risking his job for him. But only a little.

Lyle climbed in the front and started the engine. "Where am I taking you?"

"The studio," Will said. "I'll be lucky to make it on time for the show."

"All right."

The minute Lyle pulled out into traffic, he started talking. Mostly work stories—busts, cases he'd been handling, other cops. Will tried to sound engaged. He offered the occasional *mm-hm* and *wow, really*. But he had no interest in Lyle's life anymore. He used to care, way back in the beginning. The idea of being a cop had seemed so exciting.

He'd stopped giving a shit somewhere between the first black eye and the last round with the belt.

Eventually Will realized he didn't recognize the neighborhood outside the windows anymore. They were moving through a run-down, graffiti-covered area that he thought was Uptown but couldn't be sure. Had Lyle been talking to distract him? "Damn it, where are you going?" he demanded.

"Relax, Will. Traffic's bad around the park. I'm just going around."

There was an edge to his voice that Will didn't like. He bit his lip and looked around the car with an eye for a fast exit. Wasn't going to happen. A metal grate separated the backseat from the front. Like a regular squad car, the back doors had no interior handles or locks. "Lyle," he said carefully, trying to quell rising panic. "Look, just pull over and let me out, okay? I'll take a cab back."

Lyle didn't answer. He turned the car down a narrow one-way street and punched the gas.

"Lyle!"

"Cab sniffing around back there," Lyle muttered. "Bastard's following me."

Panic swelled through him, urging him to scream, kick, break glass. Will made himself breathe. "There's cabs everywhere," he said. "Nobody's following you. Just let me out."

"They can't find out. What they do to gay cops…"

"What the hell?" Will blurted. "Lyle, you're not making any sense."

He slowed to a crawl. Turned and drove into a parking garage. Orange-and-white-striped sawhorses blocked the entrance. Lyle drove over them. Wood dragged on pavement, crunched under tires.

"Stop it!" The panic was an animal now, gnawing at him with tiny, sharp teeth. "Jesus, let me out, you crazy son of a bitch, what are you *doing!*" He scooted along the seat, pressed himself into a corner as far from Lyle as he could get.

Lyle parked in the back of the place, far from the entrance. There wasn't a single other car. No sign of life. Crumbling concrete, excessive graffiti, and grated blue-white security lights instead of overhead neons. Whatever Lyle planned to do, he'd have no witnesses.

Once the car stopped, he just sat there. Gripping the wheel. Will's heart drummed at a furious pace, and his shaking hands rattled the cuffs behind his back. "Lyle?" he whispered. "Please. Don't do anything stupid."

"It's your fault. Nasty little cock-tease." The ragged voice sounded nothing like Lyle's.

"Okay." *Play along with him. Find a way out of this.* "Okay, okay, it's my fault. I'm sorry, Lyle."

More silence. Then a hoarse, shuddering sob. "You *bitch.*"

"I'm sorry," Will repeated. He could taste his own fear. "Come on. Let's go somewhere else. Somewhere nice, so we can talk—"

"*Shut up!*" Lyle held his head in both hands, like it would explode if he didn't. "You deserved it. Sneaking around like that. Why couldn't you just learn your lesson?" Another sob, a ratcheting breath. "I can't let them find out. I can't go to jail. I'm a cop."

"Lyle, please. Nobody knows."

"Liar." The word fell flat. "You told Tess."

Oh God. Had Tess said something to him, or was he just speculating? Either way, denying it would make things worse. So he didn't say anything.

After a minute, Lyle said, "That gun wasn't stolen."

"What?"

"It's registered to Tess. But it's stolen now. Temporarily." Lyle held something up in front of the grate. The gun. He'd wrapped a bandanna around the handle—probably to keep his prints off. "I haven't decided yet. It might be suicide. Or maybe I'll frame the bitch."

Will's bladder grew hot and heavy. It took everything he had not to piss his pants.

Lyle got out of the car. He came around and opened the back door, holding the gun in one hand. "Get out," he said. "I don't want a mess in there."

Will's first instinct was to refuse. But that would only get him killed faster. He inched across the seat, fighting for time to think. Lyle's eyes were moist, reddened. Wild. But he thought there was a glimmer of hesitation in them, or even regret. Maybe he could talk his way out of this.

"Hurry up." A finger curled around the trigger.

Will climbed out awkwardly and stood, holding the frame for balance. "You'll be in jail a lot longer if you kill me."

"I won't get caught." He motioned with the gun. "Over by the wall."

"Wait…"

You liked it.

He swallowed and dropped his gaze. It was his only chance. "You were right, Lyle," he managed to say. "I liked it."

"You what?"

Will made himself look up. "I liked it. And...I did deserve it."

Lyle's eyes narrowed. "Prove it."

"How?" Jesus. Was he really doing this? "Anything you want."

"Ask for it."

Shaking again. He had to go through with it. "Please..." His breath hitched. He couldn't do it. Couldn't say any more. *Damn it, do you want him to kill you?* His mouth moved without sound. At last he managed a choked drawl. "Please punish me, Lyle."

"Oh, Will. Do you really mean that?"

"Y-yes," he stammered. Playing the game. Buying time. "I wasn't ready before. I am now. I'll learn my lesson."

"I knew it." His smile was absent, haunted. "I knew we could be happy together. And you won't tell anyone about us."

"Never." If his heart beat any faster, it would explode. He gulped in breath after breath in a desperate bid to keep from hyperventilating. "Can you please take the cuffs off?"

Lyle's eyes flashed dark. "Eventually. If you behave."

Despite his best efforts, a mewling cry escaped Will's throat. Lyle might have lost his mind, but he still wasn't stupid. He wasn't taking chances.

Whether or not Will survived the night, he was getting another beating. Right now.

* * *

If Cobalt continued to cancel his appointments, his customers would stop coming and he'd no longer have a business. At the moment, though, he didn't care. He doubted anything would matter to him for a very long time.

Will would be safe. And out of his life forever.

He'd no idea what Uriskel had said to make him leave. He'd not asked for elaboration. Cowardly of him, yes. But he hadn't wanted to drive Will away himself. He could not have been that cruel. So when Uriskel told him that he'd ensured Will would no longer speak to him, he had let his heart break—and let it go.

Or so he'd thought. But Will refused to leave his mind. He could no longer sleep in his bed. Could barely sleep at all. Food, drink, rest, companionship—he wanted none of it. He desired only the one thing he could not have.

He was vaguely aware of potential problems. Uriskel had gone out earlier and not yet returned. Darkness had fallen, and the moon was near-full—meaning Uriskel could be killed if Eoghann found him. Malik had protested his cancellations and nearly begged him to attend to one appointment he'd rescheduled when Will had arrived injured.

He'd done nothing about either situation. Everything seemed pointless.

At the least, he'd resisted retiring to his loft. He sat locked in his office behind the booths with the radio on. Waiting to hear Will's voice, needing reassurance that he was real and alive. Five more minutes and he'd have it.

Someone pounded on the door.

"Not now," he called. "Leave me be."

"Cobalt, you've got to take this." Malik sounded breathless, almost angry.

"No. I don't." Whatever it was, it didn't matter.

"She's going to call the police."

Sighing, he got to his feet and reluctantly approached the door. It wasn't fair of him to burden the boy with so much of the business. And whoever was causing trouble might respond better to him than his assistant. He should have simply closed the shop tonight. He opened up.

Malik thrust a cordless phone at him. The business line. "Here."

Cobalt frowned and accepted it. He'd thought the problem to be in the studio. A phone call could have been returned later. He turned his back on the ruffled boy and lifted the damned phone to his ear. "Yes," he intoned.

"Is this Cobalt?" An unfamiliar female voice.

"It is."

"Where's Will?"

Shock doused his blood with ice, and the cloud in his mind evaporated. "Who is this?"

"It's Tess. I'm his producer…his friend." Desperation and the beginnings of fear edged her words. "Please tell me he's with you."

His throat tightened. "No," he managed to say. Then, dreading the answer: "Why?"

"Because he's not here. And he should be. Shit!" Something clunked in the background. "Any idea where he might be?"

"No." But he did have an idea. One he didn't like at all.

"Shit," Tess said again. "Look. Will wouldn't tell me much, but I know you guys have a thing." Her voice dropped. "Do you know about Lyle?"

The bastard who'd beaten him. "I do," he whispered.

"Well, that son of a bitch's been calling, looking for Will. And now Will's not here, and he's not answering his phone. I think…I think something might've happened to him."

No. His mouth went dry as cotton. "I'll find him."

"Thank you." There was no relief in her voice. "Please call me when you do."

"Yes."

Cobalt dropped the phone without bothering to turn it off. He left the office, stalked through the studio. Ignored Malik, Nix, and Shade, everyone who hailed him. Damn the Grotto. Damn the moon and Eoghann. Only Will mattered.

He'd start with Will's apartment. And if he discovered nothing there, he'd scour the city, the world, until he found him.

Chapter Twenty-one

"Had enough, babe?"

Lyle's voice rang hollow in the garage and in his pounding head. Will could only sob.

He lay on his stomach across the hood of the car. Lyle had used the cuffs he already wore, and his own set, to attach his wrists to the side mirrors. He'd also stuck a floodlight on the roof and turned it on. All the better to see where he was hitting and to watch Will writhe and contort with the blows. *Babe.*

Lyle wasn't a sadist in overdrive. He was a monster.

Tears and mucus puddled under his cheek, gummed his skin to the metal it rested against. He tasted salt with every harsh breath. His ass and his thighs burned, throbbed. Lyle had skipped using his hands this time and gone straight for the belt. At least the bastard hadn't taken his pants off. Yet.

"Please," he finally rasped, knowing Lyle expected a response. Still playing the game. It had to end soon.

Didn't it?

Leather whistled and snapped. Will screamed.

"That wasn't an answer, Will." His voice, heavy with lust, turned Will's stomach. "I'll ask again. Have you had enough?"

Deep breath. Play along. "Nnnnn. No…" *More*, he tried to add. *No more. Please no more.* But his tongue wouldn't cooperate.

"No? You want more? How brave of you." Lyle moved closer. "You really do like this, don't you?"

"Yes," Will whimpered too late. Yes, had enough. Please stop. Learned my lesson.

"All right. But we have to stop soon, so I can…make it up to you." Lyle rubbed the bulge in his pants.

Fresh tears slipped from Will's eyes. Of course he was going to rape him.

"I'll tell you what." Closer. The doubled belt dangled from his hand, a snake ready to strike. "You'll get ten more. Behave yourself, do what you're told, and I'll unlock you after we're done."

Will nodded. Anything. Just make it stop.

"I want you to count these."

Oh God. He couldn't do that. He could barely speak. And the more deeply Lyle dug into this twisted fantasy of his, the harder Will's subconscious resisted.

But his will to survive won out, and he said, "Yes."

Lyle moved out of his line of sight. Will's body tensed, and his head buzzed sickly. Tess was probably furious right now. Worried too. He couldn't think about her. It was too easy to envision her tears when she found out what he'd gone through.

Cobalt. Had he ever really cared? Twice he'd offered to kill Lyle for him. But Will had just been a distraction for him, a way to relieve his frustrations with his real love.

It hadn't felt like a distraction, though. Not once.

Why wasn't Lyle hitting him?

"There's one more condition." Lyle was behind him. He couldn't turn enough to see what the bastard was doing. He stared to the side, and something moved in the shadows beyond the glare of the floodlight.

Hallucination. Had to be.

He sensed Lyle leaning over him, felt the heat of him. Hands slid under his waist and fumbled with the button on his jeans.

Will couldn't even scream anymore.

Lyle freed the button, lowered the zipper. Will concentrated on the shadows, biting back sobs while Lyle tugged his jeans and underwear down. Cool garage air collided with his heated backside. He gagged.

The hallucination approached the light. A tall silhouette, a shadow against shadows.

"My God, Will. This must hurt like hell."

Bastard-bastard-bastard. Do it. Get it over with.

Shuffling steps. Lyle positioning himself. "Ready, babe?"

Fuck you. "Yes."

The hallucination left the shadows. Cobalt. Silent, expressionless. Still beautiful. Will would watch this vision, draw strength from it while Lyle beat him. While he tried to remember how to count to ten.

A listless slap behind him. Leather on pavement. "Who the fuck?" Lyle snarled.

Will's heart seized. If Lyle could see him, then he wasn't a hallucination. "Cobalt?"

"Get out of here." Lyle came around, stood between Will and the not-quite-hallucination. "This is police business."

"Is it, now?"

It happened fast. Cobalt moved in a blur. He grabbed Lyle's head, twisted hard. Produced a sickening, wet snap, like knuckles cracking underwater. Lyle dropped in a heap.

Game over.

"No!" Will jerked and tugged at his bound wrists, ignoring the pain. "You can't. I had things set up. He was going to let me go." Hot white flashes exploded behind his eyes. He heard Lyle's neck snap. Saw him die. Snap. Dead. "You killed him. He's a cop. Christ, they'll shoot you like a dog..."

Cobalt bent to the body and came back up with Lyle's keys. He unlocked Will's wrist. The sudden loss of support sent him sliding down the car. Cobalt caught him.

He moved to the other side and repeated the process. Will, wrapped in a cocoon of shock, felt like he'd been forced out of his body. He watched himself struggle to stay upright, watched Cobalt help him inch his clothes painfully back in place. Watched as he wavered and dropped to his knees in front of Cobalt—and then he returned to agonizing awareness.

"You killed him!" His chest hitched hard, pain and relief. Utter confusion. Cobalt saved him. Cobalt murdered Lyle.

Cobalt wasn't speaking.

Will looked up at him and got a sense of...*wrongness.* The silence. The odd set of his jaw. The blankness in his eyes. The missing lower-lip stud. Maybe he was a hallucination after all.

But hallucinations couldn't kill people.

"Will." Even his voice seemed wrong. Detached, unfamiliar. "Come with me."

Will shuddered. "Where?"

"Away. I'd like to take you...away."

Cobalt held a hand out. In a daze, Will took it. His grip felt strange. Almost...ridged. Cobalt helped him to his feet, and Will staggered back. What the hell was going on?

"I'd drop that if I were you."

Will recognized that dry, sarcastic tone. Skelly.

Cobalt's eyes narrowed. He released Will's hand with a quick frown. "You," he said. "Following me?"

"Seems that way." The redhead came up behind Will, passed him, and stood next to Cobalt. Fury blazed from Skelly's features, along with something else. Fear?

Will stared. Something about seeing the two of them together screamed *wrong.* But it wouldn't click.

The grin that spread on Cobalt's face was not pleasant. "You are a bold one," he said.

"No. I'm a fool." Skelly shivered—or had Will imagined it? Cool green eyes turned in his direction. "Run along now, Master Will. Go home. *Cobalt* and I have...business to attend."

"Indeed we do," Cobalt said.

A compulsion came over Will, powerful and demanding. Overwhelming. *Run. Now.* He obeyed without thinking.

He didn't look back.

* * *

The cab sailed along, weaving in and out of traffic. Will huddled in the backseat. Hurting. Confused. Losing his mind.

"*Go home*," Skelly had said. And he went. Like he was a machine and Skelly had programmed the order into him. No questions. No protests.

And Cobalt. Did he have an evil twin? Will's eyes acknowledged that was him, but his heart cried foul. Maybe he just hadn't accepted the relationship with Skelly. It was the first time he'd seen Cobalt act like there was something between them.

He shifted on the seat, and the movement made his eyes water. At least the beating hadn't been as bad this time. It was shorter. He'd been clothed.

Lyle was dead.

He still couldn't believe Cobalt had killed him. Hadn't even broken a sweat doing it. Just snapped his neck, with no more effort or emotion than opening a can of soda. Yes, Lyle was a monster. But maybe Cobalt was too.

Something was wrong back there. Skelly standing next to Cobalt was the key to his disconcerted impressions. What bothered him about it? The two of them, side by side. Implied intimacy. The way they'd been at the Alternative Asylum, looking at shirts.

It hit Will hard. Cobalt was taller than Skelly. Had at least an inch on him. He remembered noticing it at the Asylum. But in the garage, Skelly had been taller—by two inches, maybe a little more.

Jesus. Nothing made sense.

The cab pulled over. Will hadn't even realized where they were. There was his building, and the driver was telling him the fare. He glanced at the digital display on the dashboard up front. Eight or nine something. His eyes, blurred with pain and exhaustion, couldn't make the numbers pull together.

He found a twenty, handed it over. Got out.

Will limped to the door of the building. He keyed in the code, pushed it open, and stood at the foot of the stairs. A tiny spot of yellow on industrial gray carpet stuffed in the top corner of the first riser caught his attention. He blinked at it. A flower petal from the sorry-I-beat-your-ass bouquet Lyle had sent him. He wouldn't get any more flower deliveries.

It seemed to take him a week to climb the stairs. By the time he reached the third floor, his legs were throbbing lumps of jelly. He shuffled down the hall, head bent, eyes burning and watering. He'd go in and collapse. On the bed, if he made it that far. Maybe he'd die. Then he wouldn't have to think about this madness anymore.

His apartment door was open.

The lack of surprise on his part bothered him in a vague way. He should have been nervous, even terrified. But he didn't care. Couldn't be Lyle—he was dead. Maybe he was being robbed. Maybe the burglar had a gun and would shoot him. That wouldn't be so bad. At least then his head wouldn't feel like it was splitting in half.

He dragged himself inside and closed the door just as a tall figure stalked into the living room from the bedroom hallway. The remaining shreds of his sanity ran screaming for the nearest exit.

Cobalt.

"Will!"

The voice brought him halfway back. At least he sounded like Cobalt now. But he couldn't possibly be here.

"Thank the... Oh, Will. What's happened to you? You're hurt." All the warmth and tenderness he remembered. "Was it that bastard Lyle? I swear, Will, give me your word and I'll kill him for you."

Will barely heard him. The floor rushed up, and blackness swooped down.

Chapter Twenty-two

Cobalt's relief at finding Will died violently when he crumpled to the ground.

He rushed to him, knelt beside him, and brushed the hair from his face. Dark circles under his eyes. A fresh bruise on his cheek. Lips moving without sound.

"Will," he whispered. "Tell me what's happened."

A long, shuddering exhale. "Not here…"

"All right, love. Let's get you off the floor." Will was feverish, barely conscious. Moving him likely wasn't what he'd meant, but Cobalt could think of nothing else to do. He slid an arm under Will's shoulders, the other beneath his thighs.

Will jerked and cried out.

"No." The idea, the certainty that someone—Lyle or Eoghann—had gotten to Will, after he'd turned his back on him, was a hot knife in Cobalt's gut. "Oh, no, love. What've they done to you?" Gods, he should never have let him go.

He'd not make that mistake again.

Cobalt lifted him, cringing when he sobbed and stiffened against him. He carried him to the bedroom and laid him gently on the mattress. Will curled instantly on his side, whimpering, clutching himself like a babe in the womb. "Not here," he murmured, eyes closed and fluttering beneath his lids. "You're not here, not here, not here..."

Slipping away. Sliding into madness.

Please. Not Will. Cobalt settled beside him, stroked his sweat-drenched hair. "Come back to me, love," he said in shattered tones. "Please come back. I can't lose you."

He called on his magic almost without thinking. Just a breath, enough to break the fever and restore awareness. *Please come back to me.*

Will shivered. Clenched and relaxed with a sigh.

"Will." Cobalt touched his face with trembling fingers. "Talk to me."

His eyes opened. They were bright, shot with red. "Thirsty," he croaked.

"Yes. Of course. I'll get you a drink." Torn between relief and dread, Cobalt went to the kitchen, filled a coffee mug with tap water, and brought it back to him. Will struggled to sit up. "No. Be still, love. Let me help you." He sat down, held the mug to Will's lips.

Will managed a few sips, then slid back down. He closed his eyes again. "You killed him."

Cobalt started. Water sloshed in the mug, almost spilling. "What?"

"Lyle." Will grimaced. "You can't kill him for me again. You already did that."

Something deep inside Cobalt cracked and bled. He was mad. Hallucinating, like the others. "I didn't, Will," he said, knowing it would do no good. "Your friend Tess called me looking for you, when you didn't come for your show. I left the Grotto and came straight here. You arrived a few minutes after me."

"No." Will pushed himself up to his knees. His eyes were still red, but his gaze was clear and direct. Lucid. "Do you have a twin?"

The question was so bizarre, Cobalt couldn't articulate a response. He shook his head.

"What the hell's going on, then?" Not insane. Angry. "Lyle was going to kill me. I talked him into beating me instead. He was about done, and then you showed up and broke his neck. Only you weren't you…" Will buried his face in his hands. "Shit. How could you not be you? How did you get here first?"

It should have sounded like the ramblings of a madman. But there were no wild gestures, no shifting eyes, no stunned repetition or rocking. Will truly believed whatever he'd seen. Cobalt put the mug aside with a frown. "Tell me what happened," he said slowly. "Perhaps there is an explanation."

"Jesus." Will scrubbed his hands down his face. "I got arrested," he said. "It's a long story. The short version is Lyle basically kidnapped me, and he was beating me because I told him I liked it so he wouldn't kill me. He was going to let me go when he was done. And then you—" He stared hard at Cobalt. "Somebody who looked a fuck of a lot like you killed Lyle. Snapped his neck. Just like you said you would."

"There is no one—" Cobalt cut himself off with a gasp. Would he dare? "Will. Why did you doubt it was me? I'll assure you it was not, but…there must have been something not right."

"There was a lot of not right," Will said. "You didn't have this." He pointed to his own chin, indicating the labret piercing. "You didn't *know* me. I mean, you said my name, but it was like you were reading it from a name tag. You were so...blank. And there was the thing with Skelly. That's the big one."

"Skelly was there?"

"Yeah. He sent me home. Told me to run along. The thing is, though, he was taller than you there. But he's not. You're taller."

"Eoghann," Cobalt ground out.

Will stared at him. "So you do have a twin?"

"No." Cobalt closed his eyes. The bastard must've formed his glamour to imitate him, so he could get close to Will. But he'd not succeeded—apparently thanks to Uriskel. Still, there was no mistaking Eoghann's intentions. Whether he stayed with Will or left him, the ruthless Unseelie would not leave him be.

He'd not allow further harm to come to Will. And that meant he must tell him the truth.

"I've a confession for you, Will."

"Great. And things'll make sense after you confess, right?"

"Yes." *I hope.* He drew a long breath. "Skelly and I—"

"I already know about that," Will cut in sharply.

"You do?"

"Yeah. Skelly told me you two were soul mates. In no uncertain terms." He scowled, looked away. "He told me about the others. Said I was just a distraction for you, and you were using me to make him jealous."

"That snake. He'd no need to—" Cobalt stopped himself. Uriskel had been trying to protect Will, in his own insincere and twisted way. Just as he'd unbelievably done tonight, at the risk of his own life. And Cobalt had done nothing to correct the halfling's falsehoods, so the blame was as much his. "I'm so sorry, Will. I'd not thought he'd said such hurtful things."

"So it's true."

He laughed bitterly. "Soul mates? With him? I'm surprised he's familiar with the concept. No," he said. "It's not true at all. In fact, we've been enemies for a very long time."

Will's expression suggested he'd no intention of believing that.

Cobalt sighed. Regardless of whether he'd lost what he shared with Will, he had to confess the truth. It would be the only way to protect him from Eoghann. "What I'd meant to say was this." He met Will's eyes. "Skelly and I are not human."

Will couldn't figure out if his shock stemmed from the biggest, most ridiculous excuse he'd ever heard in his life—or the tiny part of him that believed Cobalt instantly. Not human. What a crock. "All right," he said. "I'll bite. What are you, then? Aliens?"

"We're Fae."

"Uh-huh. Am I supposed to know what that is?"

"The Fair Folk. The Good People?" He slumped, and muttered, "Fairies."

"Fairies." Will laughed. "Hey, what a coincidence. I'm a fairy too."

"Will…"

"Oh, come on, Cobalt. I'm too old to believe in fairies." A sneer tried to surface on his face, but he fought it away. "I can handle you and Skelly being lovers. I'm a big boy."

"His name is Uriskel. He is not my lover. He is Fae." Cobalt's eyes flashed, and his skin appeared to turn an impossible shade of glittering green. It was gone in a blink. "And so am I."

Will rubbed his eyes. "Did you just change color?"

"Yes," he whispered. "What you see of me is an enchantment. A glamour. My true form is…not human."

The glimmer of belief in him returned, stronger this time. But this was crazy. Impossible. "Show me."

"I can't."

"Then you're full of shit. How long since you escaped from the nuthouse?"

Cobalt stood abruptly. "Blast it, Will! I can't show you, because you'll lose your mind. Few humans react well to an eyeful of Faekyn. And I'll not drive you to insanity."

Jesus. If this was a lie, it was a well-constructed one. He'd either practiced it a hundred times, or he actually believed he was a real, honest-to-God fairy.

Or he's telling the truth.

Will shook himself. "Look," he said. "I'm sorry, but I can't believe you unless you show me. You have to admit it sounds crazy. I promise I won't go white-haired and drooling nuts on you, all right?"

For a long time, Cobalt didn't reply. At last he stepped back and straightened with sorrow in his gaze. "I'll hold you to that promise, then," he said.

It started with his eyes.

The deep blue darkened to black. Green flecks surfaced in widening irises, and gold rings formed around them where the whites had been. The corners turned up slightly. Dark lashes thickened, lengthened.

Will's stomach fluttered. He forgot how to breathe.

His skin changed. Pale golden green was the nearest Will's mind could come to grasping a shade he'd never seen before. The lines of Cobalt's face shifted, forming narrow and graceful angles. His lips kept their sultry shape, but the flesh was forest green. And the tattoos along his jaw remained the same. Fierce and fluid, more natural now than before.

Streaks of green tangled in his coal black hair. They looked like vines. Tiny points protruded from the sides—the tips of his ears. His arms and legs were longer. Fingers too. Three joints in each of them. Two in his thumbs. His nails were thorns.

Beautiful. He was impossibly beautiful. Wild, ethereal, *magical.* Will ached with the effort of looking at him.

"What's your name?" Will said. "Your real name."

He blinked. His head cocked like a bird's. "Ciaràn."

"Ciaràn." Speaking it aloud sent a warm shiver through him. "I believe you."

"Seen enough, then?"

No. "Yes."

In seconds, Ciaràn the Fae became Cobalt the Artist. "You're not mad?"

"No. Not angry. Not drooling in my drawers." He smiled. "Not exactly what I expected either. I thought fairies were this big, with little wings." He held his thumb and forefinger apart. "You know. Like Tinkerbell."

Cobalt shook his head. "Those'd be sprites. And they're nothing like your Tinkerbell, apart from the size."

"Are you...?" *Serious,* he had almost said—then decided he didn't want to know that yet. "Never mind. You're beautiful. Both of you."

"Oh, Will. You've such strength in you."

Will snorted. "I don't think so. If I did, I'd never have gotten involved with Lyle, or any of those other bastards."

"That you did, and are still whole, is testament to your strength."

"Yeah, right." Will crumbled the whole abuse subject into a mental ball and shoved it in a corner of his mind. He'd deal with it later. Right now he had a thousand questions that he wasn't sure should be answered. He hadn't quite wrapped his head around the Fae thing yet. One step at a time, he decided, and asked the most important question first. "So who's the guy that looks just like you?"

"His name is Eoghann." A curtain of disgust drew across Cobalt's features. "At least, I'm forced to assume that was he.

Eoghann was…my lover, before I was banished from the Fae realm. Or rather, I was his. Eoghann loves no one but himself."

Will frowned. "Banished?"

"A tale for another time," Cobalt said with a sad smile. "It seems he's decided to desire me again. When I refused him, he attempted to use Uriskel to get to me. And now he's on about going through you." His lip curled, baring teeth. "The bastard's mimicked my glamour to get to you, Will. I've no idea what he'll do with you, but I'll not let him have the chance. And…that's why Uriskel said what he did to you."

"The lover thing?"

"Yes." Cobalt dropped his gaze. "He tried to drive you away, so Eoghann wouldn't harm you. And I let him. I wanted you safe, and I thought if we'd nothing between us, you would be."

Will went cold. "Why didn't you just tell me the truth before?"

A bitter smirk. "Would you have believed me?"

He almost said *yes.* Thought about it. Tonight, after watching Lyle die, after experiencing things that warped the fabric of reality—yes. He had no problem accepting that Cobalt was a fairy. Hell, he'd seen the evidence. But yesterday, when he was still wrapped in the afterglow from the best sex of his life and more than willing to believe a man like Cobalt would never actually want him, that his attention had been a fluke?

"No," he finally said. "I wouldn't have."

Cobalt moved toward him with burning eyes. "Come to the Grotto with me," he said. "Please. You'll be safe there. Eoghann can't enter the building."

Will started to refuse. He was exhausted, overwhelmed, and wanted nothing more than to sleep for a week, and maybe get good and drunk when he woke up. But then he remembered the wet crunch of Lyle's neck breaking, the cold expression on the face of the killer. He didn't want to be next in line.

"All right," he said. "Let's go."

Chapter Twenty-three

Will called Tess from the cab on the way to the Grotto. After she stopped screaming, he explained, as quietly and with as few words as possible, that Lyle was dead, and he was going to stay with Cobalt while they worked some things out.

She cried. Made him swear to take care of himself and call her tomorrow. He promised he would. They hung up, and he tucked the phone reflexively in his front pocket.

The awkward movement sent pain screaming through him from the waist down. Tears pricked his eyes, and he managed to turn the startled cry that formed in his throat to a closed-mouth grunt. The adrenaline of the last few hours must've dampened his nerves for a while. But he was crashing now, and his ass let him know it.

Beside him, Cobalt flinched. Alarm suffused his face. "Will," he whispered urgently. "What's happened?"

"Nothing new," he said through gritted teeth, trying to shift and take some of the pressure from his backside. "I'll live. Be better when we get there."

"Oh, love." Without asking, Cobalt seemed to understand his desire not to mention anything about beatings in front of strange cabdrivers. He turned sideways on the seat and reached out. "Come here."

Will shuffled toward him, not sure what he meant to do. Before he could ask, Cobalt gripped his waist and lifted him onto his lap.

His surprise gave way to heat and badly timed desire. Public displays of affection, even for an audience of one disinterested cabbie, had never been part of Will's relationships. And something in him, something he'd refused to acknowledge, always insisted it was his fault. He wasn't good enough, and they'd been ashamed to be seen with him.

Cobalt put an arm around his shoulders and drew him down to rest against him. "Better?" he murmured near his ear.

"Mmm." Will slid down a bit and laid his head on his chest. Cobalt's ragged gasp when he brushed what was definitely an erection had him practically drooling. Briefly, he entertained the fantasy of fucking Cobalt in the back of a cab. But his ass wouldn't take it right now.

"Won't be long, love." Cobalt's low voice vibrating under him soothed better than a hot bath. "I'll fix it for you."

Will smirked. "More gunk?"

"Perhaps I've something better."

The husky promise in the words almost burned him.

Will let himself relax as much as possible. Cobalt's warmth, his slow breathing, and his arm curled protectively around him conspired to leach consciousness from him. He knew nothing until Cobalt shook him gently and whispered, "We're here."

Will climbed from the cab, blinking and bleary. The Grotto stood dark and silent. Either they'd closed the place early without Cobalt there, or it was later than he'd thought.

He let Cobalt lead him inside, through the dim and deserted main room, up the stairs, and into his bedroom. Cobalt closed the door. "How bad is it?"

Will shrugged. "Not as bad as the first time. He didn't... Well, I had clothes on." Until the end. But he wasn't going to think about what could've happened. "If you have any more of those drugs, a couple of them'll probably knock it down."

Cobalt drew a breath, like he was about to say something he'd regret. "I can heal you. If you'll let me."

"What? How?"

"Magic."

Will resisted the urge to push his own jaw back into place. "You mean like real magic?"

"Yes. We've healing abilities. Some of us, anyway." He moved closer. "But I'll have to see your injuries to heal them. And I'll understand if you'd rather I didn't."

"Well, you've seen me worse than this." Will's mouth twisted. "It won't do anything weird to me, right? I mean, since I'm...uh, human."

A pained look came over him. "No. Nothing strange."

"All right."

Will turned away, working his shoes off first. He'd have to strip. And did he really just agree to let Cobalt magic his injuries away? Maybe he had gone nuts. So Cobalt was a Fae. Okay. He had green skin and pointed ears and triple-jointed fingers. Fine. But magic?

He tugged his shirt over his head. Cobalt gasped. "He's burned you."

"What... Oh." He'd just about forgotten the Starbucks incident. After everything else, getting arrested barely registered as important. "No, Lyle didn't do that. Some self-important bitch spilled hot coffee on me." He unbuttoned his jeans, hesitated, pushed everything down. "This was Lyle's contribution," he said.

The silence behind him was frigid.

"Cobalt?" Will turned his head.

"Lyle was fortunate to encounter Eoghann instead of me." Fury tightened his voice, crackled from his eyes, and made the lines of his body rigid. "I would not have been so merciful as to simply snap his neck."

Will swallowed. "It's done now," he said. "And I'm glad it wasn't you that killed him."

"Yes. It's done." Cobalt blinked and relaxed visibly. He gestured to the bed. "If you'll lie down..."

Nodding, Will stepped from the rest of his clothes and stretched out facedown. The mattress dipped as Cobalt sat beside him. He tensed in anticipation.

"Breathe, Will," Cobalt murmured. "I'll not have to touch you for this."

Will wasn't sure if he was relieved or disappointed.

For a moment nothing happened. Just as Will thought Cobalt had changed his mind, a warm and tingling pins-and-needles sensation blossomed in his shoulders. The feeling cascaded down his body like hot oil, soothing, easing the pain from him by degrees. When it reached his backside, the tingling flared to white-hot intensity. He squeezed his eyes shut. The sensation cooled and erased the last of the aching from him.

The bed rocked. Cobalt groaned.

Will looked at him. He'd gone pale and sat with bowed head, arms propped on his thighs like he was about to collapse, or puke. Maybe both. "Cobalt. You okay?"

He stirred and sent a tired smile. "Yes. Healing exhausts me, but I'll recover. How do you feel?"

"Amazing." Will sat up and stretched. No part of him throbbed or twinged. There wasn't even residual soreness. "I'd ask how you did that, but I doubt you'd be able to explain it."

"And you'd be right there." His smile wavered. He turned away, stood. "I imagine you'll be wanting to rest. I'll leave you to it, then."

"Are you kidding? I couldn't sleep right now if you paid me."

Cobalt faced him with an unspoken question.

"Finding out magic is real doesn't happen every day, you know." Will grinned and patted the mattress. "If you leave now, I'll die of curiosity."

"Very well." Cobalt sat. Reluctantly.

Will bit his lip. "What's wrong?"

"Don't…"

His scent pounced like a jungle cat, powerful and hungry. Wind and water and smoke. Summer heat, a tangled field of wildflowers carried on a breeze over a rushing waterfall. Will breathed in deeply and let out a moan of pleasure. "Can you tell me now?" he whispered.

"Tell you what?"

"Why you smell like that. Like…heaven."

"By the gods, Will. You astound me." Cobalt swallowed hard. "It's my mating scent. All the Fae have one, but it's rare for humans to detect. Even when they're aware of our existence."

"So you do that when you're turned on?"

He gave a slow nod. "I'm not able to stop it. Particularly when I'm near you."

"Jesus. That's the sexiest fucking thing I've ever heard."

Cobalt looked like he'd been sucker punched. "But you'll not want me now," he said.

"I won't?"

"You know I'm not human." He tensed, closed his eyes. "I'll not force myself on you, Will. I may not be able to have you, but I know you'll be safe from Eoghann here. That is enough for me. I'll ask for nothing more."

He was too stunned to respond. Cobalt—beautiful, sweet, almost too damned perfect—thought he wasn't good enough for Will? He wondered whether it was snowing in hell right now.

Cobalt seemed to take his silence as an affirmation. He stood to leave.

"Wait," Will rasped. "I don't care."

Brief hope lit his eyes and fizzled. "You've no need to lie and spare my feelings." He started walking away.

Will climbed from the bed, caught up with him, and grabbed his wrist. "Cobalt. Look at me." When he turned, Will nodded down at his erection. "Does it look like I don't want you?"

Cobalt made a strangled sound. "No. But…"

"But nothing. I want you. God, I want you so bad it hurts." He loosed his grip, stepped back. "Let me prove it."

"How—"

"Take everything off. Your clothes. Your glamour." His cock twinged at the thought of touching Cobalt in that beautiful, exotic form. "Let me have you, the way you really are."

"Ah, Will. How you tempt me."

His scent rose again, filling the room. Will groaned. "Don't make me beg you."

"Never. You'll never beg for what's yours." Cobalt peeled off his shirt. "Promise me you'll tell me if it's too much. Please."

"Shut up and strip."

Cobalt complied with quick, sure movements. His eyes flashed black, then blue again. His skin quivered. "Will…"

"Do it."

He changed in a blink. Will let his gaze wander over him—gold-ringed black eyes, pointed pixie features, dark green lips. Lithe and slender body. The cock jutting from his groin was still long, still thick, rounded at the top with a seamless head. A shade darker than the rest of his skin. Finger-width veins stood out, curled around the shaft like vines.

Will reached out and traced the scarring on his chest with his fingertips. He could feel Cobalt's heart hammering just beneath the surface. He moved up, touching the hollow of his throat, his tattooed jaw. Skin like silk. He brushed a thumb over his lips. "You're beautiful."

A low rumble simmered in Cobalt's throat. "Will. Can't wait…"

"You don't have to be gentle all the time," he whispered.

In a heartbeat, Cobalt closed the distance between them. He wrapped his arms around Will, crushed him against his chest, lifted him. Hands cupped his ass. Lips pressed his mouth, firm and hot and demanding.

Will hooked his legs around Cobalt's waist and kissed back. Dizzying heat filled him head to toe. The world spun around him.

Cobalt carried him a few steps, pressed him against the wall. "Bed's too far," he panted. "Here. Now."

"Yes." Will arched against him. "Fuck me."

Fingers brushed his entrance, spreading something warm and wet. Will didn't ask where it came from, didn't care. Cobalt steadied him, paused, entered swiftly with an explosive groan.

Will gripped his shoulders and rocked with him. Sweet pressure, steady thrusts. Hands on his waist, lifting and pulling, faster, the arc increasing. Animal sounds—his, Cobalt's.

Through a haze of bliss he stared down at the slender face, full dark lips, eyes fluttering under closed lids. Not human. Still beautiful. He reached out and stroked the thick, silken tangles of hair. "Cobalt," he groaned. "Look at me."

Black and gold eyes opened. They burned.

"Oh, *God.*" Will clenched his legs tighter around Cobalt and bent to his mouth. Lips met. Tongues entwined, slipping and thrusting, teasing. Cobalt tasted of everything beautiful and wild in the world, everything right. Whimpering, Will worked his hips faster, impaling himself on the thick, rock-hard shaft that filled his ass so perfectly.

The pressure built too fast. Will's cock throbbed painfully, and he came with a cry that wrenched his gut and left him breathless. Cobalt climaxed seconds after him, thrusting deep, grinding Will's name from his lips like a prayer. He pinned him to the wall. Shudders racked them both. "Easy, love," Cobalt whispered. "I have you."

"Yes." Will curled into him. "Always."

Chapter Twenty-four

Will slept.

Cobalt watched him for a time, content to revel in the aching thrill his reaction to the truth had caused. He'd accepted, believed, demanded to be immersed in it. When Will had asked him to drop his glamour, to take him in true form, Cobalt had been certain he'd die of ecstasy. Never in his life had another being, human or Fae, stirred him so strongly.

Even with as much restraint as he could muster, the taking had been rough.

Eventually he rose and made his way to the loft. The lingering warmth in him chilled as he forced himself to face the facts. He'd not be able to shelter Will forever. Even if Will agreed to stay, to be caged here and kept like a favored pet, he'd no desire to keep him that way. But Will would be vulnerable to Eoghann every time he left the safety of the Grotto.

Uriskel had not yet returned. The moon displayed its cold face above the city, whispering a deal of death for any Fae cruel enough to take it. He wanted to believe Uriskel could care for himself, but the torments he'd already suffered at Eoghann's hands suggested otherwise.

How had the Unseelie come to desire him so badly? It was a question he had to answer, because as long as Eoghann continued attempting to have him, Will would remain a target. If he could dissuade Eoghann from pursuing him, he and Will would be free.

A thought came to him that was so simple, it could not possibly work. But he'd try anyway. If Eoghann could manipulate a phone to call him, then he could do the same. And then he'd ask the bastard about his fixation.

He got his cell phone, turned it on, and stared at it. How would he go about finding Eoghann? He moved through menus to the incoming-call log and scrolled to one he knew had been the Unseelie. *Unknown caller.* Summoning his magic, he willed the device to reopen the circuit it had already known.

Ghostly tones drifted from the phone's keypad. Seven digits. The line rang.

Cobalt held the phone to his ear and waited.

After three rings, the line clicked open. "I'm occupied." Eoghann's voice, tight with annoyance.

"Are you, now." Cobalt couldn't help wondering who he'd been expecting to call. "No time for an old acquaintance, then?"

"Ciaràn." A grunt in the background. A dull thud. His tone shifted to mocking pleasantry. "Have you changed your mind?"

"No." Cobalt closed his eyes, certain the backdrop sounds had been Uriskel. "I've a question for you."

"Ask. I reserve the right not to answer."

"Why me? Why *now?* I've been gone a decade." He decided to attempt a bit of flattery, appeal to the Unseelie's immense ego. "You're powerful and attractive, Eoghann. Any Fae in the realm would be honored by your attentions."

"Perhaps. But it's you I'll have on my arm, Ciaràn."

"You'll not have me."

"I will. Voluntarily or not, you'll return to the realm with me."

"Are you mad? I'm banished."

Eoghann's laughter cut to his bones. "And that matters not where I'm concerned. He'll not dare say a word about your return, and I'll be free of his cursed spies."

"Who's this he, then?" Cobalt blurted, not understanding a word of his raving.

"Your father."

Weight settled in Cobalt's stomach, slick and dull. "My father is dead. He died before I was born. You are mad."

"Ah, Ciaràn. You've been lied to. How fascinating."

"What?"

"I'll tell you this, since what's mine has come back to me." Another dull thud. A spate of weak, lung-rattling coughs. *Uriskel.* "Your father is very much alive, and the reason you'll return at my side. There's one other who knows what I know. Don't you wonder, Ciaràn, why he's never told you?"

"Uriskel." He finally managed to speak the halfling's name. "Let him go, if it's me you want."

More chilling laughter. "Ah. Perhaps he has told you, then. He'll pay for that as well."

"He's told me nothing, Eoghann. I've no idea what you're talking about."

"Why the concern, then? He is a snake, a traitor. And he despises you."

"Perhaps," Cobalt said quietly. "But he's no love for you, either."

There was a long pause. At last Eoghann said, "Keep your precious human close to you, Ciaràn. I'll not wait much longer. I'll take him. I'll hurt him. And if you still refuse to return with me, he will die."

"Bastard! If you—"

His threat fell on an empty line.

* * *

Will sat at the table nearest the entrance and watched the Grotto come to life.

He'd spent the day with Cobalt. They had stayed in, talked. Made love. It was a dream, broken only by the occasional reminder of Cobalt's concerns that Uriskel still hadn't come back, and that the asshole who'd copied his glamour and killed Lyle would hunt Will down. Cobalt wanted him to stay here forever.

Right now, that was fine with him. He didn't want to think beyond the moment.

Within half an hour of opening, the place was near full. It wasn't hard to figure out the main attraction—Cobalt, center stage, working shirtless on a scarified back piece for a pretty, dark-haired girl. Most of the audience here were fans, not customers, and Cobalt was playing to them tonight. Making up for his absences. But Will wasn't jealous. Cobalt had made sure he didn't doubt his feelings. Besides, none of the fans would be sleeping in Cobalt's bed. That place was reserved for Will.

He felt more than a little guilty not doing his show tonight. He'd planned on it, but Tess insisted on his taking a few more nights off. She was convinced watching Lyle die had scarred him for life, and he had to agree that they should at least wait for the news to blow over. It would fade soon. After all, it was just another New York murder.

Will closed his eyes and listened to the music that pulsed from the speakers and wound through the conversations around him. He heard Malik's cultured tones as the shop assistant chatted with someone in the front room. A moment later, a chair scraped across the floor close to him. He cracked a glance and blinked at Nix, who was in the process of sitting across from him with a wide grin.

Shade had already taken a seat, silent as a locked room. She smirked a greeting. "Something's different about you tonight, Master Will," she said. "Can you find it, Nix?"

"Not hard to miss, is it, love?" Nix leaned forward and waved a hand in the air near Will's head. "Practically a line running from here to Cobalt's booth. And frankly," he added in a conspiratorial whisper, "you smell of sex."

"Is that it?" Shade actually smiled. It was a little creepy.

Nix furrowed his brow. After a moment, his mouth gaped. "He knows! Bloody hell. What a treat this is." He leaned back and folded his hands on his stomach. "Welcome to the lot, Will. Glad to see your gourd's not flipped."

"Thanks. I think." He grinned. For some reason, it was impossible to hate Nix.

"Hey, I feel for you, mate. You've not had an easy time of things, if you're still in possession of your faculties." For half a second Nix looked serious, and then his impish smile returned. "Where's our friend Skelly, then? We've not driven him off."

Will frowned. Before he could say anything, Shade cut in. "Trouble," she said. "Of the dark variety. Strange, that. Most times he's the trouble himself."

"Poor bugger," Nix said. "I was getting to like him."

"You're touched, Nix."

"You'd know best, love."

Something unsettling passed through Will. The sensation that he was being watched. He looked around the dark-lit room but didn't see anything out of place, anyone paying particular attention to him.

Shade tipped a grimace. "I'd trust your instincts," she said. "Stay in tonight."

Will stared at her. "Are you...?" Psychic, he thought but didn't say.

"Yes."

"Oh. Okay." He cleared his throat and tried to think bland, boring thoughts.

"No need for that." A corner of her mouth lifted. "I can only read what you intend for me to hear. Your private thoughts are still yours."

"Right. It's just a little weird when you answer me before I ask anything."

"Tell me about it," Nix intoned.

Shade glared at him. He pantomimed zipping his mouth shut.

Her expression for Will was kinder. Almost indulgent. "All right, then," she said. "I'll try and let you get a word in now and again."

"Appreciate it," Will said.

She nodded. "Though I do enjoy the look on your face. Like you've a sprite caught in your pants."

"There's a nasty thought." Nix gave a dramatic shudder.

The conversation turned to Cobalt. From Nix, Will learned that he loved the ocean, loved New York, and hated spiders. The story he told about a time one of Cobalt's customers had brought a pet tarantula to the studio, complete with a prolonged girlish yelp that was supposed to represent Cobalt's reaction, got Will laughing until his stomach ached. Shade was less forthcoming, but she spoke of his skilled artistry and his fierce loyalty and dedication to those he cared for.

Will sensed a gentle warning beneath her words. She acknowledged it with a nod. "Not to worry," she said. "I know his heart's safe with you."

Always. Will looked across the room to where Cobalt worked. As though he'd felt the attention, Cobalt glanced up and smiled before returning to his task.

Time passed, until eventually Nix stretched and yawned. "About time we nipped off, isn't it, love?"

"Leaving already?" Will said.

"Already!" Laughing, Nix pointed at a clock on the side wall. "We've been hours, mate. Cobalt's wrapping up. Place is clearing out."

Will blinked and shook himself. "Damn. Guess it has."

They said good-byes, and Will settled in to wait. Tonight he'd relax and pretend that life was good and there were no crazy fairies out there looking for him. Tonight there was only Cobalt. He didn't need anything else.

Watched. He was being watched. Eyes looking through the walls.

He bolted upright. Cobalt still in the booth, talking to his customer, laughing. People in various stages of leaving. Malik in the entrance room, murmuring something. *Come in...* He couldn't make out the rest. A dull thud sounded. Someone grunted in pain.

Will's skin crawled. He stood and walked to the entrance. Glanced out. Malik was alone in the small outer room, standing by the table with slack features and a glossy, blank stare. He didn't look hurt. "Hey," Will said. "You okay?"

Malik's head swiveled in his direction. "I stubbed my toe. On the table."

"Um. Right." The kid acted like he was seriously strung out on something. If that were the case, Cobalt would be pissed. He vaguely recalled something about Malik being in college, the same place as Tess's brother, and hoped he was just exhausted.

Unable to shake his unsettled feeling, Will made his way to the booths. Being near Cobalt calmed him some. After a minute, the customer emerged. Cobalt held a finger up, put a few things away, and came out. "I see Nix and Shade have taken to you," he said with a smile.

"Huh? Oh, yeah. They're…" Will frowned. "Cobalt, I think there's something wrong with Malik."

His smile sank. "How do you mean?"

"I don't know, really. He seems kinda…well, stoned."

"Where is he?"

Will pointed toward the entrance. "Out there."

Cobalt strode off. Will followed, not sure what to do with himself, hoping he hadn't just gotten the kid fired. He seemed decent enough. But at least Tess couldn't blame this one on him.

"Malik," Cobalt said when he reached the room. "Everything all right?"

"Yes." He looked a little better. Still slow to react, but at least his eyes had lost that weird blankness. "Things are fine. This is my place too."

Cobalt's brow furrowed. He shot a glance at Will, turned back to Malik. "What was that?"

Malik blinked and shivered. "Cobalt. Everything all right?"

The kid's apparently unconscious echo of Cobalt's words creeped Will out almost as much as Shade.

"They're fine," Cobalt said slowly. "And you?"

"Yes. I suppose…I must be tired."

"I see." Cobalt moved past him and went to a door at the side of the room that Will had never noticed before. He tried the handle. Locked. "Perhaps you should go home, Malik. Get some rest."

The boy nodded. "I'll do that. Good night." He walked outside.

Will shook his head. "Sorry about that."

"You've no need to apologize." Cobalt came back into the studio and moved aside to let the last few people out. He closed the door and locked it.

"Where does that other door go?" Will asked.

"To my loft." Concern clouded his features. "That was…unusual."

"Yeah. I hope everything's okay with him."

"Mm. Yes." Cobalt blinked and faced Will. A slow smile spread across his lips. "Alone at last. Care for some wine, love?"

"Yes. Among other things."

"Ah, Will. You're insatiable."

"And you're not?"

Cobalt kissed him hard. "Sex first. Wine later."

"I'll second that."

Will reached the stairs first, with Cobalt a few steps behind. The lights were on low in the loft. He headed straight for the bedroom—and froze when a slight movement in the living area caught his eye.

"Excuse me. Do you have the time?"

Impressions registered like lightning. The scarified creep he'd seen outside stood beside the couch, one hand clutching a kneeling, hooded figure beside him by the back of the neck. The other hand held a small wooden box, balanced on his palm like he was offering a gift. The creep grinned, whispered something.

The box opened and unleashed hell.

Chapter Twenty-five

Cobalt barely registered the fact that Eoghann had managed to gain entrance to the Grotto before the bastard released a swarm of sprites. The nasty little creatures headed straight for Will, enveloping him in a cloud of buzzing wings and gnashing teeth.

"No!" He glared at Eoghann. "Call them off."

"They'll not harm him. Yet." Eoghann shoved the figure huddled beside him. "Up, dog. You've a job to do."

"I won't." Uriskel, his voice splintered and raw.

"Still resisting? How utterly tiresome." Eoghann yanked the hood down and clamped Uriskel's neck with one hand. His fingers dug into the flesh.

Uriskel rose in jerks and spurts. His glamour was gone. Oozing claw marks raked his cheeks, his forehead. His bared needle teeth glistened crimson. Blood lined his lips and drizzled from his mouth, dark streaks on blue skin. He turned and spat a mouthful of blood in Eoghann's face. "I won't," he said in a cracked whisper. "Kill me."

Eoghann swung the wooden box hard against his face and shoved him to the floor. "Halfling worm! Tell him. You know what'll happen if you don't."

"Stop," Cobalt said weakly, looking from Uriskel's crumpled form to Will, surrounded by a pulsating skin of sprites. He couldn't save them both. So far Will hadn't moved, but if he tried to run, they'd be on him. And a full sprite attack could easily drive a human mad. At the least, he'd be crippled with the injuries they could inflict.

"I'll warn you now, Ciaràn. Move any closer to your human, and I'll set them to him."

"Bastard! What do you want from me?"

"You know what I want."

Cobalt closed his eyes. How in the gods' names had the Unseelie managed to enter the building? He certainly hadn't been invited. He thought of Malik, of his strange behavior and his unresponsive stare. The words he'd said. "*This is my place too.*" Cobalt had thought little of the statement, believing it gibberish borne of exhaustion. But hadn't he told the boy to consider the Grotto as much his place?

His stomach dipped. "Malik invited you in," he said.

"He did indeed." Eoghann grinned. "Tragically, the boy's affections are not returned. But it's likely that he's beyond caring by now."

"You..."

"Broke your toys? Of course. They crumbled like dust, except for that one. So far." He gestured at Will, then gave a mocking bow. "Why should you be permitted to enjoy being banished?"

Cobalt couldn't even speak. The enormity of the revelation, the rage of it, burned in his throat and cauterized it closed. He hadn't driven his lovers insane. Eoghann had. Likely while wearing his stolen glamour.

"Ah, but you've not heard the best of it." He lashed out and kicked Uriskel. A gesture forced the halfling roughly to his feet again. "Tell him. You're not clear of it yet."

Uriskel's eyes rolled in his head. He opened his mouth, and a fit of coughing seized him, racking his body with shudders. When it stopped, he drew a great gasping breath and met Cobalt's eyes. His own swam with defeat. "Bastard you are," he croaked. "But not lowborn. Not you, Ciaràn of the glen." A sneer half formed on his lips, but he couldn't hold it. "You were fathered by the highest of nobles. The Seelie king himself." He flinched as though he'd been struck. "And so was I."

"What devilry is this?" Cobalt snarled, looking to Eoghann. "You're forcing him to lie to me. I'll not believe it. Traitor or not, he'd have told me if we were...brothers." The word emerged a whisper as a memory surfaced. Uriskel's urging him to speak with Will. Displaying concern for his feelings, however minor. "*Tell him we're family. Brothers. That should sound about right.*"

"I'm forbidden to tell you." Uriskel flinched again. "Part of my...terms of service. One of many rules, for the breaking of which I can be put to death. And I'm told it will be slow in the coming."

Cobalt's heart shattered. "But you've just told me."

"Yes. In exchange for a quick death." Twitching, shivering, Uriskel turned to face Eoghann. "Now do it, you preening backbiter. Kill me."

The smile on Eoghann's face was cold as the ages. "I rather enjoy you alive."

Before Uriskel could react, Eoghann sliced another gesture in the air. Cobalt felt ripples from the surge of power that knocked the halfling flat.

"Now, then." Eoghann started toward Cobalt, passing Uriskel without a glance. "You'll return to the realm with me. Your pretty human pet will live out his short, pathetic life. And should your dear brother attempt to interfere with the high court again, he'll be granted a long and painful death. Everything is perfect."

The last shreds of hope in him died. "Very well," he whispered. "I'm yours, Eoghann. Call off your sprites, and I'll return with you."

A wounded-animal cry filled the room. Uriskel launched himself at the Unseelie and bore him down, pinning him to the floor. "Destroy him, Cobalt," he said through his teeth. "Destroy us both if you have to. Hurry. Your Will can handle a few insects."

Nodding once, Cobalt called on his magic. He'd thank Uriskel later.

Through the mad buzzing of the leathery, black-skinned *things* flying around him, Will heard snatches of the conversation between the Fae. He understood that Malik had let Eoghann in. That Uriskel was Cobalt's brother, and Cobalt hadn't known. And that Cobalt had agreed to go somewhere with Eoghann so he'd call off the creatures.

The last thing he heard, before the floor started vibrating like an earthquake under his feet, came from Uriskel. "*Your Will can handle a few insects.*"

Insects. Was that what these things were? In that case, no way in hell he'd let Eoghann take Cobalt from him because of a bunch of oversize bugs. The creep would have to do better than that.

He reached into the swarm, grabbed one, and almost dropped it in revulsion. Cobalt was right. Sprites didn't look anything like Tinkerbell. It did have arms—four of them, jointed like a praying mantis—and two thick legs with tiny, claw-toed feet. Its face was mostly mouth stuffed with teeth, with a slit nose and eyes like drops of oil. A massive insectile abdomen bulged behind the distorted humanoid form. Double sets of clear dragonfly wings sprouted from its back. Its flesh was hot, dry, a small, pulsating chunk of muscle.

It squirmed and shrieked in his grip. Teeth sank into the meaty part of his palm. Its abdomen swelled and glowed, scarlet under black-veined flesh. Cringing, Will closed it in his hand and squeezed.

The thing burst like an overfed leech. A teaspoon or so of liquid splashed his hand and burned him on contact, a flash of intense pain. Tendrils of smoke rose from his skin. He could hear it sizzling. With a startled cry, he wiped his hand on his shirt—and watched a hole smolder through the fabric.

Jesus. Fucking fireflies from hell.

A handful of sprites left the swarm and dived for him, latching onto his arms, his chest, his back. One landed on his shoulder and bit his neck. He swatted it hard, grunting in pain when it popped and sprayed him with fiery liquid. Two on one arm, one on the other. Their guts, or whatever the stuff was, dripped down and left blackened rivulets etched in his skin. He couldn't reach the ones on his back, but he felt their teeth in him, their bloated bodies hanging from his flesh.

One of them skittered across his shirt, looking for a place to sink its teeth. It wasn't glowing. He crushed it—and it didn't burn him.

The little bastards were using his blood for the scalding stuff.

A fresh bunch attacked. He batted them off, smacked them, pounded them flat with fists. The bites stung, the burns throbbed. He clenched his jaw and kept going, one after another. His gut churned every time with the squelching sensation of burst flesh. And there were still more, still dozens more circling him in a chittering frenzy.

This one-at-a-time shit took too damned long.

Will reached out and scooped as many as he could in both arms and crushed them to his chest. Some of them managed to bite. Not all, though. He did it again. It hurt like hell, but he could take the pain. He liked it. He'd welcome it, if it meant killing these awful things.

A few more passes, and only a handful remained. They kept diving, kept biting. Not too smart, sprites. He kept swatting and crushing. The last one in the air went straight for his throat. He raised his chin, inviting it, and waited until it landed to pluck it off and pop it in one hand.

He stood still, breathing hard. No more buzzing. But the back of his shirt felt heavy. He pulled it over his head and off, brought it around to look.

Two sprites clung to the fabric. Their glowing, pulsating abdomens stretched like balloons—golf-ball sized, acidized stolen blood swirling just beneath the taut surface.

Will dropped the shirt and stomped it flat. Two rough black circles blossomed and sent smoke spiraling up from the sprites' remains.

Shuddering, holding back bile, Will lurched away from the carnage. Now he could help Cobalt.

Or not.

The earthquake he'd felt had apparently been floorboards coming to life and tearing free to wrap themselves around Eoghann and hold him down. Cobalt stood over him, holding a hand palm down, fierce concentration etched on his face. He gestured. Another floorboard ripped itself out and curved across the trapped Fae. If anything was going to drive him insane, this would be it.

And then he saw Uriskel.

Will guessed this was his true form. Light blue skin, a grasshopper-shaped face, teeth like curved bone needles. Black and gold eyes like Cobalt's. He looked like he'd been rammed headfirst into a paper shredder. He held one of Cobalt's wine bottles upraised and smashed it on Eoghann's head.

Eoghann let out a gurgling hiss. "You dare strike me, you mongrel breedling?"

"Shut up and die," Uriskel said.

The boards trapping Eoghann began to creak and pop. A series of snaps burst from them like fire. Blackness and rot seeped through them. They crumbled to dust.

Cobalt stumbled back with a gasp. He glanced in Will's direction. Stopped and stared.

"I'm all right." Will nodded at Eoghann. "Finish him off."

Cobalt managed a smirk. "Stay back. Please."

"Blasted human!" Eoghann shook free of the debris and shot to his feet.

Uriskel flew at him.

Eoghann's reaction was too fast for Will to follow. Whatever he did, it lifted Uriskel a foot from the floor and flung him across the room to crash against the far wall. The impact shook the building. Uriskel slid down and collapsed in an abrupt heap.

Cobalt screamed something in a language Will didn't understand. Eyes blazing, he held his arms out like Moses parting the Red Sea. A groaning sound rebounded from the walls and filled the room. Plaster cracked, crumbled, sloughed away from beams. Faint metal pings peppered the breaking sounds—nails raining on the hardwood floor.

"Fascinating strategy." Eoghann folded his arms and regarded Cobalt with an indulgent sneer. "Pull the place down on us all. I'll wait until you're through. At least then we'll be rid of the human."

The urge to bolt passed quickly. Will trusted Cobalt. He glanced at Uriskel, who still hadn't moved, and saw the plaster breaking apart from the wall above him. Steeling himself to move fast, ignore the pain, he ran over and dragged Uriskel to the far side of the couch.

Thick boards and beams pulled loose from the walls. They danced and clattered and floated together, coalescing like they were magnetized. The wood flexed, bent, knotted itself together. It formed a skeletal creature, a wooden ogre with creaking, splintered joints and sheared points at the ends of its clublike arms. The mass shambled toward Eoghann with a dull, groaning roar.

"Really, Ciaràn. I'd expected better of you." Eoghann raised his arms and gestured.

The thing kept coming.

Eoghann displayed a split second of confusion. Anger replaced it quickly. He gestured again, and black rot blossomed in the ogre's legs, slowly spreading. Bits of wood crumbled away. The monster wavered—but it moved forward, step by ground-shaking step.

Eoghann opened his mouth. Whatever he planned to say was lost in a scream when a splintered stake plunged into his chest, through it, pinning him down.

Will wasn't surprised that he failed to die. Blood soaked his shirt and bubbled from his mouth, but his arms kept moving in frantic gestures. The rot spread faster through the creature. It wouldn't be long before it fell apart completely.

Cobalt groaned and sank to his knees. "Get out, Will," he panted. "I'm tapped. Can't stop him. Need you...safe."

"I'm not leaving you."

"Please."

Will shuddered. If he left, Cobalt would die. If he stayed, Cobalt might die anyway—and he'd probably die too. *No. Not fair.* There had to be another choice.

"Will…"

Uriskel's voice barely carried past his lips. Will bent closer to him. "Can we do anything?" he whispered.

"Not me. You."

"What?"

Uriskel's hand stirred debris until he found a nail. He held it in his palm. His flesh scorched, and smoke rose from the edges.

Will snatched it away from him. It was cold to the touch.

"Cold iron," Uriskel murmured. "Fae…powerless."

"Right."

Will scurried across the floor on hands and knees, grabbing every nail he could find. He risked a glance at Eoghann. Most of the wooden ogre lay in a crumbling heap. Eoghann started to stand, his furious gaze riveted to Cobalt. "You'll return to the realm as a corpse," he snarled.

Cobalt shivered in place. He couldn't even lift his head.

Heart pounding like a pile driver, Will stuck nails between his fingers and formed tight, spiked fists. He waited until Eoghann turned fully away, toward Cobalt. Then ran at him. The first swing hit home and drove four of the nails in between his shoulder blades.

Eoghann whirled with a hiss. His glamour fell away. Reptilian features. Blue-black skin. Fangs and claws. A living, breathing nightmare. Guaranteed insanity.

Will pounded the other fist into his stomach without hesitation. "I've seen worse, shithead," he snapped. "I dated a cop."

The shock on Eoghann's face stiffened to a rigid mask. He sank down and curled in a steaming ball at Will's feet.

Chapter Twenty-six

Cobalt watched Eoghann fall, his eyes refusing to believe what they'd seen. Somehow, Will had brought the bastard down.

At last he saw the nails skewering the Unseelie's back and understood. Cold iron. This building was old, erected long before drop-forged nails became the standard. But how had Will known to use these against Eoghann?

It mattered not. The Unseelie was poisoned, paralyzed, but still alive. Cobalt would kill him. Kill him for the humans he'd tormented and condemned to madness, for the anguish he'd heaped on Uriskel, for Will. For no other reason than he was a monster who did not deserve life. He struggled to his feet and prepared to deal a death blow.

"Don't, Cobalt. Stay your hand."

He froze. Uriskel was kneeling beside Will in a posture echoing his earlier subservience to Eoghann. "Y-you want him spared?" Cobalt stammered.

"No. If the decision were mine, I'd let you have at it, and piss on his grave alongside you." Uriskel rose to one knee, winced. "I'm to bring him back alive. The Seelie king has a lengthier punishment than death in mind for him." A haunted grin crossed his bloodied lips. "Bastard thought I'd die in the attempt. Won't he be surprised to see me."

"Uriskel…"

He waved a dismissive hand. A nail-shaped burn scored his palm. "I'll not stomach any grousing at the moment. Attend to your Will, you thick dolt."

"Thank you."

Uriskel snorted. "Thick, *deaf* dolt."

"I am that."

"Cobalt," Will said. "I think we're going to have company."

Cobalt looked at him. Shirtless, covered with oozing bites and sprite burns and plaster dust, clear eyed and focused. Fearless. Gods, how he loved him. "Company?"

"Yeah. I kinda thought we might need help, and I figured if I thought loud enough, maybe Shade would hear me. So I think they're on the way."

Somewhere downstairs, a door banged open. Cobalt's jaw went slack, and then he laughed. "You've known for a day, and already you're better than I at handling the Fae."

Uriskel let out a groan. "Keep the Sluagh away from me. I've enough wounds already, without her cutting tongue."

Footsteps on the stairs. Shade came up first, with Nix right behind her. She stopped and stared at the torn walls, the debris-scattered room. Her gaze landed on Eoghann's frozen form, and her eyes widened.

"Bloody spectacular mess!" Nix came around her and strolled toward them, hands in his pockets. Wood and plaster crunched under his feet. "I'd fire the decorator. Nice to see you're still drawing breath, Uriskel." He stopped, tipped his head at Will. "I see someone's had a bit of a row with sprites. Told you they were nasty buggers."

"Be quiet, you daft bit." Shade seemed to materialize at Nix's side. "We've enough to heal one of you. Who's the worst of it?"

"I'm only just drained," Cobalt said. "Will…"

Will shook his head. "I'll live. Take care of Uriskel."

Shade raised a cool eyebrow. And nodded.

"Blast the lot of you! I'll not be handled like a spoon-fed fledgling." Uriskel lurched to his feet, turned his back, and managed a few wobbling steps.

Cobalt rushed after him and caught him just before he toppled. "Easy, Brother," he said, low enough for only Uriskel to hear. "You've a journey to make. I'd see you face the bastard who calls himself king on your feet and not your knees."

Uriskel stiffened. After a moment, he said, "Odd, that."

"What?"

"You called me brother. And I've not been cast into the fiery pits of hell."

Cobalt's eyes burned. He blinked back tears, knowing Uriskel would despise seeing them. "I've a question for you."

"Ask it quickly."

"Why…" Cobalt wasn't sure he wanted the answer, but he had to know. "Why did you follow Eoghann, when he went after Will? He might have killed you."

"Perhaps I wanted to die." A shudder racked him. "And perhaps I've too few brothers who are not mincing noble scum to let one of them get his foolish self enslaved by that sadistic piece of filth."

Despite his best efforts, a few scalding tears escaped Cobalt's eyes. He swiped them away. "Can you stand?"

"I damn well can, if my alternative's you holding me like a wilting female."

Cobalt eased back. Uriskel took a step away and turned with a smirk. "Well met, Ciaràn of the glen."

Cobalt knew it was the closest he could come to thanks or acknowledgment, and enough for the moment. A lifetime of hatred couldn't be overcome in hours. "I suppose you'll stay in the realm, then," he said, unable to keep the slight tremor from his voice.

Uriskel sighed. He reached in a pocket and produced a small leather pack with a flap closure. "Here. Great softhearted fool," he said, pressing it into Cobalt's hand. "I'll come back for these. Don't lose them."

Brow furrowed, Cobalt lifted the flap. A deck of playing cards nestled inside the pack.

"All right. Call the Sluagh and her pet shape-shifter here. Tell her I'd prefer to keep what blood I've left inside my body, if it's all the same."

Cobalt grinned and went to deliver the message.

While Nix and Shade attempted to heal Uriskel, who reacted with all the grace of a cornered tiger, Cobalt led Will as far from the destruction and Eoghann's still-smoldering form as possible and embraced him hard. Will returned the gesture, and they stood without speaking for long moments. At last, Cobalt said, "I must apologize to you."

Will looked up at him. "Don't even think about it. None of what that asshole did is your fault."

"No, love. That's not the reason." Cobalt brushed a curled finger along his jaw. "I've underestimated you. Your strength is boundless."

"Right. I should join the circus or something."

"What?"

"Never mind." Will flashed a lopsided smile. "I did kick some sprite ass, though."

"You did. And you defeated Eoghann. You saved my life, Will."

He shrugged. "I guess we're even, then."

"I've not saved you. Eoghann killed Lyle." The memory of Will's torment burned through him. "Though I'd gladly have done so myself, had you asked me."

"But that's why you did," Will said. "I told you no, and you respected that. Even though you didn't like my answer." He caught his lip. "Without you, I'd have gone back to him. And I'd be dead right now."

"Ah, Will." Cobalt groaned and leaned down to murmur in his ear. "Do you suppose it'd be rude of us to retire to the bedroom?"

Will grimaced. "Probably. But I can guarantee a rain check. I'm not going anywhere."

"If I've my way, you'll not leave my bed for a month."

His smile was the sun. "I can live with that."

* * *

Will cut the line. "And that was Doctor…uh, Jay, with an interesting take on the psychology of relationships. Thanks for your time, Doc." He gave himself a mental pat on the back for saying *interesting*, instead of a few other words that had come to mind. *Creepy*, for one. The guy sounded like being on the air was the last thing he wanted to do, and he was going to kill somebody the minute he hung up. Maybe he'd lost a bet or something.

"Ready?" Tess in his ear.

He smiled. "Bring it on."

Three lit lines. Will rolled a sweeper and repositioned the mic. "All right, people. We're open for calls. You've got questions; I've got answers."

"Line two," Tess said. "Fade your in-vee. He's a breather."

"Oh, thanks." Will tweaked the volume and opened the line. "Hey, you're on *The Truth*. Question or confession?"

"Uh, hi. Yeah, I got a question?" Some breather. The guy was practically panting.

"I figured you did, pal, or you wouldn't've called me." Will rolled his eyes. What a genius. "What's up?"

"So I got this date tomorrow, right? It's our third, and I sucked him off last time?"

"Way to go. Hope you brushed your teeth."

A wet, sloppy breath. "So he says he'll do me this time. But he's bigger than me?"

"Ouch, man."

"Yeah. So I want to look bigger? How do I do that?"

"Well, outside of surgery, you could try turning the lights off. Better yet, shave."

"You mean my pubes?"

No. Your pits. "That's right. Shaving makes the tree stand taller." Will paused for a beat. "Seriously, buddy, don't worry about it. If he has a problem with the meat, you're gonna want him to shop another store anyway. Love means never whipping out the ruler."

Tess blipped in. "Nice one. Oughta be a bumper sticker."

Will turned toward the studio camera and stuck his tongue out.

The caller mouth breathed again. "Thanks, Will. You're great."

"Nah. I'm just a guy with a mic. Thanks for calling." He cut the breather.

"Three," Tess told him. "Somebody slipped her a happy shot."

"Squealer?"

"Giggler."

"Fun." He hit three. "You're on, sweetheart. What've you got for me?"

"Hi, Will! We all missed you last week."

"Well, it's nice to be missed. Who's we, darlin'?"

"Everybody in the place. I work at Body Pop on Fifth."

"Sounds painful."

She giggled, a high-pitched, nervous sound. "We do piercings and stuff, you know? I'm the tongue girl."

"I hope that's on your business cards."

"Oh my God!" Another giggle. "I'm totally doing that."

"Make sure you send me one. So, what's your question, tongue girl?"

She took a deep breath. "Is it true about you and Cobalt from the Grotto?"

The question threw him off, but he recovered fast. "That depends on what you mean by 'it,' sweetheart."

"Are you guys...you know. Together."

Damn, were they ever. On the bed, on the couch, in the shower, on the floor. Together in more ways than Will had ever thought existed.

"Will," Tess barked. "DA."

He shook himself. Dead air. Dragging ass. "That's a big ten-four," he said. "In other words, yes. We are." He felt no shame in saying it, no fear that Cobalt would fly off the handle.

"Oh. My. God. That is *so* hot!" The girl covered the phone, but her next words came through anyway. "Told you so, Peej! You owe me a shot."

"I'd recommend taking it orally," Will said.

"Shit! Oops. Can I say that?"

"You can say anything you want, darlin'."

"Wow." She let out a contented sigh. "That's so awesome. Congrats, Will. I mean, everybody in New York wants that guy, you know?"

"I don't know about everybody. There's gotta be someone out there who doesn't want him. You know, all those people who had their sex drives amputated back in the sixties."

More laughter. "Are you gonna have Cobalt on the show?"

"That'll be up to him." Will bit down on his lip as the words invoked a different image than what she'd had in mind—Cobalt fucking him right here in the studio, while the whole city listened. That'd probably be terrible for ratings. But with his audience, maybe not. "Thanks for calling, tongue girl. I'll look for that card."

"Bye, Will!"

Tess came through again. "There's some hot guy here looking for you."

"Oh, yeah?" Will rolled a thirty-second fill. "Tall, dark, and knock-you-flat?"

"I'm drooling."

Will glanced at the clock. "I'll take one more, and I'm out."

"Gotcha." A pause. "Line two."

The fill faded. Will punched the line. "Hey there. Welcome to *The Truth*. How can I fix your bitch?"

"This is Will Ambrose."

"No, *this* is Will Ambrose. You're calling me. Query away."

"I've a problem that I've not been able to solve, and I hear you've particular experience."

Will frowned. The voice was unfamiliar, but the guy's cadence sounded like Cobalt, and Uriskel, and every other

Fae he'd met. "Maybe, maybe not," he said. "I won't know until you ask."

There was a pause. "I've a partner," he said slowly. "I love him more than life. And he's quite sick. Possibly dying." A quick, shuddering breath. "I may be able to...help him. But I'd have to confess certain things, and I fear I'll do him more harm that way."

Will's heart thrummed in his ears. Definitely Fae. He pushed his initial how-the-fuck reaction aside. "Tell him the truth. We—" He stopped himself before he could say *humans*. "He can probably handle more than you think. And trust me...real love is worth saving, any way you can do it."

"Thank you, Will." The caller hung up before he could disconnect.

Will let his breath out slowly. "Well, folks, it's about that time. Good night, good luck, and we'll be in touch tomorrow." He snapped on the closing roll and killed the lines. The on-air light flashed off.

"That was extremely weird," Tess said in his ear. "Touching, but weird."

"Yeah." No way in hell he'd explain things to Tess right now. She wasn't nearly drunk enough. "So where's my visitor?"

"Right outside your door."

Grinning, Will took the cans off and headed across the studio. He opened the door. "Come on in. Just have to take care of a few things."

Cobalt stepped through with a smile. He ducked and kissed him, hot and hard. "Be quick, love. I'm anxious to show you."

"I can't wait." He knew Cobalt had finalized the design for his scarification piece. By mutual agreement, his sessions would be private. Will had a feeling he wouldn't be able to keep from jumping Cobalt right in the booth, no matter who was watching. "Hey. Did you happen to hear that last call I had?"

"I did."

The reserved note in his voice made Will look hard at him. "And I guess you don't have any idea how he knew that I...well, know?"

A teasing grin slanted his lips. "I've a suspicion. But it wasn't me, love. I'm not the mischievous kind."

"Nix." Will groaned.

"He means well enough."

"Great. Now every Fae in New York's going to call me with their problems. How many of you guys are there, anyway?"

Cobalt offered a slow shrug. "I've not counted lately."

Will shook his head. "It's cool. I can deal with it." He smirked. "But if I'm going to give out sexual advice to the Fae, I think I'll need more...experience."

A visible shudder worked through Cobalt. "I believe I can help you with that."

"Perfect. Let's get started. I'm thinking backseat of a cab."

"You are wicked, Will."

"Nope. I'm just a guy with a mic—and the hottest lover in New York."

He smirked. "My lover is hotter than yours."

"Come on." Will grabbed his hand. "We'll go set something on fire."

He was surprised the studio didn't burn down on the way out.

ᘔTHE ENDᘔ

S. W. Vaughn

S. W. Vaughn lives and writes in upstate New York, a nice place to visit during the two months it isn't snowing. When not writing, Vaughn spray-paints graffiti art on the walls of the writing cave, collects movie posters, and double-checks the dark corners of the house with a flashlight for mice, snakes, and the occasional possum or visiting horse from next door. Vaughn works in multiple genres but prefers urban fantasy and erotic romance.

CPSIA information can be obtained at www.ICGtesting.com
Printed in the USA
BVOW031420200812

298349BV00001B/40/P